The Whole She-Bang 3
A collection of Canadian crime stories by Toronto Sisters in Crime

Edited by Janet Costello

Toronto Sisters in Crime, Publisher

Toronto Sisters in Crime, Publisher

The characters and events in this book are fictitious. Any similarity to real persons, living or dead, is coincidental and not intended by the authors.

Library and Archives Canada Cataloguing in Publication

The Whole She-Bang 3: stories by Sisters in Crime: Canada; edited by Janet Costello

ISBN 978-0-9880936-5-2

Detective and Mystery stories, Canadian (English). Costello, Janet

Also issued as ISBN 978-0-9880936-2-1 and 978-0-9880936-7-6 (e-books)
Cover Art and Design by Chris Lang

Praise For The Whole She-Bang 2

The Sisters in Crime anthologies showcase some known and many (as yet) unknown writers. This new one includes a great piece by the late much-loved Lou Allin, as well as a batch of good stories from writers Catherine Astolfo, Melodie Campbell and Jill Downie. There's humour, plenty of suspense and some real drama here and it's great for filling in those moments while you're waiting for the gravy to thicken or the potatoes to boil and you don't want to get too involved in a long book.

The Toronto Globe and Mail

In the 24 stories ... we get countless small pleasures. A story by Linda Wiken gives us a Toronto Police DI named Anne Mason whose understated but shrewd style would make her welcome in a whole novel. Susan Daly presents a juicy story of confrontations between characters based on Rob Ford and Margaret Atwood. Elizabeth Hosang's story examines the possibilities of justifiable homicide in the case of two neighbours who have different ideas about gardens. Enough other treats along similar lines make the collection a Sisterly success.

The Toronto Star

For my Dad, Stan Tench, the first to show me that you can take what some consider a hobby, apply your strengths to it and make it an integral part of your life.

Acknowledgements

Thank you to the members of the Toronto Chapter of Sisters in Crime. Your volunteer work, for more than twenty years, has provided inspiration, support and motivation for so many.

Thank you to Dorothy Birtalan, Linda Cahill, Teri Dixon, Deanna Dunn, Kate Freiman, Robin Harlick, Jeannette Harrison, Nathan Hartley, Rayna Jolley, Lesley Mang, Arlene McCarthy, Helen Nelson, Steve Shrott, Renate Simon, all Sisters to this project. Your countless hours volunteered, accepting the stories, judging, proofreading, fact-checking, editing, providing legal help, formatting and marketing this anthology are very much appreciated.

Thank you to Chris Lang, our new and exciting cover artist.

Janet Costello

Janet Costello is a long-time supporter of short mystery fiction. When she isn't earning her living to finance a steady supply of quality reading materials, she is watching films, doting on her cats, Audrey and Humphrey, or spending quality time with friends. The Whole She-Bang 3 is the third anthology she's edited. Janet's next project? She is co-chair for the Toronto Bouchercon in 2017.

Table of Contents

Introduction
by Lesley Mang
Chapter President, Toronto Sisters in Crime

This collection of stories continues the tradition of excellent writing, intriguing plotting, and splendid characters shown in our first two anthologies. We do indeed have a deep well of talent to draw on in producing this new book. And that well is by no means exhausted.

The rules we established when we produced our first anthology were applied here. Again, we did not establish a firm number to be included and the judging was blind. The judges selected stories they thought deserved to be published.

Here are twenty-two stories for your reading pleasure. A few of the authors have appeared in the previous collections, *The Whole She-Bang* and *The Whole-She Bang 2*, but there are many new voices, some published for the first time.

In these stories you will read about the seminal relationships in human experience and how they go awry. Many of the stories feature conflict in families: sibling rivalry, marital infidelity, parent/child disagreement, marital and parental abuse. Other stories focus on academic, business and sports rivalry, power struggles between women and the men who want to control them. Some feature the frightening abuse of strangers and the depravity of sexual jealousy.

You'll meet a wide range of unusual characters: a shoplifter with a proven technique for getting away with it, a betrayed wife who uses her rival as a murder weapon, an amateur crook whose self-indulgence leads to his demise, a resident of a seniors' home who is fed up with being treated like a child, an innocent young girl who inadvertently witnesses a murder, a hockey player with good reasons to kill his rival, a young academic accused of murdering an older colleague with whom she has had an affair, a good Samaritan who unwittingly stumbles on a murderer. And of course there are many more.

The quality of the storytelling is outstanding. You'll find all the hallmarks of excellent writing, fine description, irony and humour in the plots and characters. And satisfying conclusions to fraught situations.

Congratulations to all of the authors for their fine stories. We hope that this sample of your work leads to many readers in the future.

Again this anthology was produced in record time (under a year) by a team of volunteers who put in hundreds of hours collecting, judging, editing, proofreading, formatting and planning a marketing strategy. A very big thank you to all of them.

And a very big thank you to Sisters in Crime, a volunteer organization devoted to promoting the recognition of female writers of crime fiction, for inspiring this collection.

Steve's Story
by Cathy Ace

Cathy Ace was born and raised in Swansea, South Wales and immigrated to Canada in 2000. She uses her knowledge of the cultures, history, art and food she encountered during decades of travel in The Cait Morgan Mysteries—a series of traditional closed-circle mysteries featuring a globetrotting professor of criminal psychology. Ace's other series is set in her native Wales; The WISE Enquiries Agency Mysteries feature four female PIs, one of whom is Welsh, one Irish, one Scottish and one English. They tackle quirky British cases from their base at a Welsh stately home set in the rolling countryside of Powys. Cathy lives in British Columbia, where her ever-supportive husband and two chocolate Labradors make sure she's able to work full-time as an author, and enjoy her other passion—gardening. Bestselling author Ace won the 2015 Bony Blithe Award for Best Canadian Light Mystery.

Steve found the kind words and sympathetic glances bestowed upon him while he sat shiva for his father a lot tougher to stomach than bashing in the old man's skull with a crowbar. True, battering him to death in their diamond-cutting studio had been upsetting, and pretty messy, but it had allowed him to instantly achieve his goal of an independent and wealthy future, so he'd put his mind to the job and had powered on through.

Compared with those few, strangely exhilarating moments, the seven days of mourning seemed endless. His mother having died when he was just eleven years old, Steve's Aunt Rebecca assumed the role of chief supplier of food for those who arrived at his late father's home to pay their respects. He wasn't surprised to see all the women arrive with more platters of edibles when they accompanied their husbands, and dragged their suitably-dressed children, to sit still and somber in the darkened, claustrophobic rooms his father had called home for almost fifty years. By the sixth day, there was no space left in his father's fridge, and the freezer was overflowing. When the final services were held, he cleared out the disgusting messes squashed into tubs or flattened beneath plastic-wrap on disposable plates, and headed back to his own house.

Once there, he luxuriated in the longest shower of his life and indulged in a fresh blade for his razor. He found the entire process to be liberating in a way far beyond that which he'd originally imagined. It was like a little rebirth, as a rich orphan.

The police investigation had been fruitless, as he'd planned. The cops theorized his father had opened the workshop's security door for the unknown assailant; the best they could come up with was someone dressed as a delivery guy had managed to gain access that way. They believed the attacker had broken the old man's hands in an attempt to make him give up the combination to the company's safe which his father had bravely, if foolishly, not done. He'd then crushed the almost-octogenarian's skull in a fit of anger, but failed to remove the safe from its housing, or to open it, so had left, empty-handed, after completely destroying the security cameras and everything they'd recorded. There were no substantive forensics at the scene and no stolen goods to track, so the case remained open, but without any real leads. The cops had been surprisingly gentle when dealing with Steve, who'd discovered he was able to cry at will as he'd opened the safe for them to prove the business's stock of gems was still stored, untouched, inside.

He made a heartfelt plea on the local television news channels for anyone who knew anything to come forward with information, and he, together with his family's synagogue for the past seventy years, even put up a reward as an encouragement for people to do so.

After a month of following up on tips that produced nothing of consequence, the cops regretfully hinted they might never discover the perpetrator. The Family Support Unit's offer of grief counselling was something Steve thought it better to decline, but he'd been gratified by the very real sense of frustration he witnessed when the lead detective on his father's case had shaken him warmly by the hand and had encouraged him to try to move on with his life.

Steve wasn't ever suspected because everyone knew he'd been horribly sick with the flu at the time. He'd made sure his cover story would hold up by carefully laying the groundwork. He'd called his doctor's office to arrange for the delivery of flu medication and had prepared dozens of used tissues to dump on the floor beside his sofa where he'd set up a makeshift bed in which he'd slept, with hot water bottles to make him good and sweaty, for a few days. He'd even posted a couple of photographs of a thermometer showing his 101.7 degree temperature on Facebook. The most painful part of the whole thing had been gouging the edges of his lips to form scabs that looked like cold sores, and rubbing the skin from his nostrils with an emery board to make sure they looked good and raw when he blearily answered the knock at the door to be informed of his father's demise. When he swooned and collapsed—sweating profusely from the laps he'd been running around his kitchen, then peeled open his eyes—red from the lemon juice he'd rubbed into them, he knew the reactions he saw meant he'd convinced the cops he was extremely sick. Far too sick to have been out and about, let alone bashing in his own beloved father's skull.

Doing the deed itself had involved several calculated risks, but had turned out to be a breeze. It was winter, so almost dark by 4 p.m., and he'd snuck out of the back of his house appearing shorter than usual by hunching over his tall six-three frame, wearing a ball cap pulled down over his eyes, a scarf wrapped around his face and bulky outer clothing, the bloodstained layer of which he'd removed at the scene and stuffed into a bag that he'd carried home. He knew his father wouldn't be missed until he didn't show up for evening prayers, and even then it would take some time for him to be found because no one would go to check on him until after the services, and they'd likely start at his house before going to his workshop.

There wasn't anywhere else to look—the old man's entire life revolved around his workshop, synagogue and home. Steve counted on the process giving him a few hours to get rid of the evidence, clean himself up and prepare for the inevitable knock at his door, which it did. He burned everything he'd worn to do the job in the fireplace upon his return, while he allowed the crowbar to sit in the dishwasher for two full cycles before making it grubby again with some grease and tossing it back into the toolbox in his garage.

While the police on TV shows used every type of technology available, and some that wasn't, to check alibis and reveal suspects, in real life they didn't do any such thing—something he'd learned from talking to a couple of off-duty cops who hung out at a bar he sometimes dropped into after work. If he was honest, it was this insight that had started him thinking about how he could get rid of his father. Indeed, he reckoned it was partly the fault of those two detectives that he'd done it at all, because, without their curse-laden condemnation of the way forensics work was portrayed in fiction, it would never have occurred to him that he could have gotten away with it.

If only his father had handed the business over to him as he had promised when he was forty, or even when he'd turned fifty, he might never have so much as contemplated killing him. However, Steve could see the old man had no intention of retiring, and certainly didn't have the good grace to die, so he'd decided to help him on his way and get his hands on what was rightfully his—what he was owed—while he still had the energy to enjoy it. It had taken him half a year to think it all through, but it had been time well spent, and he'd even begun to relish the grim enjoyment of looking across the workbench at the man he could visualize crumpling beneath his blows one day soon.

Some weeks after the official mourning period ended, friends and extended family members began to urge Steve—who'd eaten hardly a thing for weeks, and was looking decidedly peaky—to get away; their shared sentiments were that the whole thing had been a terrible tragedy, a huge shock to his system, and he deserved a break from everything. Of course he had to stick around while the police investigation continued to grind along, so he used the time to sort out his father's affairs, even managing to sell the house to a couple who planned to gut and flip it. All the while he made sure he told everyone who would listen he couldn't face going back to work in the place where "it" had happened. After all, he was a grieving son, so why should he be expected to return to work? No more long hours spent hunched over the bench for him, peering through lenses so strong they made his eyes water. No more knowing his father would scream at him for the tiniest miscalculation in a facet, or striving for unacknowledged perfection every second of each tedious day.

Eventually, Steve let it be known he was going to take a cruise, and a few of his great-aunts were surprised when he told them he planned to travel to China, via the Caribbean, Panama Canal, Hawaii, the Polynesian Islands and Australia. It would be a three-month trip that demanded pretty much an entire closet full of new clothes, not only because he'd lost so much weight—the effect of the shock and grief, of course—but also since he'd booked a suite on one of the most exclusive cruise lines to sail the seas; that was a little detail he chose to keep to himself.

"Penny for them," whispered a breathy voice close to Steve's ear as he stood at the rail watching the ship's wake foam in the turquoise waters off Cartagena.

The sun was hot on his back and the wind ruffled his neatly trimmed hair as he turned. "Ah, Barb." He smiled.

A first-time cruiser like himself, Barb had been assigned the same dinner table as Steve for this part of the journey; he'd elected

14

to share his meal-times with other cruisers because, after all, he was a single man in his fifties, travelling alone, and could do with some companionship.

A somewhat naive and impressionable woman, only just into her forties, Steve had decided to make the most of the chance handed to him by Fate; Barb was also cruising alone but was only booked to sail as far as San Diego, where she lived. He aimed to win her over long before that, and have some real fun. He liked that she was short—he preferred them compact; it made him feel even more of a man. A pocket-Venus was just his type. Raven-haired too. Perfect.

He allowed his eyes to slide down her desirable body in its form-fitting outfit as he sucked in his paunch and straightened his spine to realize his full, and considerable, height. "Just thinking about... you know...." Steve bit his lip and squeezed out a tear.

Barb looked up at him, her heart-shaped face distraught. She touched his arm gently, sending a shiver of anticipation through Steve's eager loins. "I'm sorry," she said huskily. "Of course, your poor father. I know you said last night how much he would have enjoyed sharing this trip with you. He must be filling your thoughts. I apologize, I didn't mean to bother you."

Steve wiped his wet cheek, then took the woman's hand in his own, her flesh feeling cool and pliable between his sweating palms. "Don't worry. No bother at all. I'm happy to have some company. Stay?"

Barb's dark, limpid eyes were full of sympathy. "Whatever you want," she said meekly.

The previous night at dinner, Steve had told Barb about his much-loved father, and his tragic loss. He'd wondered afterward if he'd maybe talked up the size of their business a little too much, but he wanted to impress her with his wealth, and let her know he could afford to spend a little on her while they shared each other's company aboard. Barb had been tremendously supportive. She was a wonderful listener. And that body? She didn't even know how good-looking she was, and she was also still reeling from ending an un-happy relationship. Perfect. Ripe for the picking.

Of course Steve knew there couldn't be anything long-term between them because she was from the west coast and he from the east, but he had decided to put some effort into overcoming her defences, and make the most of his opportunities. He suggested a Piña Colada in his suite away from the heat of the late afternoon, and where they could enjoy the view of the sunset from his private deck. If he got her started on the cocktails early enough, he reckoned this would be the night she'd respond to his advances.

The news of Steve's disappearance from a cruise ship somewhere off the coast of Colombia sent shockwaves around the synagogue he'd attended his entire life. Both men in one family gone in less than three months? It was a great loss to the community. It was some time before the lawyers finally got around to opening the safe built into the floor of the workshop Steve had inherited from his father, and confusion reigned when it was found to be empty. Everyone in the small diamond-cutting community was aware the gems his father had owned at the time of his death had never been sold on or liquidated, and they certainly weren't in the safety deposit box the company had used. Diligent searches throughout the banking community failed to uncover the stones in any of their storage facilities. They had disappeared.

For weeks rumours circulated about the value of the stock stolen from the workshop, and the cops finally released a figure of six million dollars to the press. It was generally agreed Steve would have been sensible to remove the diamonds to the safety of a bank's vault before he'd headed off on his trip, but it was also widely acknowledged he'd probably been too grief-stricken to have been thinking rationally at the time. Quiet conversations among groups of saddened men after prayer meetings suggested he'd also probably been lulled into a false sense of security by knowing his father had invested not only in a building that was accessible through just one door, which the thief had somehow managed to open and relock, but also in the world's least-crackable safe. Heads nodded knowingly as all agreed that if only Steve had reinstated the broken security cameras smashed at the time of his father's murder, the cops might have had more than they did to go on—which was nothing.

Barb, aka Bree, aka Bella, reckoned the diamonds she'd liberated from Steve's safe could comfortably finance her for the next few years or so, cruises included, even though she'd had to shift them for a fraction of their real worth. Half a dozen voyages in the past eighteen months had taught her you couldn't possibly guess whom you'd meet aboard those sumptuous floating palaces, or what they might tell you over dinner. She'd also learned a well-kept figure, a cleverly adopted persona, and a readiness to listen could produce great opportunities for the right sort of woman.

Before meeting Steve she'd relied on a few variations upon a couple of themes. She'd selected her mark, then justified her presence on the ship by claiming to have won the trip as a prize in a charity lottery that she'd been unable to exchange for cash—something she'd have preferred. Eventually she'd let the man in question draw out of her a heart-wrenching tale about a desperately sick mother who needed cash to pay for life-saving surgery (that one was usually good for up to twenty grand) or the one about the addicted, violent man who was stalking and threatening her so she had to disappear, leaving everything behind. A couple of times she'd been able to drag almost twenty-five grand out of men with that one, and once she'd even scored a pick-up truck.

In any case, as she inevitably ended up rolling around with them in their cabins letting them do whatever they wanted to her—which was usually very little, and almost always pathetically predictable—she told herself it was better than turning tricks in parked cars or cheap motels, and the payout was not only a great deal more rewarding, but all her own; no pimp to share it with, no cops to pay off to allow her to stay on the streets.

With Steve, it had been different. She'd met him at the dinner table the first night out and right away she'd spotted he was too cheap to part with any cash, however good her story might be. But when he'd boasted to her about what he and his late father had done for a living, she'd known he was the best mark to ever fall into her highly accommodating lap. All she had to do was keep him talking until he gave her what she wanted. And he had, of course. It made her laugh that his father had used his only son's birthdate as the combination to the safe where he kept all their gems, and she'd waited patiently for Steve to invite her to his accommodations. They always did. Once there, she'd easily talked him into showing her his passport photo, which had allowed her to see his birthdate, and she'd even managed to lift his keys without him being any the wiser. Then she'd been ready to put the rest of her plan into action. At least, that was what she'd hoped. Sadly, things hadn't gone exactly as she'd envisaged.

As she sat in her condo overlooking San Diego Harbor painting her nails, she tried to work out what it had been about Steve that had revolted her. She'd done so much with, and for, so very many men over the years that it unsettled her to realize she couldn't work out why this particular one—an otherwise unassuming man with a paunch and bad breath—had made her skin crawl when he merely brushed against her. She'd seen pretty much every emotion from lust, to shame, to anger and even disgust in the eyes of men, but in Steve's all she'd seen was a blankness that filled her soul—assuming she still had one, of course—with dread. It had been like looking into the eyes of a shark; nothing there at all. Of all the men she'd known, he was the only one who'd freaked her out a little. And she didn't know why.

Maybe that was why she'd pushed him. She certainly hadn't planned it, and it hadn't even been much of a push. He'd been cavorting about on the oh-so private deck leading from his suite at the aft of the ship, plying her with cocktails while he showed off his woeful dance moves, then he'd lunged for her. She'd given him no more than a little shove. He'd half-pirouetted before his tall, heavy frame had tipped over the rail that was only hip-high to him, disappearing into the churning sea below. He'd fallen silently, and it had been dark. There wasn't even a splash. She'd left his suite without anyone knowing she'd been there, and had been gratified it had taken almost two days for anyone to realize he wasn't on the ship any longer. Even then they didn't make a fuss about it. Indeed, it made her wonder how often people simply vanished from cruise ships without it being widely reported.

Despite this one little hitch, Barb had pressed on with her over-all scheme: she'd headed east on the first possible flight, used Steve's keys and then the combination to get what she wanted, and hadn't been spotted by a soul. Besides, who would notice a short, rotund, bald guy wearing a hoodie and jeans in that sort of area? She'd sliced the latex bald-cap into tiny pieces, dropping bits into garbage cans all around the museum district the next day, and she'd dropped off the clothes she'd worn at a charity shop. She was out of the city seventy-two hours later with a purse full of tickets to local attractions in case anyone in a uniform asked why she'd made such a long trip for such a short time. She'd mixed the gems in with a collection of glass beads she'd bought at one of those stores so popular with folks who liked to make their own jewelry, and she'd even picked up a couple of magazines about arts and crafts to support her tale about being a fanatical fabricator of all things glitzy if anyone questioned her. They didn't.

Barb flicked through the glossy brochure she'd brought home from the ship. Where next she wondered? Transatlantic? Or the Panama Canal again? Always rich pickings there—men ticking off a bucket list item and more interested in engineering than women.

Sad little men realizing time was running out. Easy marks. It wasn't as though she needed the money, but she truly enjoyed the travel. And the inventing of a new backstory. But she told herself she didn't want to become mixed up in more than one disappearance at sea—that was the sort of thing it was easy to spot and cops, of whatever type, might be dumb, grasping, and untrustworthy, but they usually caught on to a pattern, as they'd told her in so much pillow talk over the decades. No, it was back to the old stories for Barb; she'd gotten away with it once, but twice? That would be pushing it.

Ha! *Pushing it!* She laughed at her own little joke as she picked up the phone to call the cruise line.

Power Play
By J. A. Menzies

While J. A. Menzies would hate to stumble on a real body under any circumstances, she has a thing about noticing the "perfect" locations for finding mythical bodies. In order not to waste this fascinating (and hopefully, unusual) skill, she decided to write mysteries. Her stories, including the Paul Manziuk & Jacquie Ryan Mysteries, are set in Canada and feature intriguing settings, compelling characters, and intricate, dynamic plots. Reviewers, including Publishers Weekly, *have compared her novels to the best of Agatha Christie and Georgette Heyer.* Library Journal *called her a "master of plotting." J. A. Menzies lives in Markham, Ontario, and is a member of Sisters in Crime, Crime Writers of Canada, The Word Guild, and The Writers Union of Canada.*

For a short time last winter, I thought I'd found a little bit of heaven right here in Toronto. Then came the Monday morning when our general manager traded two first-round draft picks and backup goalie Page Bryant, one of my best friends in the entire world, for much-sought-after forward Denny Callaghan and a young goalie from Calgary. Bubble popped.

When I arrived at the rink that morning, Coach McGee told me Denny would take my spot on the first line, and I'd centre the second line. I'd known that from the minute I heard about the trade so, while it hurt, it wasn't unexpected. And since I was twenty-eight, not eighteen, I was used to the fact that hockey is a business. Trades happen. So do moves up and down the line-up. And although I'd been playing well and the team was winning, we needed a boost to get us into contention for the Stanley Cup. So, if the only thing Denny's arrival had affected was my job as a hockey player, I could have lived with it. But there was more to come.

What can I say about Tami Stafford that hasn't been said many times before about Cleopatra, Helen of Troy, Mona Lisa and a lot of other beautiful women? I met her at a charity event for a women's shelter. She was one of the event organizers. While I was signing "Blessings, Miles Borden," a couple of hundred times, I was thinking about skin the colour of a pecan, silky black curls, and dark eyes that made me want to leap tall buildings. Yeah, I had it bad.

At the end of the evening, Tami thanked me for coming. If anyone from the press had been watching, the headline would have read, "Tongue-tied hockey player ensnared by local beauty."

And ensnared I was. From that moment, I began to think about settling down. Wife, kids, house in the suburbs, dog, bikes in the driveway... the whole nine yards.

The day the trade for Denny came down, I was actually getting up my nerve to propose to her. But with all the hoopla, extra practice, and so forth, I didn't see or speak with Tami that day. Just a quick text to say I wouldn't be able to make it for our dinner date.

The next day we had a home game, and Tami was in her regular seat with the other players' wives and girlfriends. I waved, but that's about it.

Two days later, with the ring burning a hole in my pocket, I arrived at a welcome party for Denny and found Tami, her arm linked with his, laughing as if he'd just told the funniest joke in the world.

In case you haven't seen Denny Callaghan, we're talking six-foot-three, 220-pound Adonis with sculpted muscles, longish blond hair, and piercing green eyes. Plus he came with a well-deserved reputation as a first-class lady killer.

When I saw Denny with Tami that first time, the last of the air in my little happy bubble just kind of gurgled away. I forgot all about the diamond ring in my pocket.

Sure, when Tami saw me, she came over and talked to me a bit, but I'd have had to be blind not to see she was another moth caught in Denny's bright flame.

The ensuing weeks just made it more obvious. Denny had won a different kind of game without even trying. Which made me a three-time loser: my best friend, my position on the first line and my girl.

All this to explain why, when they found Denny's body, two cops came for me. One of them was an older guy with an East Indian look. He was dressed in dark jeans, a black turtleneck and a parka. The other was a petite redhead in a parka, a skirt and knee-high boots. She didn't look old enough to be out of high school.

The guy said they were with the Homicide Squad, and the redhead asked if it was true I had a grudge against Denny.

I've read thousands of crime novels and watched even more TV crime shows, so I said I wasn't opening my mouth unless my lawyer was present.

The cops acted as if my saying that meant I was guilty, but I shut my eyes so they couldn't see the fear lurking in my baby blues.

Sitting on a hard chair in a tiny room, waiting for my lawyer, I tried to process it all. Denny was dead. And from the little I'd been told, it seemed he'd been beaten to death with a hockey stick. Unreal!

My lawyer showed up eventually, and with him there to advise me when to shut up, I told the cops half a dozen times that I knew nothing about Denny's death because I hadn't had anything to do with it. Unfortunately, I had no alibi. During the time he was killed, I was in my condo, by myself, sleeping.

Somebody told the cops that Denny had stolen my girl. I countered that Tami wasn't "my" girl; she was her own girl, and since no commitment had ever been made, she was free to do what she chose.

The cops finally told me I could go. But not before the redhead asked me for my autograph. For her nephew.

On the sidewalk outside the police station, my lawyer told me the cops hadn't charged me because they only had circumstantial evidence. The way he said it gave me chills. Like he was congratulating me on covering my tracks. I said, "How could they have concrete evidence when I didn't do it?" and he looked away.

When I got home, I called my buddy and former left winger, Nate Cannon.

"You heard?" I asked.

"I heard the cops arrested you for it," he said.

"Not yet." I sighed. "Wish I knew what's going to happen now."

"The cops will keep hanging around until they find somebody to arrest."

"You have any idea who did it?"

"It wasn't you?"

I hung up.

After kicking a pillow around the living room, I sat down. Clearly, I needed to figure out who killed Denny Callaghan before the police decided circumstantial evidence was enough. Not only did *they* think I'd done it, but so did my lawyer and apparently my teammates. Which left my parents and Tami.

I called Mom and Dad at their Florida winter home, but got no answer. Likely in the swimming pool or on the golf course. I'd made sure they both had cellphones, but I hadn't managed to convince them to carry them at all times. I left messages.

That left Tami. Never one to fail to follow through when I'd decided on a course of action, I called her. "Hi," I said casually.

"Oh, Miles!" There was a sob in her voice. "Isn't it terrible?"

"Yeah," I said. "Terrible."

"He was so young and so full of life. I can't believe anybody would do that to him. Why, Miles? Why would anybody be so cruel?"

"I don't know."

Tami was still talking. "They're saying you did it, Miles. But I don't believe that."

"I'd hope not."

"You didn't, did you?"

"Not you, too?" I hung up.

I made myself a cup of strong coffee. If I wanted to stay out of jail, I'd need to figure out who really killed him. Or at least find a way to prove it wasn't me. But how?

I realized I also needed to know what was happening with our game tomorrow. I phoned Coach McGee.

"Miles?" he said. "Where are you?"

"Where should I be?"

"I heard—well, the cops—"

"Yeah, they took me in. But since I didn't do it, they let me leave." Okay, a bit of a white lie. They let me leave because, as my lawyer so kindly pointed out, all they had was circumstantial evidence. "So what's happening with the lines tomorrow?"

There was about a minute of silence. Then Coach said, "I figured you did it for the girl, not to get back on the first line."

My third time hanging up on someone I'd phoned.

I paced around my living room. Who else had a motive? It had to be someone who could hold a stick up in front of Denny without causing him to be suspicious, or someone he'd turn his back on without a second's thought.

Who, other than me, didn't like Denny? No, scratch that. I didn't *not* like Denny. I mean, I didn't know him well enough to dislike him. I even felt kind of sorry he was dead. Sure, I wasn't crazy about his taking my spot on the first line, but not only did he have nothing to do with the trade, he was a better player than me, and he could've helped us win games. The truth was, whoever killed Denny likely ended any chance we had of making the playoffs. And that sucked.

Yeah, I wasn't happy about the fact that the girl I was about to propose to had latched onto him the minute he'd arrived, but it's not as if she was the only girl in the world. And I hadn't actually proposed to her yet, so who knows? She might still have said yes.

Really, when you thought about it, I had no motive for killing him.

Who benefited from Denny's death?

In books, they look for things like money, power, and love. So, who would get his money?

I had no idea about his personal life. Resorting to Google, I found out he and his wife had divorced a year ago. No kids. Which meant that, unless his will said differently, his parents or some other family member would probably get his money.

I couldn't image the nice couple I saw in the pictures killing their son for his money. Nor his other family members. They looked so... so normal.

And it's not as if Denny was a jerk, either. He'd bought his parents a new house. He'd bought his older brother a top of the line SUV. His younger sister got a Prius. I was ready to scratch them off.

I'd need to follow up on the wife, just in case. Maybe she still got his money when he died. Or maybe the divorce wasn't enough because she really, really hated him.

I needed to find out why his wife divorced him.

Wait a minute. My buddy Page Bryant had just been traded to Calgary. Could he—would he—help me get in touch with her? Or would he, like everyone else, assume I was guilty?

I could but try.

I sent him a text. Five minutes, later, my phone rang.

"Miles?" Page's voice. I could picture him, his black eyes the size of Frisbee discs in his dark brown face. "I heard what happened. You okay?"

"So far."

"Who do they think did it?"

"Me."

"No way!"

Finally, someone who thought I wasn't a killer.

"No, but I don't have an alibi. As in I was home alone."

"Bummer. So who did it for reals?"

"No idea. That's why I'm calling you. Can you ask around and see if anyone on your team has a clue? Like did he have any enemies? Somebody with a motive? Like a teammate, or his ex-wife? Why did Calgary trade him? Why the divorce? All that stuff."

"Yeah, okay." Page's voice sounded distant. "I've got a few ideas." He took a deep breath. "Not sure how easy it will be to find out more, but I'll ask around a bit."

"Great! I can't do much about the Calgary links from here."

"Miles, how well did you get to know him since the trade?"

"Not well at all. I mean, I saw him at practices and games but we never hung out. But because he took my place on the first line, everyone seems to think that gave me a motive. And, well, Tami was kind of gaga about him, so that doesn't help."

"Okay, one thing I *can* tell you. He divorced his wife. Not the other way around."

"Interesting."

"Also, from what I've heard, women fell for him. Hard."

"So was he cheating on his wife?"

"This is only hearsay so it might not be worth much, but apparently he has—had—a great line, and he didn't seem to be able to keep himself from using it. Even after he was married. Or even if the woman was married."

"So there might have been a few people with motives?"

"Yeah, here in Calgary," Page said. "But he was killed in Toronto."

"Right."

"Unless you can find somebody who flew to Toronto recently."

I thought for a minute. "Can you get me a few names?"

"I'll see what I can do."

"Thanks."

"Hang in there, buddy."

While talking to Page, I'd decided this had to be a long-term thing. Denny had only been in Toronto for three weeks. Too little time to make someone mad enough to kill him. It was possible that somebody who lived in Toronto had been stewing about something Denny had done a long time ago, and finally saw the chance to get even. But who? And how could I get more information?

What were the chances the cute redheaded cop who'd asked for my autograph would talk to me? When she'd first met me at police headquarters, she'd given me a card. What had I done with it? Not in my wallet.

I have a bad habit of stuffing things like receipts and other stuff in the back left pocket of my jeans. Sure enough, it was there. Crumpled, but there.

The card read "Detective Constable Jennifer Lindsay," and there was an email address and a phone number.

I texted her. *Would you and your nephew like to have supper with me?*

Ten minutes later, she responded. *My nephew can't make it, but*

I can.

I suggested we meet at a restaurant I frequent. It's a pretty nondescript place with great food where a lot of Toronto's professional athletes hang out with their friends. And no, I won't mention the name. By "friends" I don't mean groupies, although of course some athletes have trouble telling them apart. Not only the young ones.

I arrived a few minutes early and was standing out front when Detective Constable Jennifer Lindsay arrived. "What do I call you?" I asked. "Detective? Constable? Both? Neither?"

She smiled. "Why not Jennifer?"

"Is that what your friends call you?"

"They call me Jen."

I grinned. "Maybe we'll get there yet. After I've met your nephew."

She blushed.

"There is no nephew, right?"

"There is, but he's eighteen months old. I don't think he's seen you play yet."

I realized that from this exchange she may have formed the impression that I was a ladies' man. Not so. Tami was the first woman I'd been serious about. Partly because my parents raised me to treat women right, and partly because I've always been sensitive about the whole "hockey players get girls" thing. That wasn't my scene. And yeah, I get ribbed about it a lot. Which is why I tend to hang out with the guys who are happily married. So it was very unusual for me to banter with a woman I barely knew, especially a homicide detective. But banter I did.

When I'd made the reservation, I asked for a table for two in a back corner, and that's what we got. No need to worry about people overhearing us easily.

I told her what was good, and we ordered. Then I said, "So you're a hockey fan?"

"Yes. Good hockey, not the fighting or blindside hits."

I nodded. *Me, too.*

"You play?" She seemed too tiny, but you never know.

"Goalie."

"Really?"

"Yes. But my real game is soccer."

"You fast?"

"Very."

I nodded. She was wearing a sweater that kind of clung, and I could see the muscles on her arms.

"So," she said, "let's cut to the chase. Tony, my partner, likes you for Denny Callaghan's murder, but he doesn't know you. I do. At least, I've watched you play. Whoever killed Denny slammed him with a hockey stick at least eight times. That means a great deal of anger was involved. I don't see you for it because I don't see you getting in a rage."

"Thank you. You win the accuracy prize."

"So who did it?" she asked.

"I thought solving that little problem was your job."

"We need someone to help us understand the dynamics."

"You asking if I think someone on the team killed him?"

"Is it possible?"

"Possible, I suppose. Not likely though." Before she could ask another question, I leaned forward. "So, how about you tell me something? He really died from being hit with a hockey stick?"

"Yes."

"People get hit with hockey sticks all the time and don't die."

"It *has* happened. Maybe they were lucky to hit the area of the brain they did. Or unlucky, if you look at it from his perspective."

"Did he have defensive wounds?"

"No."

"So he stood there while they hit him?"

"We think he was taken by surprise from the left side. He fell forward and was then hit again and again. Now you tell me, did he talk about his life outside of hockey?"

"Not to me."

"You weren't friendly?"

"I didn't see him outside of the rink."

She looked around the room. "Did he come here?"

I shook my head. "He preferred rowdier spots."

"For instance?"

"A high class strip joint."

"You don't go there?"

"My mother would kill me."

"How old are you again?"

"Twenty-eight."

"And you still worry about what your mother would like?"

"Well, if she didn't kill me, my dad would."

Detective Jennifer burst out laughing.

When she finally stopped, I said, "Look, I'm from a small town and I wasn't raised to treat women like they were commodities. I wouldn't respect myself if I went to places like that."

"Why aren't you married?"

"Up until today, I hadn't met the right person." With a start, I realized that was true. If I'd really been in love with Tami, I wouldn't have shrugged it off when she latched onto Denny.

"Well, good luck with that," she said.

There was a lump in my throat as I asked, casually as possible, "You married?"

She shook her head. "Up until today, I hadn't met the right person yet, either."

I held back a grin.

"Can you give me the names of places he frequented? People he hung out with?"

I did my best, and she wrote it down.

"Okay, Tami Stafford. You were dating her?"

"Yes. But it wasn't serious."

"I heard it was."

"I thought it was. But when she started to hang with him, I lost interest."

"So you don't want her back?"

I said, "No chance," and realized my words were one hundred per cent accurate.

We had dessert and then she left. I thought I knew where she was going, and part of me wanted to tag along, but I knew I'd only cramp her style. She was a police detective. Tiny as she might be, I had no doubt she could look after herself. Plus her partner Tony, who'd been sitting alone at a table across the room, would have her back.

Not long after I got back to my condo, Page phoned. He'd talked to some of Denny's former teammates. No one he'd spoken with could think of any reason why someone would want to kill Denny. They hadn't all loved him, but they all thought he was a great hockey player, and they said that what he did away from the rink was his own business.

Page had Linette Callaghan's phone number, but since someone had given it to him, he had no idea if she'd talk to me. He also had names of two of the women Denny had allegedly had affairs with.

After we hung up, I phoned Linette. She didn't say much. Just that they had divorced more than a year ago and she'd moved on. I asked if it was true he'd divorced her, and she said that he was a first-class jerk. She added that she could prove she wasn't in

Toronto on the day Denny was killed.

I asked her about other women and she said that while she knew there were some, she didn't know their names.

I called the other two women, but one of them yelled at me and the other one said she wasn't talking to anyone. So much for my interrogation skills.

The next morning, Detective Jennifer texted me. *Breakfast?*

We met at a place a few blocks from my condo.

"What's up?" I asked after we'd ordered crêpes.

"I've got a question or two."

"So do I. What about the crime scene? Don't you have some evidence?"

She gave me a funny look. "I said *I* have a few questions."

"I just—you know, wondered if you have any clues."

"I get it. You watch the forensics shows. Okay, the only fingerprints on the hockey stick are his. Whoever hit him with it wore gloves. There are a few unknown prints on the door and the walls and so forth, but they're smudged or overlaid with Denny's, so they could easily belong to a maid or a former guest of the hotel. The door knobs had been wiped clean."

"So you have nothing concrete to link anyone to the murder?"

"Your turn. Why did you give Tami Stafford a black eye?"

I'd been sitting easy, but now I jerked to attention. "What are you talking about?"

"She has a black eye. She says you did it."

"Tami says I hit her?"

"Yes."

"I don't believe it."

"Ask her."

"I never."

"So you say."

I got up and walked away. Then I went back. "Tell your partner he can have my breakfast. I assume he's here."

She looked past me for a second, then brought her eyes up to meet mine. "Yes, he is."

"What's this all about?"

"I told you. Tony thinks you did it: I don't."

"So have you been testing me or trying to get information from me, or what?"

"Or what."

"Well, have a good one."

I left the restaurant. My head was spinning. I hadn't even been alone with Tami for over two weeks. I could only think of one reason for her to lie. I grabbed a cab.

Tami opened her door a crack. "Miles, what do you want?"

"Someone just asked me if I'd given you a black eye."

"So?"

"I came over to see it."

"Go away."

She started to shut the door, but my foot, in its stout black winter boot, was wedged in it.

"It was Denny, wasn't it?"

"I walked into a door. They didn't believe me, so I said my boyfriend hit me."

"And you said I was your boyfriend?"

"They assumed it. Somebody else must have told them. Nobody hit me."

I let her shut the door.

Even if Denny'd hit Tami, it didn't mean she'd killed him. But the fact that she'd lied about it opened up a world of possibilities.

Still fuming, I texted Detective Jennifer: *Can you find out where Linette Callaghan was the day Denny was killed?*

She got back to me right away: *Calgary.*

You're sure?

According to the interviews by the Calgary police, she was at her parents' home. They verify that. No sign of her buying an airline ticket.

I've got news for you. Not all hockey players' wives buy tickets. Ever heard of charters?

On it.

We had a home game that night. Since I hadn't been arrested yet, Coach McGee and the rest of the brain trust decided it would be okay for me to centre the first line. We actually won. I scored a goal and assisted on two others. Being angry was working for me.

The next day, Detectives Jennifer and Tony dropped by my condo to tell me they had proof that Linette and seven other women had come to Toronto in a chartered airplane. It had been hired by the wife of one of the hockey players on the Calgary team. The eight women had split the cost.

So Linette's family had lied. She hadn't been at their house on the day Denny died. Hadn't been in Calgary at all.

Apparently, Linette had left Denny more than a year ago and gone to a women's shelter in Calgary. Which likely explained why Denny had divorced her.

Later, Linette began working as a volunteer for the shelter.

She met Tami at a conference for people who worked with women's shelters. Phone records showed they'd been in touch for nearly six months, and that there had been a flurry of calls since the trade was announced.

The police theory was that every one of the women involved had a reason to hate Denny, and they'd come up with a plan to get even.

I wore a wire when I knocked on Tami's door that evening.

She looked surprised to see me. "What do you want?"

"You dumped me for Denny. Now that he's gone, I thought we should talk."

"I don't think—" She looked down. "You'd better come in."

Once we were seated in the living room with cups of coffee, she said, "I don't really know what to say. I—I—like you a lot, Miles. But..."

"But you're not sure I should date a murderess?"

She turned white. "I'm not—"

"Don't bother lying. I figured it out. Starting with the black eye."

"Denny didn't give me a black eye. I was trying to get away from him and I ran into the bathroom door. Just like I said."

"Was that when you killed him?"

"I didn't kill him. But if I had, it would have been justified."

"How's that?"

"Denny was a narcissist. Everything was about him. Linette told me that he was proud of his reputation for being an elite player who never got penalties. But that was partly because he didn't want to get hurt, and partly because he scored a lot of his goals on power plays.

"Off the ice, he got his kicks from going after women who were weaker than him. He'd turn on the charm, shower them with gifts, and make them think he was in love with them, and then he'd start being verbally abusive in between the compliments and the gifts. Then physically abusive. But not punches or kicks. He did things that wouldn't leave bruises and that weren't obvious abuse. Like with a hockey stick. He'd use it to contain them in a corner; to choke them; to hit things at them. Demeaning, and hurtful, but not typical abuse."

"So you and Linette came up with a plan to get even with him."

"You know about Linette?"

"Yes."

She began to cry. "You don't understand. He was evil."

"So why not call the police?"

"Do you know what happens to women who accuse men of abuse? They get abused all over again for everyone to see. It's even worse when the guy is someone like Denny. A so-called hero, right? Somebody little kids look up to."

"How did you do it?"

"He invited me to his hotel suite, so I agreed. When he went into the kitchen to get ice, I propped the outside door an inch open before following him. I kept him busy while the other women came in and hid in the bedroom. Then I got him to follow me to the bedroom, and as he entered, they attacked."

"Why the hockey stick?"

"Poetic justice."

"Had he hurt you?"

She looked down. "Not physically, but verbally."

"So each of you hit him at least once?"

"Yes. But we didn't mean to kill him. Just make him think twice next time he approached a woman."

"You may not have meant to kill him, but you did. And no one has the right to take the life of another person—no matter how much of a monster he might be."

Tami's eyes flashed. "If we didn't have that right, who did? No one would have believed us. If we'd done nothing, he'd just keep hurting more and more women. Who else would have stopped him?"

I left her standing there looking like an avenging angel.

A bunch of cops were waiting outside.

I went to Jennifer. "You're going to have to charge a lot of people: Linette, her family, Tami, and seven other women, some of whom have young kids."

"Yes. It's going to be big news."

The following day, Detectives Jennifer and Tony met me for lunch at my favourite restaurant.

"What's going to happen?" I asked.

Tony answered. "The women are claiming self-defence. They say one woman died from suicide because of his abuse, and insist there could, or would, be more. They also say his violence was escalating."

"Any chance they'll win?"

"I doubt it," Jennifer said. "But they're going to get a lot of press. Maybe it'll do some good. Change the way women who report abuse are treated. Who knows?"

"I have a fair bit of money," I said. "Who's the best lawyer around?"

"I can give you a few names."

"Jen, I've got to get going," Tony said. He looked at me. "No hard feelings?"

"None."

"Okay, then."

When he'd gone, I looked over at Jen. "So tell me, what's it like to date a cop?"

"About as challenging as it is to date a professional hockey player."

"I'm up for it if you are."

She gave me a little smile. "You're on."

The Lake Effect
By Andre Ramshaw

Andre is a copy editor by trade, working for the Postmedia chain. Before that he was for many years a reporter, covering news, sports and features for newspapers in Canada, Britain and Australia. As well, he has been an auxiliary police constable for the past ten years in Toronto and Hamilton, worked as a special constable in the U.K. and trained as a recruit constable with the Calgary Police Service. For many years he worked as a private investigator in his home province of B.C., conducting surveillance operations, interviewing witnesses and testifying in court. He continues to write non-fiction, contributing travel features and columns, but in the past two years has been trying his hand at fiction. He has written several short stories but his two in this anthology are his first to be published.

Fred Fluellen wasn't sure what tipped him over the edge. It could have been killing the neighbour's dog while driving drunk. Or watching from behind the curtains as children wailed in the street and old Mrs. Sorensen from No. 47 pumped her cane in his direction like an arthritic piston. Or seeing the bawling children claw the air as the dog's legs hung lifeless from their daddy's arms. Or staggering to the bathroom and vomiting until it hurt to breathe.

Fluellen thought of all this as he thumbed another .40 calibre round into the magazine and loaded the gun. He racked the slide and lifted the gun to his right temple, its heft catching him by surprise. It had felt so much lighter in training, just two weeks ago. A sheen of sweat made the gun feel like an oiled barbell in his hands. He tried to steady his breathing but the nervous tremors rattling his body intensified with each breath. His gun hand danced. It was no use. He lowered the pistol onto a newspaper and pushed back his chair, his arms hanging limply. The perspiration from the gun transferred to the newsprint in a slow bleed. He studied it as if it were the most fascinating thing in the world.

He cast his eyes around the one-room cabin. It was built in the 1960s, two hours north of Toronto, on a lake in the Muskokas that hadn't yet been turned into a year-round wellness retreat for 60-hour-week hedge-fund stress cases in fleets of X5 Beemers. It featured split-log construction, single-pane windows, a pot-bellied wood stove and an outhouse. In the southeast corner was a kitchenette partly cordoned off by a Japanese folding screen, behind which a hotplate, mini-fridge, a few pots and pans and a skillet were arrayed in a state of benign neglect. Along the remaining walls were haphazardly stacked piles of paperbacks, fishing gear, boxes of manuscripts, correspondence, yellowed newspapers and a milk crate strained to capacity with photo albums. All of these looked in an equal state of neglect. At the centre of the room, atop a Persian carpet that had seen too many cats' claws, rested a dimpled oak desk not much bigger than a drinks trolley upon which sat the pistol and paper, a half-dozen pens and pencils, and a yellow legal pad. To the right of the desk stood a low side table that supported a portable typewriter and a six-inch stack of foolscap. These completed the general air of indifference.

Fluellen leaned back in the cushioned banker's chair, one of the few unneglected items in his inventory, and gazed distractedly out the cabin's expansive front window. The cabin, in all its humble disarray, had been passed down through generations of his family and he had resolutely avoided changing or modernizing it beyond the basics. The girlfriends that he'd maintained had consistently agitated for change—"just think what it could be worth!"—but had slowly given up and drifted away when it became clear he was no more a committed handyman than he was committed to the concept of settling down.

He eased the chair forward again and dropped his eyes to the gun. He reached for it but jerked back at the sound of tires on gravel; the sound carried to him as clearly as a doorbell. His driveway was at the end of a cul-de-sac, with signs warning of NO TURNAROUND and NO ACCESS TO LAKE. Bear sightings were more common than cars. He slipped out from behind the desk in time to see a middle-aged man in a yellow and red uniform ambling toward the front door with a large padded envelope under his right arm. Fluellen scurried back to the desk, folded a newspaper over the gun and yanked open the door as his visitor was mid-knock.

"Oh! I'm sorry, sir. I'm with DHL Courier, looking for a 1168— No. 7 Sideroad. Says here it's at the end of the road."

Fluellen grinned. "Common mistake. This is No. 6 Sideroad. Sign blew down years ago. No. 7 is the next one down, about half a mile along Highway 11."

The courier was a man of Fluellen's age, mid-forties, with a kindly face and eyes and a slouch that suggested he was not one to be rushed. "Nice little spot you've got here," he said.

"It has its charms."

"A man can put the world behind him out here," he said, nodding appreciatively.

"Permanently in my case."

"Sorry?"

Fluellen forced a mirthless laugh. "Just saying, I'm in no rush to go back to the city."

The courier chuckled. "I hear you, my man, I hear you."

Fluellen flicked his eyes toward the gun, resisting an urge to unload his burden on this stranger.

"Are you all right, mate?"

"I'm fine, thanks—just drifting. Are you okay with the directions from here? I'm pretty sure that address you're looking for is the last place on the street, much like mine."

The courier glanced at his clipboard. "Yeah, I got it. Thanks a lot."

He walked back to his van, but turned abruptly as he reached the driver's door. "By the way, did you hear about the convict that broke out of Gravenhurst Medium yesterday? Cops are asking everyone in cottage country to keep an eye out."

Fluellen frowned. "No, I had no idea. I've got limited cellphone coverage in this spot, and I've only got an old transistor radio for company. Packed away somewhere in here."

"I wouldn't worry about it," the DHL man said with a shrug. "He's probably headed for Toronto."

Vaguely unsettled by the news, Fluellen sidled back to his desk. He picked up the gun, now dry, and held it in his lap. He'd got it about ear level when he was again interrupted by a visitor, this one tap-tapping on the window.

The head peering through the glass was that of a small boy, perhaps nine or ten years old, with surfer-dude blond hair combed back. He stumbled backwards, clattering onto the rotting slats of the verandah as he caught the older man's eye. A strangled yelp followed. Fluellen rolled the gun in the newspaper and was out the front door before the boy had finished dusting himself off.

Fluellen stifled a grin. "You okay?"

The boy looked askance at his ripped shorts. "Yes, sir."

"What can I do for you?"

"I was wondering if you want a boy to do some yard work for you. Just ten bucks an hour. I live just over there." He pointed to the pink stucco palaces along the far shore, beyond the row of Scots pines that shielded the Fluellen bolt hole from what surely would become its eventual fate.

"You're a long way from home, aren't you?"

"I come down here all the time. Me and my friend Ethan found an old canoe over by the Point." He hooked a thumb over his shoulder. "We see bears down here all the time. And foxes. Ethan even saw a wolf."

Fluellen felt a stab of shame. He thought of the dying dog and the neighbour's distraught children. How many near misses had there been? How long before he sat in a jail cell fashioning a noose out of smuggled socks?

"You okay, mister? You look sort of pale."

Fluellen drew in a lungful of lake air. "Just gettin' old. You had me scared with that talk of bears and wolves."

The boy examined his shoes with a bashful shrug.

Fluellen threw out his hand. "My name's Fred. What's yours?"

"Darien."

"Darien, eh? Nice to meet you. Listen, I don't have any yard work that needs doing right now, but why don't you come back in a few days and we'll talk."

In a few days, thought Fluellen, the only work around here would be for the coroner.

Darien skipped off the steps and bounded to the shores of Lake Rubicon with a jaunty wave. He darted through a stand of pines and disappeared.

Fluellen turned with a sigh, took his seat at the table and hoisted the pistol.

The next time it was the back door. Heavy shuffling sounds on the porch. Then the groaning of old wood. A bear? Fluellen braced himself against the rear wall, gun in hand, listening intently. For a moment that seemed an hour, all he could hear was the blood thumping in his ears. No window gave onto the back. No way to see what was out there. More scuffing noises now, closer this time. Fluellen saw the door knob rattle. He tightened his grip on the gun, leaned over and threw open the door with his free hand. A grunting force plowed through and landed on the floor in a cloud of dust and splinters. It leapt to its feet. "Don't shoot!"

The two men studied each other. The intruder was a solid six feet, a good half-head taller than Fluellen, and thickly built around the chest with a beer drinker's paunch that heaved like ocean waves. His hair was close-cropped steel-grey over a lined face that was winter-pale and hid grey eyes that had sunk into shadowy folds. He wore a navy blue work shirt, khaki cargo shorts and hiking boots.

"Hey, man, put the gun away. I'm just looking for something to eat."

Fluellen shoved the gun in his waistband. "You're the guy on the run from Gravenhurst jail."

"What? What are you talking about?"

"Don't bother lying. I'm not calling the cops."

Having been roughly arrested for public intoxication two summers ago, Fluellen was no fan of the Muskoka Regional Police, which attracted burnouts from the Toronto force and semi-retired underachievers with a flair for speed traps.

"You got any food?"

"Have a seat. I'll see what I can dig up."

A few minutes later Fluellen plunked a platter of cold ham, cheese and rolls in front of his uninvited guest, who ate wordlessly from a corner of the desk as wind rattled the window panes with tetchy insistence.

Having devoured the meal, the intruder pushed his chair back, pulled a toothpick from his shirt pocket, let it roll between his lips.

"I ain't on the run from no jail. I don't know anything about this guy from Gravenhurst. That ain't to say I ain't wanted by the law, you understand."

Fluellen returned the gun to the desk but kept it close.

The stranger raised his chin in the direction of the gun. "You thinkin' of offing yourself, Mr. Freddy Fluellen?"

Fluellen jolted, his hand darting for the weapon. "How the hell do you know my name?"

"Whoa! No need for gunplay, Fred. Can I call you Fred? You can call me Nick. For now."

Fluellen moved his hand from the gun but kept his eyes locked on Nick, whose eyes glittered with sadistic excitement.

"I know a lot about you, Fred. I have friends on the wrong side of the law who do me favours once in a while."

"Why? What do you want with me?" Fluellen felt his stomach knot with tension.

"Let's just say we have some unfinished business. See, I'm a bit of a drinker myself, and I've sat with a forty-five in my lap looking for a reason not to put it in my mouth and squeeze the trigger. But I've never killed anyone. At least not yet...."

A bead of sweat threaded down Fluellen's back. He opened his mouth to speak but his jaw quivered uselessly.

A malicious grin spread across Nick's face. He bundled his seat forward with a harsh scraping that pierced through Fluellen like a klaxon. He planted his elbows on the desk and steepled his fingers. Nick spoke quietly, his eyes blazing. "You killed more than a dog, my friend."

Fluellen fought to contain his panic.

Nick read it in his face. "Yeah, you remember," he growled.

"You're crazy." Fluellen's voice was reedy, his hands fluttering. "You've had your fill of food. Now get out of here."

"It's not that easy, Freddy."

Fluellen let the silence build like prison walls. Finally he cracked. "How do you know so much about me?"

"I know you used to be a writer."

Fluellen snorted. "'Used to be' is right."

"How 'bout a drink?" Nick pointed to the unopened bottle of Jack propping up a desk leg.

Fluellen glanced down. His adversary had keen observation skills, which was both frightening and impressive.

"Put that there so it would be out of temptation's way," Fluellen muttered. "But not too far to make a man die of cravings."

The smaller man hauled up the bottle, opened it with shaking hands, filled two tumblers. The men talked and drank, Fluellen unburdening himself with the zeal of a Catholic convert. Priest, DHL man, invading lunatic—who the hell cared at this point? Confession felt good. And maybe the booze would lower Nick's defences, give Fluellen a chance to get rid of him, get back to his own escape plan.

"You and me got a lot in common," Nick said, his cruel eyes flitting between Fluellen and the gun. "I think you and me...."

A frantic pounding jerked both men's heads toward the front door.

"Sir! Sir! It's Ethan—come quick, he's drowning!"

Fluellen opened the door to find a shivering Darien, sopping wet, his face clouded with terror.

"Where is he, Darien? Show me." Fluellen sprinted toward the lake, Nick close behind, trailed by the frantic Darien.

"He's there!" the boy shouted, pointing to a spot about fifty feet offshore where Fluellen could make out the lines of a capsized canoe amid frothing whitecaps.

Nick was already in the water when Fluellen's eyes focused on the thrashing arms of the drowning Ethan. Even in his drink-sodden confusion, Fluellen noticed the tattoo on Nick's neck—crossed pistons and a dagger. A biker's tag. Where had he seen it before?

"You gotta help him. Please!"

Darien's cries pierced the twilight as Fluellen plowed knee-deep into the churning water, Nick now but a few strokes from the boy's flailing arms.

"I've got him!" Nick croaked as he twisted his lanky frame and began stroking backwards to the shore, Ethan limp across his chest.

To Fluellen he spluttered: "Take him—can't hold on...."

Fluellen, now chest deep in the water, looped his arms under Ethan's and drifted with him to the pebbly beach.

Ethan's body lay lifeless as Fluellen fell to his knees, shook his head, and began chest compressions. He couldn't let this boy die.

A cough. Then a retching sound. Fluellen leaned his ear to Ethan's mouth, felt a damp puff on his cheek, saw his chest rise. The kid was alive. And Nick had vanished.

"The boy's going to be just fine thanks to you, sir." The MRP sergeant clasped Fluellen on the shoulder with a friendly squeeze. "I'm sure the detachment will be putting your name forward for a community bravery award."

Fluellen felt sick. It was the mysterious Nick who deserved the praise.

"There's just one thing, though," the sergeant said. "The boy's friend, Darien, seems to think there were two of you who went into the water to rescue Ethan. We can't get much detail out of him. He's still pretty shaken up. Poor kid."

Fluellen decided it was best to leave Nick out of the picture. Chalk it up to the whiskey.

"No, Sergeant, there was no one else around. I generally come up here to get away from people. And I haven't seen anyone except for Darien and Ethan and the DHL courier guy."

"Not to worry. I'm sure Darien is just a little confused, what with the panic and all. Plus it was getting dark and the wind was picking up pretty good at the time. Still, I wouldn't mind a look-see inside the cabin, just to put my mind at rest. After all, this Gravenhurst escapee is still on the loose."

"Of course, Sergeant, follow me."

Fluellen shot straight for the desk, scooped up the plates and glasses and dropped them in the kitchen sink, still filled with soapy water. "Apologies for the mess. Came up here to do some writing, and domestic chores kind of fall by the wayside."

The sergeant waved a hand. "Not at all, sir. You should see my hideaway after a fishing weekend."

He shuffled to the rear of the cabin, Fluellen following nervously. "Use this much?" he said, pointing to the back door.

"Hardly ever. Too overgrown back there."

"Mind if I have a peek?"

"Be my guest."

The MRP sergeant opened the door wide and swept a flashlight beam over the back steps. "These your boot prints?"

"Er, yes," Fluellen replied. "Had to scare off a bear the other night."

"Yep," the sergeant drawled, "they're getting bolder all the time. Had one poking around my pool the other night. Scared the kids near to death."

Fluellen sighed with relief. Clearly Sergeant Mason, as his nametag indicated, was typical of the MRP—never look for complicated crime if you can avoid it.

As Mason continued his poking about, Fluellen raked his eyes across the desk. The gun. Where the hell was the gun?

"Everything all right, sir?"

"Oh, yes, Sergeant. Just, er, wondering what I did with my cellphone. It's my only form of communication. Anyway, I'm sure it'll turn up. Are we all done here?"

"Yes, I think so," Mason said. "I don't see anything out of the ordinary. I'll take your details and we'll put this one down to youthful excitement, eh?"

In the weeks that followed Fluellen became something of a minor celebrity: fêted by the neighbouring town, honoured by the constabulary, written up by the local rag, even invited to hedge-fund parties. Best of all, though, was news from his publisher—his latest novel had been accepted for publication and there was talk of selling the film rights. Thoughts of suicide were banished.

But then there was Nick. Not only had Fluellen whitewashed him from his rescue-redemption narrative, he had refused to confront Nick's final words: "You killed more than a dog."

What did he mean? Killed what? What had he done in one of his blackouts? And where and how does Nick fit in any of it?

Fluellen poured himself a scotch. Just the one. What was the harm? He raised the glass in silent salute to his success, downed the contents in one draught and shuddered with pleasure as the warm liquid got to work. Why stress over Nick? Probably drowned out there in Lake Rubicon. Problem solved. Even if a body turns up, there's no connecting it with him. And the gun? What would that prove? He'd bought it black market, serial numbers shaved off. No, there was really nothing at all to worry about.

And then came the letter. It was delivered by courier, a small white envelope inside a DHL package. No return address, no indication of its origins.

Fluellen tore it open and began to read:

Dear Fred, I'm no writer like you so please excuse any mistakes in this. I read about you being a hero saving that little boy. But we know who really did the saving. Anyhow, I'm writing to you cause we never finished our chat. I came to see you to extract—is that the right word?—some revenge on you for what you done to my old man. You probably don't remember. I guess you was pretty drunk, but you clipped my dad one night in your fancy car. You probably didn't even know it. My dad was pretty lit up at the time too. He fell and cracked his head. I was a wanted man so I stayed in the shadows while the cops and ambulance men came. But I got your licence plate and tucked it away in case it might come in handy. Anyway, losing my old man was no great loss. I was trying to get some finance help from him to get back on my feet but he pretty much blew me off and I was mighty sore when we left the bar that night. Figure I might have pushed him in front of a car if you hadn't saved me from the trouble. I found out next day that my father had passed on and I figure I put all my anger and stuff into tracking you down and making you pay. I figured you was pretty well off cause of that car you was driving and I thought I could make me a nice score by keeping you off the cops radar—in exchange for a little finance help. I got friends in low places (heh heh) and it wasn't no problem getting your address info from your plate. So I staked out your place for days and days, waiting for a good time to make my move. Maybe you seen me—I was there when you smoked that poor little pooch. Then I followed you to your cabin and when I was pretty sure you was alone and didn't have no visitors to speak of I decided to pay you a call. But that kid kind of messed up my plans. I seen you was in pretty bad shape though so I swam away after I seen the kid was safe and laid low for awhile till I could get me some clean clothes and get back to the city. I took your gun, hope you don't mind. Figured I was doing you a favour what with you trying to top yourself and all. I been there. You could probably turn this letter over to the cops and they

42

could track me, but I think we got a bond and I know you won't do that right? Anyway I expect a little 'donation' for my troubles, you being a famous writer again now, and I have put a address down below where you can send it. I know you won't disappoint me old buddy. Imagine if I told the real facts about your being a so-called hero—heh heh! Best regards, Nick.

Fluellen shivered. Then he tore the letter into dozens of tiny pieces and watched them flutter down over the kitchen scraps, like snow falling gently on a crime scene.

He caught his reflection in the kitchen toaster and recoiled at the haggard stranger who stared back at him. He sat at the big desk in the middle of the cabin, tried to work. He pushed thoughts of Nick to the far recesses of his mind. But every time he closed his eyes he saw a pair of crossed pistons and Nick's sadistic face.

The book launch was a typical affair—a big-box store, pretty young publishing PRs flitting about, large table stacked with signed special editions, expectant readers clutching hardcovers and permanent markers, and, in the middle of it all, a slightly uncomfortable author silently praying for closing time.

"How much of the book is based on real events, Mr. Fluellen?" The question was posed by an attractive woman in her forties whose seductive smile eased three hours of writer's cramp in a toothsome flash. "Make it out to Renata," she purred, "with an 'a.'"

Fluellen reached for the book and began scribbling. "Well, Renata, Redemption Lake is certainly inspired by real events in my life, but I dare say all writing is at its heart autobiographical. Wouldn't you agree?"

"Yes, I've heard that," she replied, "but the Nasty Nick character—he just seems so, well, real. I do hope you will feature him in future books. He's... how shall I put it? Deliciously dangerous."

She turned on her heels and threw Fluellen an over-the-shoulder grin that would have warmed all the cats in Cheshire.

He squirmed in his seat and surveyed the remaining queue of signature-seekers. From the corner of his eye, he noticed a man who looked vaguely familiar.

"Last call for book signings, ladies and gentlemen. Line up here, please."

One of the PRs whispered into Fluellen's ear that he might want to scribble more and chat less if they were ever going to clear the backlog of book-lovers.

Fluellen accepted the hint graciously and began working swiftly through the queue.

"You don't remember me, do you?"

The man in front of Fluellen held two books in his arms, one of which he placed carefully on the table, sliding it forward so that it lay squarely under Fluellen's gaze.

"Go ahead, open it. It belongs to you."

Fluellen peered up at the man briefly, then opened the book. Inside was a hollowed-out cavity. Inside that was a gun. His gun.

Fluellen slammed the book shut. "What the hell is this?" he hissed. "Who are you?"

"Easy, old buddy." The man leaned forward until he was just a few inches from the author's face. He whipped off his hat and sunglasses. "It's your old pal Nick," he said, pulling back a mangy beard to reveal his tattoos. "I didn't have the whiskers when you seen me last."

Fluellen's head swam. That bloody biker tattoo. He forced himself upright. He could sense the crowd growing restless.

Nick leered. He leaned closer to his prey, his breath hot and rancid. "I figure you'd want your gun back as a reminder of our little adventure together. A reminder of what might have been. And what might still be...."

Nick brandished his second book, waved it in the air like a circus-tent preacher. "Redemption Lake! I love it. And buddy, I tell ya, that Nick character is something else. Can't wait to read the sequel, my man. I can just see those fat royalty cheques now."

Nick turned to the crowd. "What about it, folks? Anyone wanna see more of Nasty Nick in the next book?"

Murmurs of agreement rippled through a clump of nodding heads.

"There you go, Freddy. The people have spoken. Nick lives."

Fluellen opened his mouth to speak but no words followed.

Nick cracked open his copy of Redemption Lake, removed a black ballpoint pen from his inside jacket pocket and placed both with elaborate ceremony at the elbow of Fred Fluellen, author and killer.

"Well, sign it," Nick said.

"What do I write?"

"What else, pal? *'To Nick, who just wouldn't let sleeping dogs lie.'*"

Saturday with Bronwyn
By Judy Penz Sheluk

Judy Penz Sheluk's debut mystery novel, The Hanged Man's Noose, *was published in July 2015 by Barking Rain Press. Her most recent release,* Skeletons in the Attic, *was published in August 2016. Judy's short crime fiction can be found in* World Enough And Crime, The Whole She-Bang 2, Flash and Bang, *and* Live Free Or Tri. *She is a member of Sisters in Crime (International/Toronto/ Guppies), Crime Writers of Canada, the Short Mystery Fiction Society, and International Thriller Writers. Find Judy at www.judypenzsheluk.com, where she blogs about the writing life and interviews other authors.*

Bronwyn entered the Shack for Shoes wearing a pair of dollar store flip-flops and a floor-length Indian cotton sundress of indeterminate pattern. The Shack was having its annual Summer Madness Sidewalk Sale, and there were racks of shoes just ripe for the picking.

"Can I help you?"

Help was the last thing Bronwyn wanted, especially from this gum-chewing sales clerk with a bad case of acne. She looked at the girl's name tag. Ellen.

"Nope, I'm good, Ellen. I'm just going to try on a few pairs, walk around a bit in them. See how they feel. Hopefully I can find a deal."

"Holler if you need anything." Ellen smiled, a genuine smile, not the kind you plastered on to be polite. The mistake most people made, Bronwyn thought, is that they dismissed the sales staff, or worse, treated them as if they were invisible. The point was to make *yourself* invisible. The best way to do that was to befriend them, get them to trust you. Calling them by name was a good start. She noticed Ellen's can of cola on the counter and made a mental note to bring her one the next time she stopped by.

Bronwyn sauntered around the Shack for a few minutes before slipping her flip-flops under a stand of size tens. Barefoot, she strolled over to a selection of size seven sandals. A pair with ankle straps caught her eye. Black leather trimmed with red, they would look good with the skirt she had spotted last week at Willie's Wonderful World of Fashion.

With a backward glance—Ellen was helping an overfed young woman with plump ankles into a pair of pearl grey pumps—Bronwyn tried on the sandals and meandered around the shop, picking up shoes, checking the soles for prices, occasionally murmuring under her breath that there wasn't a deal to be had in this pile of rejects. It wasn't long before the other shoppers drifted away from her while trying to avoid eye contact. A few minutes later, Bronwyn was over and out, flip-flops long forgotten. Next stop: Willie's.

Willie's Wonderful World of Fashion was probably Bronwyn's favourite store, and not just because it had name brand designer fashions at discount prices. It was because they let you take as many items into the change room as you wanted. No four-item maximums at Willie's. This was the kind of place that counted on high turnover to turn a profit; the more women tried on, the more likely they were to overlook the occasional flawed seam or drooping hemline. Not to mention that most of the designs were rapidly approaching their best before date.

"Love your silver hoop earrings," Cindy said, when Bronwyn entered the shop. A bird-like brunette with tightly permed hair and gold wire-framed glasses, Cindy had been at the store since it had opened a couple years back.

"Thanks, Cindy, I picked them up at the Jewellery Emporium earlier this morning."

"They have nice stuff there."

"They surely do. Can't wait to see what I'll find here today. I've got twenty dollars burning a hole in my pocket."

"You call me if you need help, hon. Otherwise, I'll be in the back unpacking boxes. The new stock boy quit without notice."

Willie's employees came and went faster than the store's revolving front door, probably because he paid minimum wage and treated his employees like crap. Most were disinterested at best, dimwitted at worst. But not Cindy. Which was exactly why Bronwyn had befriended her months ago, chatted her up, and occasionally brought her a Timmy's double double. Every now and again, Bronwyn would make a purchase: a scarf, a belt, the occasional T-shirt marked down to seventy-five per cent off.

But something was different today. It took Bronwyn a minute to put her finger on it, but there they were: hard white plastic tags affixed to each piece of clothing. Security tags. That would never do, but not to worry. She had a good pair of expandable scissors in her bag. She grabbed a handful of clothes, carefully covering up the

46

black mini with the red trim, and headed into the change room.

Bronwyn had a motto: "never tell a lie when a half-truth will do." It had served her well ever since her first attempt at pilfering at the candy store. She had been six years old the day the owner had almost caught her red-handed. Well, black-handed to be completely accurate.

Not that Bronwyn was entirely to blame for her actions. How her parents expected her to live on an allowance of twenty-five cents a week when just one comic book could set you back as much as twelve cents—and then to be faced with a triple row of wooden bins filled with everything from gumballs, BB Bats and Red Hots, to peppermints, suckers and cherry-flavoured shoestrings—well, it just couldn't be done on twenty-five cents a week.

In hindsight, Bronwyn would concede that her final selection that day wasn't particularly brilliant. But the allure of blackball jawbreakers—the kind with the hard pressed liquorice powder in the centre—had been too much for her sticky little fingers to resist.

Bronwyn's blackened fingers gave her away at the cash when she handed over a small brown paper bag filled with sour sweets, a purple lollipop and a chocolate chunk. She saw the way Mr. Kennedy looked deep into the bag, down at her hands and then over to the wooden bins. He leaned forward, smelling faintly of tobacco and more strongly of peppermint, his sad eyes studying her. "Jeez, I almost forgot this blackball. Who knew it'd make such a mess?" Bronwyn pulled a tissue out of her pocket, careful not to disturb the jumble of hard candies tucked beneath. Inside the tissue was one seriously smudged black candy.

Mr. Kennedy leaned back then and laughed out loud, flecks of spittle landing on the glass-topped counter. "Let that be a lesson to you Bronwyn. Those blackballs are bad news. Just imagine what they'd do to your teeth. That one will be on the house." And with that he tallied up her purchases, handing her a dime and two cents change. More than enough to buy the latest issue of *Reggie*, with a penny to spare, but there was no need. *Reggie's Pals 'n' Gals* was already tucked inside the crook of her back, the drawstring on her track pants cinched up good and tight.

There were other instances going forward, although Bronwyn had to admit that every acquisition wasn't a winner. There was the time she'd sprayed sun lightener on her hair in the ladies' room at Seller's. She'd been stuck in that smelly stall for two hours waiting for her hair to dry, only to discover that her hair had turned a hideous shade of orange. Then there was the time she had filched a fuchsia lipstick from the Day-Mart cosmetics counter. It had turned out to be a terrible shade for her sallow complexion. But mostly, Bronwyn's little pastime had served her well, and if it meant telling the occasional half-truth....

"Cindy? I have a problem," Bronwyn called out, head peeking out of the cubicle.

"What is it, hon?" Cindy came into the change room, brushing cardboard dust off her dark blue smock.

Bronwyn tiptoed out wearing white denim jeans, security ink splattered on them like a Rorschach pattern.

"Oh hon, you tried to remove the security tag?"

"Is *that* what that white plastic thingie is? I couldn't get the waist to fit right with it on. Jeez, Cindy. I can't afford to buy these if I can't wear them and I can't wear them all inky. Does the ink come out?" Bronwyn bit her lower lip and blinked rapidly, fighting back tears.

"Now, now, hon, we have something out back that might remove that. No one need know. Stupid tags. This store is so cheap. Those tags aren't even activated. They're seconds."

"Seconds?"

"Seconds. They're just for show. Anyone can remove them with a drill bit and some patience."

There was a hardware store on Main Street. "You're the best, Cindy. I owe you one."

"Just bring me a double double next time you stop by," Cindy said. "Now take off those jeans and toss them over the cubicle door. I'll take them to the back before Willie notices. You better change quick and scoot out of here for today, though, okay?"

Bronwyn did as she was told, slipping back into her floor-length sundress. Underneath she wore a black mini with red trim, a perfect match for her new sandals. All she needed now was the purse to go with them. But first, she'd pick up a decaf-one-sugar for Peggy. Saturdays were always insane at Handbag Heaven.

The Tour Bus To Murder
By Lisa de Nikolits

Lisa de Nikolits is the author of six novels: The Hungry Mirror, West of Wawa, A Glittering Chaos, The Witchdoctor's Bones, Between The Cracks She Fell *and, most recently,* The Nearly Girl *which Jill Buchner of* Canadian Living *magazine calls "A playful exploration of human oddities. De Nikolits's latest book asks: What are the consequences when we deviate from the norm? The story builds with cinematic suspense and surprises, but one thing is for sure: The only crazy thing in this world is trying to be normal."*

"I never wanted an ordinary life," I told my mother as she lay dying.

"I am so relieved you said that," she replied. "I always thought it was my fault."

"No," I said. "It was just me."

It was my fault I was a misfit, a societal reject, unmarried at thirty-two, my life partner having amputated our relationship without so much as a by-your-leave.

I had arrived home to find a half-gutted apartment—neatly gutted, mind you, and a note that said he was sorry but he had been offered a job in New York. He wanted a fresh start he said; he wanted to try a new life without me.

He said he wanted an ordinary life and I looked at the handwritten note accusingly.

"We never were ordinary," I said, "That was never us."

I could feel him shaking his head from miles across the ocean. "It was never *you*," I heard him say.

I felt infinitely betrayed. We had grown up together, gone to the same school right from kindergarten.

Ben and Jenny. That was us, two kids who never fit in anywhere except with each other.

I stood in my half-empty apartment with the summer wind blowing in on scarves of hibiscus and jasmine and eucalyptus and I swear there was sunscreen too, and coconut and other people's happiness while I stood there, gutted and bleeding.

"But mum just died," I told the note and sat down on the polished hardwood floor. "And you didn't only leave me, you left our stained glass window of our angels and saints. I don't understand. What did I do wrong? I thought we were happy."

I read the note again.

Jenny, I am sorry. I've gone to live in New York. I got offered a job. I was going to tell you and I thought we would go together but then I didn't tell you and somehow I kept not telling you and it's not like there was anyone else who might have told you except for mum and dad and they said it would be better if I went alone and tried to be without you. So now you are reading this and I am gone.

Ben was a forensic accountant. I was a forensic scientist. It had been one of our shared little jokes.

"Let's get into forensics," he'd said after we graduated from high school.

"Okay," I said. "It does sound cool, but forensic what?"

We had chosen our respective forensic paths but now Ben had veered off on his lonesome.

I wasn't going to let him get away with it. If he could leave, then so could I. I would get a job in New York and I would follow him and he would realize that he had made a mistake and then everything would be all right again.

I grabbed my laptop and started researching jobs in New York but it seemed like my specialty wasn't needed.

I widened the search and I got a hit. There was a job in Toronto. And Toronto, I figured, was close enough to New York.

I stayed up all night, preparing my resumé, outlining my visa requirements and listing all the papers I had published, embellishing a bit here and there but not too much.

Then I called in a sickie and spent the day in bed, blackout curtains drawn, waiting for an email from Toronto, my laptop on the bed next to me. The next morning when I woke up, there it was, an email from Dr. Lee. He said he would sort out the paperwork, I needed to just get myself to Toronto, they were understaffed. When could I start?

I gave notice on the apartment and I put my stuff in storage. It only filled four boxes.

I really wanted to take the angels and the saints with me, but I couldn't exactly steal the window so I took a bunch of pictures with the late afternoon sun shining through and I printed off the best one. I had a postcard, a bookmark, a coffee mug and a T-shirt made too.

With a small suitcase, I arrived in Toronto, to find grey skies and a problem.

"Dr. Lee didn't have clearance to authorize your hire," the head of HR, Mrs. Duffy, told me. "He was let go a couple of days ago and no one knew you were coming. There's a good chance we can work it out. Dr. Lee was bad with paperwork and office protocol but the man was a genius, so if he recommended you, it should be fine."

"Is that why he was let go? Because he was bad with paperwork and office politics?" I asked. Mrs. Duffy shook her head.

"Just tightening our belts," she said. "Of course there will be legal fees and visa fees in getting your papers all sorted but don't worry."

"Don't worry?" I squeaked. The angrier I got, and the more stressed I got, the more I squeaked. It was probably better than shouting, particularly in this instance. I turned bright red and I squeaked as loudly as I could. "I flew all the way here; I paid for that. I let my apartment go, I gave up my job, I have nothing left, no one to help me and you say 'Don't worry'? I have Dr. Lee's email; you saw it. He said I must come, so I came. I don't have anywhere to stay that won't cost me a fortune that I don't have, and now I don't have a job. I am not just worried, I am *extremely* worried."

The last sentence escaped as no more than a cartoon mouse hiss from a pinpricked helium balloon and Mrs. Duffy smiled at me reassuringly.

"I will put you up in one of our corporate apartments," she said. "And really, dear, it will be fine. I just need a week to take care of the paperwork. I will look after you, poor sweet little thing, all by yourself, so brave. Come on let's get you sorted."

She made a few calls and typed an email. Then she handed me a set of keys, a scribbled address and a couple of cab chits.

"This is the address to the corporate suite. I will email you with an update as soon as I hear anything. In the meantime, do a tour, get to know your new city. I know it's not the greatest time of year to be sitting on the top of an open top bus, but you can sit downstairs and daydream and watch the world go by." She sounded wistful.

I wanted to tell her that I wasn't a tour bus person, that I had never toured in my life and that her suggestion was ridiculous but she held the power of my future so I smiled at her and pocketed the keys.

"Good idea," I said and my voice was close to normal.

I went back to my hotel, collected my suitcase and grabbed a cab.

Nothing was working out like I had imagined. I had thought that by now I would be sitting in a lab analyzing samples and being deferential to Dr. Lee but instead I found myself standing in the bland no-man's land of a corporate suite, with the sun streaming in through the tiny slats of the blinds, highlighting the fact that the corporate suite hadn't been occupied in a while.

The place was coated in a fine dusting of lint and static fibers. The décor was beige and tan. The place felt like a time capsule, snatched from the outer edges of a business trip that hovered like a satellite spaceship over suburbia.

I stuck my angels and saints post card on the wall which helped brighten up the place and I felt more cheerful.

I sat down on the bed, which didn't dent a centimetre, and I turned on my computer. I wanted to email Ben but I knew it wasn't time, not yet. I hadn't heard from him since he had left, and I hadn't sent him a single message. I wondered why I didn't feel more hurt by his absence but I realized it was because I didn't feel like we were separated, we were waiting to be together again—there was a big difference.

I got up and walked to the window and I saw a tour bus pulling up right outside my suite. I looked at my watch. It was only lunchtime.

The bus left before I could grab my purse but I locked up the apartment and stood waiting for the next one. It arrived fifteen minutes later and I paid for a day ticket and got on.

The tour bus host introduced himself as Fred and he told us we were lucky to have him, that he was a real live wire and not just a recording like all the other tour lines. I could tell he thought he was some kind of stand-up comedian and actually he was kind of funny. He was about fifty, he had a great voice, really soothing and deep. I liked the stories he told about each stop.

I decided to sit on the bus for the entire loop to hear the talk from the beginning to the end.

It was January and I decided that Toronto was just about the greyest city I had ever seen. The streets were lined with piles of filthy black slush.

But a light snow was falling; big puffy snowflakes that made me happy. Yonge Street was really cool and I made a note to return to Kensington Market and Chinatown.

We drove around the University of Toronto. Fred had become background noise for a moment but I tuned in quickly when he

52

pointed out a house and said that that was where he had killed his second wife. I sat upright and looked around but no one else on the bus had seemed to notice what he had said, or perhaps they didn't care or else they thought he was joking. I told myself that I really needed to develop more of a sense of humour and not take people so seriously.

"Last stop! That's it for the day," Fred announced and I looked up, startled. Where had the time gone?

"See y'all tamarra if you've got a two day pass and if ya liked my tales, leave a tip and smile in the box at the front of the bus," he said and he winked at me.

"What time do you start tomorrow?" I asked him.

"Nine o'clock on the dot," he said. "Glad you enjoyed yourself sweetie."

I treated myself to a feast of Chalet chicken while I sat at my computer, looking for the news of the day.

I remembered what Fred said about killing his second wife. Out of curiosity, I typed in deaths on Harbord Street. I found half a dozen mentions but nothing about Fred.

"Just silly imaginings," I told the angels and saints on my mug. "Let's get some sleep."

I put my computer away and got a good night's sleep.

The next morning, I was on the bus bright and early.

I did the whole loop again and when we got to Harbord, I sat up expectantly, but there was no mention at all about Fred's second wife.

However, when we got to Spadina, he pointed to an apartment on the third floor of a bland-looking block of flats and said, "And that is where I poisoned my first wife, Ming. Such a beauty she was, delicate looking, like a lotus blossom but a tongue like rattlesnake venom."

I looked around. The other tourists were all laughing or chatting or taking photos and I wondered if being comical about his dead wives was just part of Fred's stand up routine.

But when I got home, I searched for *Ming, Spadina, poison* and there it was. In 1983, a woman called Ming had died and while the police suspected homicide, they hadn't been able to prove anything.

This was too weird. I wanted to email Ben and tell him what I had found but Ben hadn't always believed me when I had told him things. Granted, there had been times when I had stretched things a bit here and there. I didn't even know why I had embellished. It was like little lies escaped from my mouth just like the girl in the fairy tale who had millions of tiny frogs pour from her mouth.

The next day I got on the bus, ready for round three with Fred. By now I pretty much knew his talk off by heart, and I was as familiar with Toronto as any long-time resident.

This time, Fred had killed a girlfriend, Eve, near the Casa Loma castle, and later that night, my search corroborated his claim.

"And you still think there is nothing to it?" I asked the angels and saints but there was no reply.

"I'm going to catch him," I told them. "He won't get away with this."

I sat on the bus the next day and I tried to catch Fred's murderous admission on my phone. I had to record and delete and record again. It wasn't easy but catch it I did.

"I killed a lovely girl in that park," he said, and he pointed. "For no good reason at all except that she was there and I could do it. A crime of opportunity, I suppose you could say."

The others on the bus roared with laughter and drowned out anything else he might have said. I made a note of the park's name and I took a few photos of Fred.

Later on, my research confirmed that once again Fred had been speaking the truth. A girl had been killed in the park.

I typed up all my findings and used the printer in the corporate suite to make copies.

The following day I went to the police department, the 51 Division that I had passed numerous times on the bus tour and I asked to speak to a detective in charge of homicide.

"I'm Constable Sales," a man said, about half an hour later. He was about fifty, grey-haired and stocky and I thought that he didn't look particularly intelligent. I shook his hand. I wondered if he was of a high enough rank for what I was about to tell him but having no other choice, I sat down.

I told him my story, showing him what I had, but I could see he didn't believe me. I asked him to do his own search to corroborate my findings but he just nodded vaguely and made a few notes on his pad that looked more like doodles than writing to me.

"You don't believe me, do you?" I asked and he tapped his pen on his chin, a habit I found particularly annoying—it reminded me of someone....

I stood up. "Fine," I said, "Let those unsolved murders be on your head."

I took a bus back to the suite and I logged onto my email, hoping to hear from Mrs. Duffy about my job and visa. I resolved to forget about Fred's bus tour and his murders and get on with my life. I had done what I could, if the police wouldn't listen to me, that wasn't my problem.

But my computer couldn't seem to find the Internet, which was odd. I rebooted a couple of times but it didn't help. I tried opening up browser after browser, and I received the same dead page telling me there was no Internet connection. I started to panic. I needed to be connected.

I tried for hours and I grew increasingly anxious. I wondered if the WiFi was the old-fashioned kind via a modem and I picked up the phone and found it was dead. What was happening? The tiny rooms of the suite seemed to be closing in on me, and my chest got so tight it was hard to draw a breath. I dug out my T-shirt with the angels and saints and pulled it on, hoping it would comfort me.

I finally fell asleep on the floor next to my laptop and when I woke, the corporate suite had disappeared and I was in a strange bed.

My wrists were tied.

I scrambled as much as I could, trying to escape my shackles and the thousand thoughts filling my head. It was Fred, he had kidnapped me. He must have followed me to the suite and grabbed me somehow when I was passed out.

I was next, he was going to kill me next and I would be no more than a passing mention on a bus tour and no one would hear or care. I had to get away, I had to get out of the straps that secured my wrists or I would be dead in no time.

I looked around and tried to focus. The room that Fred had me in was white, and sunlight streamed in through the windows. The sky was vivid blue.

I tried to scream for help but I could only squeak—useless mouse-like sounds, like a tiny animal trapped and frightened, in pain, incoherent.

"Ah, Jenny, you're awake."

It wasn't Fred's voice. I struggled to see who my captor was. My eyes felt like they had been smeared with Vaseline and they were gritty at the same time. I blinked and a woman came into view.

She was tapping her pen against her chin.

"Jenny? How are you feeling? We had to sedate you. It looks like we'll have to take away all Internet privileges for a while. You had another psychotic break. This time you thought you were a forensic scientist who went to Toronto and discovered a serial killer."

"I am. And I did. His name is Fred. He's a killer. Look at all the evidence I found, the facts support all my claims, just look."

"There is no Fred," the woman said.

I tugged at my straps. "Untie me, let me go. Who are you? You can't hold me here against my will."

"I can't untie you, not until you have quieted down. We need *you*, the real Jenny, to come back to us." The woman sighed. "We were so optimistic that this time you'd stay with us while integrating with the world but you still cannot separate fantasy from reality."

"What about Ben?" I asked. "Did he go to New York?"

"Ben died when you were six," the woman said and I suddenly remembered who she was. Her name was Dr. Duffy. I couldn't remember anything else except that I hated her.

"Ben was your baby brother," she continued and I looked at her suspiciously, why would she lie like this?

"You killed Ben," she said. "You were playing with him and you slammed his head on the sharp edge of a cabinet, pretending that you were playing. The nanny camera showed the whole thing. It all happened under a stained glass window depicting angels and saints. You're obsessed with that too. You are the murderer, not Fred. You find ways to invent serial killers in order to keep reliving the murder because you cannot accept that you did it. If you could just accept you did it, we would be able to help you. You've been with us since Ben died. I have been your doctor for ten years."

And I remembered. I remembered the cracking eggshell sound as I crushed Ben's head and I remembered the gold light shining down from the stained glass window.

Dr. Duffy approached me with a needle that would bring darkness.

I opened my lungs and I did not squeak.

I screamed.

A Sucker for St. Nick
By Coleen Steele

Coleen Steele is an award-winning mystery and suspense writer whose stories often find their inspiration in the era of old-time radio shows, film noir, swing music, pulp novels and war rationing. For more information visit www.coleensteele.com

It was Eileen's fault that Bert was there, and that day of all days. If it were up to him he'd be anywhere else, preferably at Flannigan's guzzling a beer. Instead, here he was, stuck in Eaton's Department Store on the day before Christmas. It was like being in the loony bin.

"Whachit, lady," Bert snapped at an old broad with a stiff silver perm and a brace of mangy martins strung over her shoulder. Her pale, heavily powdered face jerked toward him and her mouth fell open, reminding him of a floundering mackerel doused in flour. He gave her the shoulder and elbowed his way deeper into the madhouse.

What a disgusting place. Bright lights, brightly packaged toys, and bright, silly decorations—all of which hurt his eyes. Even the sales clerks' faces were plastered with bright smiles, though he took some satisfaction in seeing just how strained some of those smiles were. He couldn't think of a worse place to be. And it was all because of Eileen.

She'd taken it into her head that the kids had to get new toys for Christmas. *Store-bought* toys! The hand-me-down ones her sister had passed their way weren't good enough on their own. He couldn't see why not. Eileen had patched and cleaned till they looked almost new. And with the sweaters Eileen knitted for each of the little tykes, not to mention the oranges the grocer overcharged her for, it seemed like a pretty good haul to him. It was a good sight more than he'd ever got.

Eileen had been nagging him about the toys for the last week, and this morning when he'd slung on his coat with an eye for hitting Flannigan's at opening, she'd caught him at the door. "You bring those presents home today. One for each of them. If you don't, don't bother coming home at all. Ever."

How did she think he was going to afford presents? Turning out his pockets, he'd only found enough to cover the cost of a beer and a pack of Players; Eileen was too stingy with the dough she brought in sewing and making alterations for other women for him to have any extra. It wasn't his fault he could only pick up a few dollars here and there doing the odd bit of handyman work. When all those boys came back from the war, they were offered all the jobs, the cream of them anyways. Where had that left him? You couldn't blame him for not having joined up. With his trick knee they wouldn't have accepted him. He was almost certain of that.

It wasn't just jobs those fellas got either. His brother-in-law, Arthur, received free training and a new house. (Well, the house wasn't free, but he got it dirt cheap!) And now Artie was some big shot manager in a machine shop and driving a new Buick. It wasn't fair. What about cheap housing for a guy like him who stayed behind and slaved away in a munitions factory, at least some of the time anyway?

Bert just couldn't get a fair shake. That's why he was here in Eaton's, reduced to cramming in with all these other schmucks, waiting for the moment to stuff something under his coat. And it couldn't just be any stuff either. Eileen had been very firm about that. The kids had to get what they'd been asking for. For Fred that meant some Space Rogers gun—an atomic pistol—he'd been yammering on about. An atomic pistol? What happened to the plain old cowboy guns they had when he was a youngster? Jimmy was to get an erector set; Helen, a Chinese checkers game; and little Joanie wanted a play stove and refrigerator. Well, you could nix that last one. His coat was roomy—he'd bought it second-hand, a couple of sizes too big for just such occasions—but it wouldn't accommodate anything that big.

As Bert stepped off the escalator onto the second floor, he smiled smugly to himself. At least he had Eileen taken care of. He dug his hand into his right pocket and fingered the silver charm bracelet coiled there. Ouch! It had to be that little ballerina charm with the pointy legs stabbing his finger. He withdrew his hand and touched his injured finger to his tongue. Getting the thing hadn't been easy, not with that store detective eyeballing him as soon as he stepped foot in the jewelry department. Why did the guy zero in on him? He *could* have been there to buy something. Anyway, luckily the dick got distracted by some woman bawling about being given the wrong change, and he'd seized his chance. *Too bad sucker!*

It didn't look like there were any detectives or spotters in Toyland. There sure was a crush of people though. He pushed his way through the throng and past the line-up of brats waiting to see

Santa, and closed in on a display of guns and other artillery designed for the all-Canadian boy. Ha, they did still sell regular cowboy guns, right beside the Mountie and Servicemen gear. But no space guns.

Maybe Fred would just have to be satisfied with a pair of Gene Autry pistols and matching horsehide holsters. Bert frowned though as a memory of a similar set tugged at his consciousness. Did Fred already own a pair, or was that Jim that had a set? He knew one or the other was always waving a cap gun around and firing it off when he was trying to read the *Telegram's* sports scores or hear Foster Hewitt calling the shots in the Leafs' game. Damn. Eileen wouldn't be happy if he messed this up.

"Is someone helping you, sir? Are you looking for a gift for a young boy? We have a complete cowboy outfit—hat, vest, boots, holster, guns and even a sheriff's badge."

Uh-oh, now he'd attracted the attention of a sales clerk keen for a sale. They'd been known to hang on to a customer like a terrier with a rat once they took hold. He glanced at the perky young woman but didn't quite meet her eye. "I'm just browsing, thanks."

"I see," said the clerk, but she didn't make any move to leave him alone. "For your son? Perhaps a Lone Ranger outfit? They're very popular. I think we have one left." She started rooting through the rack of make-believe outfits.

"No, no. Really, I'm just lookin'." She truly was a terrier he thought, getting annoyed.

"Hmmm. Well, what about space toys? We have the very latest in those too."

Bingo! He was still tempted to tell her to get lost, but figured it'd be better to make use of her persistence. After all, he wasn't finding the damn things on his own. "Yeah, maybe," he conceded. "Could you show me what you got?"

"Certainly," she chirped.

He didn't feel the slightest guilt upon seeing the "I've got a sale" smile beaming back at him. He trudged after her to a display with a great big shiny aluminium rocket hanging above it. How'd he missed that?

"We have a whole selection of Space Rogers toys, as you can see."

He sure did and there was the little beauty he'd come for—the V-235 Atomic Pistol, available in two colours: gold or blue. He pulled his gaze from it, and nonchalantly picked up a couple of other toys, before putting them back again.

"No," he finally said with a sigh. "I don't think so. I think I got enough at Simpson's. Thanks, anyways."

He took malicious delight in seeing her smile curl into something nasty before she recovered. "Well, perhaps there's another child on your list you wish to buy for? I assure you Eaton's has the best prices."

Bert shook his head. "No thanks." He began walking away, then paused to throw a "Merry Christmas" over his shoulder, chuckling as he did so.

He made as if heading for the escalator, but after glancing back to ensure the clerk wasn't still on to him—she wasn't; a young couple pushing a baby carriage had already grabbed her attention—he veered off into the section displaying girls' toys. Joanie would be easier to please than Fred. She wanted a toy refrigerator and stove, but he'd fob her off with the story that Santa couldn't fit them down the chimney. She'd be just as happy with a doll. He stepped up to the display of this year's Eaton's Beauty Dolls and plucked one from the pile. He edged away, further from the cashier's desk, and pretended to drop it on the floor. Seeing no one had noticed, he yanked the doll from its box, stashed it inside his coat and kicked the empty box under a table display. *Easy as pie.*

Just as easily, he soon had a Chinese checkers game and an erector set under his coat. Now to go back for the V-235 Atomic Pistol. Then he could go home and get a nice warm welcome from Eileen.

All he had to do was avoid that little terrier of a clerk and keep his eyes peeled for store detectives, which looked easy enough as some sort of commotion near Santa's Workshop was drawing everyone's attention. Thanks, pal, he acknowledged in Santa's general direction.

Bert sidled up to the space toy display. Furtively glancing about, he judged the coast was clear, snatched an Atomic Pistol and shoved it under his coat.

Now for the home stretch. Focusing on the escalator, his path to escape, Bert doggedly headed for it, jostling past shoppers on his way. A half-a-dozen more steps and he'd be on that magical stairway that would carry him to the main floor and out.

Uh-oh. There was that store dick, the one from the jewelry department, and he was giving him the eye again. Had he noticed how much bulkier Bert had gotten?

Three more steps.

The man was starting to make a move toward him. Bert quickened his pace.

"Stop!"

Bert nearly jumped out of his skin. It couldn't have been the detective's voice. It was much too high and feminine.

"Sir, please stop!"

His head swivelled around. It was the little terrier again, barking at him. What to do? Make a run for it? With both her and the detective giving chase? Maybe he should just brazen it out. Claim he was intending to pay. Yes, that's what he'd do. After all, he wasn't too good of a runner anymore, what with his trick knee and all.

"Yeah?" he said with all the indignity he could muster, once the clerk had caught up with him.

"Sir, could you please come with me?"

"It's all right. I'll handle this," the store detective said, arriving on the scene.

"No, Mr. Rankin needs to speak with this gentleman right away. It's very urgent."

"It's all right, miss. It's my job."

"No, no. You don't understand. This gentleman needs to come to Mr. Rankin's office right away." She placed a hand on Bert's sleeve entreatingly.

"What's this all about?" Bert asked, snatching his arm back.

Looking flustered, the clerk persisted. "Sir, please. If you'd just follow me. Mr. Rankin will explain."

One glance at the scowling detective who looked like he could play halfback for the University of Toronto's Varsity Blues, and Bert's mind was made up.

"All right," he relented.

The clerk shot him a smile of relief, then, with the detective dogging them, led Bert behind a display curtain and into a tiny office crowded with Eaton's staff. The knot of people parted long enough for Bert to see what they were all gawking at. Lying on the floor with his head pillowed on a pink fuzzy doll's blanket was the store Santa, his face ashen grey.

A short little man with glasses and a neat Clark Gable moustache broke away from what was otherwise an all-female group. "I'm Mr. Rankin," he said, grabbing Bert's hand and pumping it vigorously. "He's perfect, Miss Prentice. Perfect. But we'll have to hurry."

Bert's eyes narrowed. "Whatcha mean?"

"Yeah, I'd like to know that too," the detective chimed in.

"Oh, it's terrible," fretted Mr. Rankin. "Our Santa has taken ill."

Ill? He looked dead to Bert. A low moan from the man refuted that possibility, but just barely.

"And all those children out there saw it. We've got to produce a live, healthy Santa before the little tykes think Santa has died."

And the parents take their brats home and don't buy your crummy merchandise Bert thought. "He don't look like he's going anywhere any time soon."

"No. No, he's not," Rankin admitted. "An ambulance is on the way, but...but we need you to be Santa."

"Eh?!"

"Mr., er...."

"McGowan."

"Yes, well, Mr. McGowan, if you would help us out, it would be greatly appreciated."

Bert did not like the sound of that at all. He started shaking his head. He could see the women were already stripping the clothes from the Santa on the floor.

"Uh-uh. You'll have to get yourself another boy."

"We don't have time. The children are waiting. We have to act quickly."

"What about this guy?" Bert asked, jerking his thumb in the detective's direction.

"He's too big, and I'm too small. You're the right fit for the suit. Mr. McGowan, we're desperate. We don't have time to go looking for someone else," Mr. Rankin said. "It would only take a little of your time. Just enough to show the children Santa's all right and take care of that line out there. Just give us thirty minutes."

"I don't know," Bert said, shaking his head.

"Please, Mr. McGowan. We're in a real bind here."

The wheels in Bert's head started turning. It looked like he had Mr. Rankin over a barrel. Maybe it could get him out of his own bind. "Can I speak to you alone Mr. Rankin?"

"Yes, yes, certainly," Mr. Rankin agreed. "But let's make it fast. The children."

"Uh, Mr. Rankin, I'm not sure," the detective protested as the manager began waving people out. "I think this guy's been shop..."

"This is more important. Now, please, everyone out."

The detective, the last out, gave Bert a warning glare before closing the door.

Five minutes later, Bert came out through that same door, clad from head to toe in red, white and black. He winked at the detective as he sailed past, destined for Toyland and Santa's throne-like chair. Cries of delight greeted Bert as he took his place with a hearty "Ho, ho, ho."

The thirty minutes turned into forty-five, but at the end of it, when Bert turned in the costume, Mr. Rankin handed him an Eaton's bag with four parcels in it: a Space Rogers V-235 Atomic Pistol, a Chinese checkers game, an erector set and an Eaton's Beauty Doll. The thanks the manager gave Bert for helping him out of the jam was a little grudging, but Bert didn't care. He got what he wanted, including a free pass from the store. The store dick couldn't touch him now.

Leaving Toyland behind, Bert made his way down to the Queen Street Exit, dawdling along and pausing to look at displays and finger merchandise, hoping to get up the nose of the detective who still stalked him. He sent the man a merry wave at the door and stepped out into the frosty December air. What a bunch of suckers, he thought, glancing down at the glossy Santa boots peeking out from under his pant legs. The boots hadn't been part of the deal, but, hey, why shouldn't Bert keep them? The galoshes he'd stuffed under Mr. Rankin's desk were old and battered with a hole in the left sole. He figured he was better off with these, even if they were too big for him. He'd just put on an extra pair of socks in future, just like the kids did when they went skating.

Tugging up his collar, Bert took a step in the direction of the nearest streetcar stop.

Whoops!

He righted himself from a skid that nearly saw his backside hit the pavement. The damn boots didn't have any tread! Great, Santa boots that didn't work in the snow.

Stepping a little more cautiously, Bert made his way to the stop just as a streetcar pulled up. He thrust his hand in his coat pocket, searching for the dime fare. Ouch! Something jabbed his finger. Ahh, the silver charm bracelet. He'd forgotten all about that. Ha, ha, it wasn't part of the deal either. Boy, did he take them! Luck was surely running his way, well, except for the slippery boots. Pushing the bracelet aside, he rummaged around a little more until he came up with the dime needed.

Bert stepped off the curb into the street with a handful of other travellers and climbed aboard, dropping his fare in the box.

"Merry Christmas," the driver said.

Bert ignored him. Probably one of those lucky buggers back from the war—had the cushy job thrown at him.

Manoeuvring his way to the back, Bert found an empty seat and sat down, placing his parcel on his lap. He was going to be in big with Eileen tonight. Even if she asked how he got them, he could rightfully say he got them legit; he worked. Hmmph, and it wasn't easy work either, having all those snotty-nosed brats climbing all over him. Well...actually, now that he thought about it, it hadn't been all that bad. Those smiles when he'd pulled the kids up onto his lap and asked what they'd wanted for Christmas, they'd been kind of...well...heart-warming. Wow, he was getting sappy.

Chuckling out loud he noticed the lady across the aisle giving him a look that could curdle milk. It was that snooty Mrs. Barnaby from two doors up, the one that was always complaining to Eileen about him—didn't like him flicking his cigarette butts into her geraniums or dropping his empties in her yard (how did she know they were his?). Daft woman. Now, she probably figured he'd imbibed a little too much Christmas cheer.

Ha, if she only knew he simply felt good at the notion of having brought some cheer—and not of the boozy kind—into the lives of all those kids today. Funny, he didn't usually care about stuff like that. But it *was* Christmas. Isn't that what people said? Weren't they always on about having the Christmas spirit? He'd never really understood that before. He'd always figured Christmas was a racket, one that cost him a lot of aggravation.

But this year was going to be different. This year he had wonderful gifts for his family. If the tots in the store had been excited and happy to see him, just think how his own brood was going to feel when they spied all those presents under the tree. Eileen would be thrilled too, of course. She'd be especially surprised and pleased that he hadn't forgotten her.

He hugged the bag of gifts to his chest and smiled. Christmas was going to be great.

As the streetcar came to a stop, he wiped his sleeve across the frosted window to peer out and check how far along they were. He couldn't make out the name on the street sign in the darkness, but wait a minute, there was that beer joint he stopped off at occasionally (when he knew he wouldn't be welcome at Flannigan's).

Only three more stops until home. He couldn't wait.

Hmmm. Of course, it was only *two* more stops to Flannigan's. He licked his lips. A beer would go down awful nice right now. Might even add to his Christmas spirit. Problem was, since he'd treated himself to a beer on the way to Eaton's, he knew the only thing his pockets contained were a soiled handkerchief, a book of matches, and a cigarette pack, half-empty.

Hey, maybe being Christmas Eve, he could persuade Billy

Flannigan to give him one on the house. Yeah, fat chance. Flannigan might claim to be Irish but he was as tight as a Scotsman, the cheap bugger.

The streetcar crowd had thinned out enough that there was now an empty seat beside him. He moved his package off his lap and onto the seat and dug around in his trouser pockets hopeful of finding some change he'd forgotten about. Nothing. He checked his coat pockets again on the off chance he'd missed something earlier. Nope, no such luck. Just the damn bracelet.

The bracelet for Eileen.

Hey. Wait a minute.

Why should he give her a present? Especially after the way she'd treated him of late, haranguing him about getting Christmas treats for the kids. And she was always nagging him about getting a job too. Besides, she'd only demanded he get presents for the little ones. He'd come through with flying colours on that score, so why did he have to give her anything?

The trolley bell clanged and Bert looked up to see he was at the stop he wanted.

Launching himself to his feet, he hurried to the back door just as the last person waiting there got out and the doors swung closed. Oh no! He grabbed the cord over the doors and jerked it spastically, the ensuing bell ringing like a carnival shooting gallery overloaded with army sharp-shooters.

"Hold your horses!" the driver yelled back.

The doors split open again and Bert charged out.

As he crossed the lane of traffic, he jammed his hands in his pockets. Ouch, there was that damn ballerina again. Well, not for much longer. She had to be worth three or four beers; even Flannigan would see that.

He started to step up onto the curb in front of Flannigan's. *Damn! The presents!* He'd left them on the streetcar seat. In a panic, he swung round....

Whoosh!

Bert's feet slipped out from under him, the Santa boots finding no traction on the icy cement. He felt himself falling backwards, and tried futilely to wrench his hands out of his pockets to break his fall.

Wham!

A great pain exploded through his body as something tore into his side. Then he landed on his back with a whump. His head lolled to the side and he looked into blinding headlights. Probably a new Buick, like his brother-in-law's, he thought absurdly.

Bert heard the clatter of the streetcar as it pulled away. Oh no! He had to catch it. He had to get those presents!

He yanked his hands out of his pockets and the bracelet flew out. It landed on the icy pavement and skidded away from him. He hesitated, glanced up at the receding red lights of the back of the streetcar and then down again at the bracelet. The bracelet that meant free-flowing beer and an hour or two in the tavern.

His mind made up, Bert rolled over and dove for the chain. He could rescue it and there would still probably be time to catch the streetcar.

He reached out his hand, fingers extended. A pair of boots were suddenly in his way.

"Are you all right, Mister?"

More boots. A pair of fur-trimmed ladies ankle boots stepped forward and crunched down on the charm bracelet.

"Arrgh! Get out of the damn way!" He shoved at the offending feet.

The ankle boots jumped back, catching and flicking the bracelet further away.

Bert ignored the grumbles and rebukes directed at him and scrambled to his knees. He put one foot down and started to heave himself up, keeping his eye on the bracelet. There it was, right by the fellow in overshoes. He just had to grab it and then run after the streetcar. Aah! The guy shifted and nudged it with his heel.

Oh no! Right by the sewer grate!

Bert lunged.

Whoosh!

His feet flew out from under him and again he landed with a thud on his belly, the wind knocked out of him. He lay there helpless, watching as the bracelet was jostled yet again by an errant boot. One of the pieces—the ballerina, he was sure—had slipped down between the grates. At first he thought the bracelet was still safe, still attainable, but suddenly the chain start to shift, then slowly snake toward the hole, and then with a snap, it was gone.

A cry tore from his lips and he went limp, admitting defeat. The bracelet was gone. And he knew the streetcar and the kids' presents were gone too.

His body started to feel numb, from shock, like the soldiers he'd read about who got shot or hit by a grenade.

"Stand back, stand back!"

A face appeared directly over him. A face with a policeman's helmet above it—one he'd seen too many times before.

"Oh, it's you, McGowan. I should have known. Had a few too many, did ya? Flannigan throw you out again?" The officer straightened up. "All right everyone, on your way. Nothing to see here."

The policeman grabbed Bert and hoisted him to his feet. "I should run you in for this. But seein' as it's Christmas Eve, I'll let you off this time. Now, get on home. Hopefully the cold air will help sober ya up along the way."

Bert slowly brushed himself off, wincing from the aches and pains that had already begun to set in. He gazed up at the Flannigan's sign, thinking of the Christmas that had just slipped through his fingers. The presents. The shrieks of joy. All the smiles. Eileen's good will.

"Go on," the policeman said. "The missus and kiddies will be waiting for you."

Bert cringed. Geez, the flatfoot really knew how to hurt a guy.

"And don't stop for any more Christmas cheer along the way."

Christmas cheer? Bert almost cried.

With one more fleeting glimpse at the sign, he turned and started slowly for home, slipping and sliding in his ill-fitting Santa boots. It wasn't just the boots that kept him from hurrying though. After all, he thought, what sane man would hurry to his own execution?

Bert turned on to their street and his pace slowed even more. It occurred to him that he would rather meet that Eaton's detective, the one that could pass for a Varsity Blues halfback, in a dark alley than go up against Eileen when she was mad.

He passed Mrs. Barnaby's place, resisting the temptation to give her gate a kick, and turning up his front pathway, he marvelled that it really did feel like mounting the stairs to the gallows. At his front door, he stopped to collect his nerve.

The muted sound of laughter and excited voices leaked out from within. Well, Eileen would put a stop to that when he walked in empty-handed. He sighed, then took a deep breath. *Here goes nothin'.* He turned the knob and pushed in.

The sight that greeted him was astonishing. There was Fred, blasting away with a Space Rogers Atomic Pistol; Jimmy was assembling beams and pulleys and gears; Helen was sorting Chinese checkers marbles; and Joanie was squeezing an Eaton's Beauty Doll. Bert wiped his hand across his eyes, convinced he must be seeing things.

"Look, Daddy, look!" Joanie squealed upon spotting him. "I got a dolly from Santa!"

The other children were just as eager to show off their new acquisitions. Bert just stood there with his mouth hanging open.

Eileen, seeing his confusion, drew him aside. "Isn't it wonderful?"

"But how?"

"Mrs. Barnaby brought them over. Said she found them on the streetcar. Since her own children are grown up now she figured they weren't much use to her, and she remembered how I'd told her how keen Fred was to get one of those Space Rogers guns so she brought the toys here. Wasn't that the nicest thing to do?"

"But those are the toys I got for the kids today."

"What are you talking about, Bert? You didn't get them."

"But I did. And I forgot them on the streetcar. Those are *my* toys."

Eileen had her annoyed face on now. "Bert, stop making up stories. Have you been drinking again?"

"No. I tell you, they gave them to me at Eaton's."

"Just gave them to you? Don't be ridiculous."

"But honestly, Eileen, I..."

"Bert McGowan, don't you say another word. There is no way Eaton's gave you all these toys. And if they did, how could you forget them on the streetcar? And where have you been?"

She peered at him in such a way, he knew he was sunk. She'd never listen to him and if she did, what would he say? That he'd held the Eaton's manager over a barrel and forced him to give him the toys? That he got off the streetcar early to spend his Christmas Eve at Flannigan's? That he planned to pawn her present to have a few beer? He'd be in a bigger mess than he was now.

"Now just go and get washed up for dinner and forget this nonsense."

Bert opened his mouth to protest but decided it was better to let it go. What did it matter? The children had their toys and they would all have a nice Christmas. It wasn't fair that he wouldn't get the credit but at least with the kids happy, Eileen wasn't talking about chucking him out of the house either.

"You're right Eileen, it's just a bunch of nonsense." He shrugged out of his coat and hung it on the rack. Maybe he could still find a little cheer in Christmas.

"Oh," said Eileen, "I let Mrs. Barnaby know that when the warmer weather comes, you'll go over and paint her porch for her, as a thank you for the toys."

Ouch. So much for Christmas cheer.

Strike Three
By Anne Barton

Anne Barton is a retired veterinarian and flight instructor. In her retirement, she has taken up writing mystery novels. She lives in beautiful Okanagan Valley in British Columbia where she is deeply involved in Habitat for Humanity and her Anglican Church work—that is, when she isn't riding horses or curling.

The seventh game of the World Series. Score tied. The bottom of the ninth. Two outs and the bases loaded. A lot was on the line, and not just the glory of being world champions. In the owners' box of the home team, one of the owners, a young man uneasy in his mind, paced restlessly behind the seats. The Blue Birds *had* to win! If they did, there would be extra revenue to cover the money he had surreptitiously used for an investment that had gone sour, putting off the time when the accounts would be audited. Furthermore, the celebrations and the excitement would result in delaying the day of reckoning. If they lost, the business of auditing the accounts would start right away, and he knew he would go to jail.

In the visitor's dugout, the manager, a man of talent and temper, whose players crowded to the far end of the dugout to avoid his scathing tirades but reacted to his tantrums by playing their best, was so nervous he had to spit out the tobacco he normally chewed before he choked on it. Win, and his bosses would have to let him stay on; lose, and they would have every reason for firing him. Once fired, he'd never get on with another team.

The Panthers had lifted another pitcher for a left-handed closer, but the Blue Birds had gotten to him with two walks wrapped around a single after the first two batters struck out. In the on-deck circle, a pinch hitter swung his bat to loosen tense muscles. He was an aging slugger, formerly the pride of the team, but now slowing with the wear and tear of twenty years and having been relegated to a pinch-hitter role. The Panthers' manager again signalled to the bullpen. The man who walked out to the mound this time was a young knuckle-ball thrower, whose wicked delivery could have batters fanning the air in frustration, but whose control was suspect. Considered a future star if he could become more accurate in getting the ball over the plate. Sometimes overconfidence got the better of him, but he had been told that his continued play in the majors depended upon his shaking off his inconsistency. The manager slapped the ball into his glove. "Get this guy or I'll personally nail you to a fucking cross!"

The pitcher alternated balls that barely missed the strike zone, with ones that the batter fouled off, waiting for a good fat one to blast over the fence.

The batter wasn't afraid of knuckle balls, those wicked pitches that appeared to take off at wild angles at the last moment. It was an optical illusion and he had trained himself not to go for it. But his timing had slowed; his responses were not what they had been.

A full count. One last pitch. One last chance to strike out a revered slugger. One last chance for that slugger to loft one out of the park.

The pitcher walked off the mound to settle himself. He took two deep breaths, rubbed the ball, tipped his cap to the back of his head then pulled it down over his eyes, walked back onto the mound and gripped the ball, his fingertips feeling the stitching, his nails digging into the hide.

The batter stepped up to the plate. He swung the bat around as if sighting along it straight toward the pitcher, and then swung it back to the position of readiness to address the pitch. Most of the players on the team, who had watched this slugger for years, knew one thing, one absolute. He would swing at this pitch unless it was clear over his head. Not for him the shame of taking a called third strike in the ninth inning of the last game of the World Series. Not for him walking unobserved to first while another player trotted home with the winning run. He would swing at the pitch. His teammates moved to the top step of the dugout holding their breath.

The batter watched the pitch coming at him, waiting until he could see the stitching on the ball. He started his swing just as the ball appeared to veer down and out.

The next second seemed to take forever to all the people watching; the owner who needed to cover up his embezzlement; the manager hanging onto the last job he would ever have; the young pitcher who hoped to become an instant star; the old slugger who would go down in baseball history as either an immortal hero or a bum.

I stopped reading from my manuscript and looked at my husband, Gerry, who said, "Go on. I'm listening."

"That's it. The end."

70

Gerry frowned. "Do you think a publisher will take it if you leave the readers up in the air like that?"

I felt deflated. I had worked hard on that novel, and thought the ending was really good. "I thought I should leave it to the reader to decide how the story should come out."

"I know that was your intention...."

A surge of annoyance flooded over me. I had to defend my work, my first-ever novel. I had wanted to be a crime writer since my teens, and this effort had occupied my spare time for over a year. "I felt that the readers would not really care which of the two main characters, who are sort of nasty people, won out. They couldn't empathize with a weak and greedy rich young man or with a nasty old guy who only gets results from his players by being mean. So I gave them two other characters, either of which they could root for, and let them decide which of those two they wanted to have win." I had slaved over that ending, trying to get every word just right!

"It might work at that. Actually, I like it. Who have you sent it to?"

"Darcy Belanger. He liked the bit I read at the Writers' League meeting and asked to see the whole manuscript."

As if on cue, the phone rang.

"For you, Vick," Gerry held the phone toward me.

"Hello...Oh, hello Darcy."

Gerry listened attentively, recognizing the name of the publisher to whom I had sent the manuscript. I brought up a visual memory of a tall, thin young man perpetually in motion, his head topped by a wild bush of curly red hair.

"Vickie darling, I've just read your novel. I HATE the ending! I can't stand endings that leave me up in the air! I want to know what HAPPENED!"

"Oh!" My heart sank.

"I know, I know. It's a great ending, Vickie. I hate it but I'll buy it. It will get people upset. It will intrigue them. They'll talk about it, and that will get others interested and they'll go out and buy it.

"I'll publish your book, Vickie. I'll send you a contract. Sign it and send it back."

I could hardly get the phone back into its holder. Gerry caught the excitement as my tone in talking to the publisher had changed. "He bought it?"

"Yes, yes, yes!" I flew into my husband's arms and we danced around the small living room of our basement apartment. Gerry was as delighted as I was. Gerry Rowe, a sports reporter for the Sentinel, a weekly suburban paper, had given me all the technical information on the game of baseball that had gone into the novel. He was almost a co-author. I took pride in saying, "You're always told to write about what you know. I write about what my husband knows." *Strike Three*, a novel by Victoria Radcliff, the pen name I used.

"Let's go out and celebrate," Gerry cried, hugging me again.

Two days later, the morning paper slapped against the wall of the house and bounced down the steps to our basement abode. Bleary-eyed, I stepped out the door to retrieve it, tossed it onto the couch, and went to our tiny kitchenette to pour my first cup of coffee before curling up on one end of the couch to read the paper. The news item was on page three. "PUBLISHER ATTACKED AT DOOR OF OFFICE. Darcy Belanger, co-owner of Belanger Publishing, was struck on the head with a blunt object as he left his office and his attaché case containing his laptop computer was stolen...Belanger remains in a coma and is not expected to live."

"Oh, no!"

Gerry popped his head out of the bathroom. "What's the matter, Vick?" I shoved the paper into his hand, pointing to the news item. "Good God, Vick. That's the guy who was going to publish your novel!"

I nodded. Gerry sat down beside me, wrapping his arm around my shoulder. "Maybe his co-owner will still publish your book."

"It's not just the novel. I *liked* him," I wept.

"I know."

"Maybe it was a gay bashing thing," I suggested, wiping away tears.

"I don't think so. Those guys get beat up far more than that. One blow and the theft of a computer sounds more like an ordinary mugging." But it wasn't, as we soon realized.

The next morning, the TV news reported that Belanger had died. His stolen attaché case had been found by security personnel at the Union subway station. There was no ID on the case, but on starting up the computer, they had found Belanger's name. Recognizing it, they had called the police, who reported that the publisher's partner, Kevin O'Conner, had determined that all the manuscripts stored in the computer had been deleted and some printed ones that Belanger had taken with him had also been stolen. The police considered the publisher's death to be the result of a deliberate attack, not a casual mugging.

A few days later, Kevin called me. "Vickie, this is Kevin. I'm finally getting myself pulled together enough to get back to taking care of business."

"Oh, Kevin. How awful for you. I'm really sorry." I knew that Darcy and Kevin had been partners in more ways than one.

"Vickie, I know that Darcy really liked your novel. He had several manuscripts he was looking at and had sent contracts to a couple of other authors, but yours was the only signed contract for a book that was not yet in production. I know nothing whatsoever about publishing. I'm the accountant and the only kinds of books I know anything about are entirely different. So I'm going to have to sell the business. I'll try to find someone who will honour your contract."

"Thanks, Kevin. I appreciate that. I know things are difficult for you." I tried to sound upbeat, but it was a blow, let me tell you!

But Kevin was as good as his word. Soon I received another phone call.

"Is this Victoria?"

"Yes it is."

"Do you go by Rowe or Radcliff?"

"If you're talking about books, I'm Victoria Radcliff. Otherwise I'm Vickie Rowe."

"This is Max Mitchell at Bay Street Press. May I call you Vickie?"

"Certainly."

"We are going to take over Belanger Publishing. Darcy used to do freelance editing for us, and any book he recommended turned out to be a winner. I had a very high regard for his instincts on what would sell. So I'll honour the contract he had with you and publish *Strike Three*."

"Oh, that's wonderful! Thank you so much!"

"We'll send you one of our contracts. It will be pretty much the same as the one you signed with Darcy."

"I'll get it right back to you."

It was a week before the news of Max Mitchell's murder hit the news. This time it made page one. Max had been hit on the back of the head while working at a computer in his office at Bay Street Press. He had been working late in the evening, not unusual with him. The attacker had probably gained access to the office when the cleaners were working, had hidden until they left, then slugged the publisher and ransacked his office. Printed manuscripts and contracts, including mine, were missing. All manuscripts on the computers had been deleted and the trash emptied. My manuscript, for one, was completely gone.

"Now what am I going to do?" I wailed.

Gerry hugged me and murmured in my ear. "You will find another publisher for your novel. If two publishers liked it that much, another will snap it up. What about that guy you met at the book club—the one who spoke to the club about publishing?"

"Michael Sandford? I'd forgotten about him. He read some of my stuff and liked it. I'll call him."

But when I called Sandford, his response was like a body punch.

"Vickie! I can't possibly publish your book. Word gets around, you know. Both publishers who have agreed to publish your novel, *Strike Three*, have been murdered and your manuscript stolen. What the hell did you write that someone is that desperate that it not be printed? *Strike Three*! There have been two strikes already, and I sure as hell don't want to be the third! Don't even send it to me! I don't want anything to do with it!"

I was stunned. The thought that the murderer was killing in order that my novel not be published had never occurred to me. Nor to Gerry.

"I can't think of anything you wrote that would get anyone desperate enough to try to keep it from being published," he remarked, looking puzzled. "That stuff was straight out of your imagination. There's nothing going on in baseball that resembles it in the least."

"But it means I'm blacklisted. No one is going to take it now."

"Well, you're going to that crime writers conference. You can explain to everyone you meet that they needn't worry and maybe someone will realize that and be willing to accept it."

"Not bloody likely!"

I took the GO train into Toronto on Friday evening to attend the first session of the conference. The hotel where the conference was held turned out to be one of those vast places that catered to several conventions at the same time. The only one I could find was for electrical engineers, so I went to the registration desk to ask where to find the mystery writers. A young man was checking in, and when he had finished filling out the registration card, he also asked where to find the crime writers' conference. As the clerk gave him directions, I could see the card he had just filled out and learned that his name was Bliss. Mr. Bliss did not seem to fit his name. He was nervous and jumpy and kept looking over his shoulder, literally, as if he expected someone to jump him from behind. I followed him and eventually found the registration desk for the mystery writers, though the unblissful Mr. Bliss had veered off to someplace else before he got there. I picked up my nametag and a huge bag filled with advertising, bookmarks, magazines and books—lots of books. It must have weighed thirty pounds, I thought. With nowhere to unload any of it, I was stuck with lugging all this stuff around for two days, as I was staying overnight with a university classmate who lived near the University of Toronto campus.

The first seminar was one in which the panelists discussed juggling writing with family and jobs. It was a lot of fun, with many amusing stories, and the members of the audience were doubled over with laughter. Just what I needed to undo the kinks caused by my worries.

The next morning, the panel that interested me was held just before lunch. It was about fictionalizing actual crimes. I thought it might give me some insight on why my novel, which as Gerry said, was straight out of my imagination, might cause someone enough stress to precipitate two murders. But on entering the room in which this panel was to be held, I wished I had chosen something else. One of the panelists was Joe McGrath, absolutely the most boring man I have ever met. I had heard him at several writers' meetings, telling everyone that he was writing an opus that would become the standard work in its field, the greatest story of the twenty-first century. Once he got the floor, there was no way to shut him up, as he disgorged huge globs of turgid prose. But I decided to stick it out. To my surprise, young Mr. Bliss sneaked into the room. I had seen him from time to time wandering around as if he were looking for someone. He had evidently not registered for the conference, as he did not have a nametag or a bag of books. I wondered how he had gotten into the seminar if he wasn't registered.

True to form, once McGrath got hold of the mike, clutching it with a death grip, he took over the seminar. The moderator tried to get the mike back again, but his efforts were futile, so there was no choice other than to listen. McGrath's great work was about a small town with two families in a constant feud. McGrath likened them to the Hatfields and the McCoys, and named them the Blacks and the Harpers. One day a Harper hit a Black child who had run out into the street in front of Harper's car. The police had to hustle Harper out of the way to prevent his being attacked by the Blacks. When it was determined that there was no fault on the part of Harper, and no charges were laid, the Blacks were furious. That night, a fifteen-year-old lad from the extended Black clan, took a .30-.30 hunting rifle and shot Harper through the living room window of his house. The youth, identified by McGrath as Tommy Payne, ran away and had not to this day been found. McGrath had used two chapters to detail the search for Payne.

The session eventually ended and with relief we all headed off to lunch. But as McGrath's spiel had dragged on, I felt that I had heard this somewhere before. But where? Had McGrath plagiarized some other author, or had I read something similar in the newspaper? As I walked down the hall, it came to me.

Several years earlier, when I was studying at the University of Toronto, I decided to head home to Edmonton at the end of the school year by VIA Rail, rather than flying. I needed those three nights and two days of rest in the comfort of a sleeping car, eating superb meals without worrying about what I had to study next. The train stopped for several hours in Winnipeg while the complete crew was changed and the train restocked. I wandered down to the Forks Market, but being the proverbial starving student, didn't spend much. To while away the rest of the time until I could get back on the train, I went into the Panorama Lounge and picked up a newspaper. I read it more thoroughly than usual, in order to fill the time. One item was about a murder investigation in a small Manitoba town, where two families, the Whites and the Laytons, were constantly feuding with one another. A Layton struck a teen-age White girl who rode her bike right in front of Layton's car. Layton was absolved of responsibility for the accident, but several days later a youth from the White clan took a hunting rifle and shot Layton as he walked out of his house. This was several months previously and the police were still looking for the youth, who could not be named because of his age.

I could see Joe McGrath walking down the hall ahead of me, and Bliss following a few steps behind. The similarity of the names in McGrath's story suddenly occurred to me. Black and White. Harper and Layton. Payne and Bliss? Was Bliss the unnamed youth in that Manitoba murder? Was he after McGrath to get the manuscript back—or maybe to put an end to the source of the story? I hurried to catch up with Joe, with the idea of warning him, but before I reached him, he hailed Michael Sandford, who was hurrying toward the elevator. Michael stopped, showing impatience. Joe said in his loud voice, "I've got that manuscript for you to look at." He sounded as if he were prepared to give poor Michael a blow-by-blow account of it there on the spot.

Michael replied, "I'm in a hurry right now. Bring it to my room after lunch. I'm in five fifteen. It's just to the right of the elevator." He gave these last instructions over his shoulder as he slid through the closing doors.

Joe saw me and hailed me like a long-lost friend. "Say, Vickie, I've got a lunch date. Could you take this manuscript and deliver it to Michael? Room five fifteen." As he said this, he thrust a large box into my hands. It was an old box that typewriter paper used to come in, but was crammed full of about half again as much paper as it was intended to hold and was held together by large rubber bands. And it was *heavy*!

"Hey, Joe. Don't tell me you still type your stuff."

"Yeah. I never took to these computers. I have a gal who types my manuscripts for me, but she's pretty teed-off this time. It's over eight hundred pages, and this is the third time she's had to do it."

"Why's that?"

"Oh, didn't you know? The last two publishers I sent it to got the chop. That queer and old Max Mitchell."

Joe rushed off, leaving me with the baby, so to speak. Oh well! I might as well deliver it. That would be better than lugging that much extra weight around until I found Joe again. I put the box into my bag, making it so heavy I dragged it along the floor rather than trying to lift it.

I had a brief feeling of elation. It wasn't *my* novel that was causing the problem. It was Joe McGrath's! But then, the more sober thought dawned on me that I now had possession of the document that had resulted in two murders.

A vague memory tried to thrust itself into my consciousness—a memory of seeing Bliss sidle around Joe and me and make his way toward the elevator. This gave me a sense of alarm, so that when the doors slid open at the fifth floor, I hesitated before stepping out. I didn't see anyone, so I turned quickly to the right, reaching up to knock on Michael's door.

Bliss was there all right, flattened against the wall to the left of the elevator. In my peripheral vision, I saw the weapon, a home-made cosh, in time to duck. It swished over my head. He would try again if I didn't do something, so I used the only weapon I had, my book bag. I swung it from the floor in an arc that I hoped would hit some vulnerable spot. The weight from all those books plus Joe's monstrous tome, produced a whopping impact when it hit, which it did after bouncing off Bliss' shoulder, onto the side of his head, with a satisfying thud. He crumpled like a wet dishrag and fell, just as Michael opened his door, right at Michael's feet.

"There you are, Michael!" I gloated. "There's your murderer! Now will you publish my book?"

A Death at the Parsonage
By Susan Daly

In her dewy youth, Susan wanted to be Trixie Belden, the thinking girl's Nancy Drew. Even more, she wanted to write about heroines as feisty as Trixie. For years she wandered in the wilderness, writing in various genres and non-genres. But in her heart she yearned for a life of crime. Because really, what could be more satisfying than a body or two in the library, a fistful of red herrings and a gutsy amateur sleuth with an intellectual bent and an unusual hobby. When she tasted success in The Whole She-Bang 2, *she found ridding the world of deserving victims to be so enjoyable she has developed a morbid and permanent taste for the practice. Susan is a member of Sisters in Crime (both the Toronto chapter and International) and the Guppies. She lives in Toronto, a short commute from her superlative grandkids.*

(Letter from Miss Maria Metcalf of Hunsford village to her cousin Frances Fanshawe, wife of Captain Harville Fanshawe of the —th Battalion, stationed at York, Upper Canada.)

22 September, 1823

My Dearest Fanny—

It was with the greatest pleasure I received your letter telling us of your imminent return to England after twelve years in the wilds of Canada. I must fill you in on what you may expect to find captivating our conversation these days.

I begin with the Sudden Death in the neighbourhood. Four days ago the Parson, Mr. William Collins, was found <u>lifeless</u> in the garden at the Parsonage. And there is talk of <u>Foul Play</u>. Possibly at the hands of—but no, I dare not express my own suspicions.

You may remember at the time of your departure for the wilderness, Mr. Collins was contemplating marriage to one of his five Bennet cousins (though he had not yet decided which one). Imagine our surprise when he married Eliza Bennet's dearest friend. Clearly Miss Charlotte Lucas had her eye on the long view, when her husband would inherit Longbourn (Mr. Bennet having no sons to succeed him) for no one could possibly have married the tedious man for himself, much less the dubious joys of living in the cramped and uncomfortable Hunsford Parsonage.

But—it all _Fell Through_.

It began when the last of the Bennet girls, Kitty (who was pushing four-and-twenty) astounded us all by making a match more splendid than any of her sisters'. On the day the banns were put up, Mrs. Bennet, in a paroxysm of joy, suffered a stroke and, her life's work accomplished, died with (I am told) a beatific smile upon her face.

The wedding was a subdued affair, and it was a shame Mrs. Bennet had to miss it, along with a lifetime of making frequent references to "My daughter, the Duchess of Dundee."

But mark the astonishing sequel. Barely a twelvemonth after the funeral, Mr. Bennet—who one would have thought had learned his lesson—was once again captivated by a fair face and a mediocre mentality. He married a Miss Maria Fortescue, whom he actually met _at the home of his own heir presumptive_, Mr. Collins. This time, however, he was luckier in his bride's ability to reproduce the issue demanded by the invasive and invidious laws that determine inheritance and estate succession. Ten months after the marriage, the second Mrs. Bennet produced a healthy, hardy son, followed less than a year later by equally healthy, hardy _twin_ boys.

The Collinses, who might have hoped—though let us believe they did not _pray_—for a chance illness to carry off the firstborn usurper, could not in all charity wish for some terrible fate for all three boys.

Now, as to the Sudden and Horrid death of Mr. Collins, of course I would not for a moment credit the rumours that _Mrs. Collins herself_ laid her husband low. One cannot help thinking, however, after years of putting up with a man reviled equally for his stupidity as for his toadyism, in expectation of someday becoming mistress of Longbourn, and then to have those hopes dashed by some unspeakable little social climber with the _same_ ambitions— well, it would be beyond wonderful if she did not feel herself _very ill-used_ by Fate. And exceedingly fed up with her husband.

But enough of that, dearest Fanny, or I shall be tempted to descend to gossip. I understand from my aunt that your husband will be settling not far from here...

"Eliza, thank heavens you've come." Charlotte Collins's violent embrace threatened to knock Elizabeth Darcy over the moment her friend alighted from the carriage. "I couldn't have borne another moment without your company."

Elizabeth surveyed her friend's peaked face, her colour not improved by deep mourning. "Of course I came. I'm just sorry we had to miss the funeral." She and her husband had been in Paris when the news had caught up with them, and she had been travelling ever since. Mr. Darcy would join them in a few days.

"How long can you stay? Several weeks, I hope."

"As long as you need me, Charlotte. Now, let's get inside out of this threatening weather. A cup of tea would be most welcome."

In minutes they were enjoying a copious tea by the fire in Charlotte's comfortable drawing room. It was just themselves, for Charlotte's two daughters had been invited to spend a quiet afternoon with their friend Miss Webb in the village. All other family and connections had returned home to their disparate locations.

Elizabeth reached for a piping hot scone and slathered it with butter. "Now, Charlotte, I know it's been a horrible ordeal, and I suspect Lady Catherine de Burgh hasn't been making your life any sweeter." The rich, controlling old lady who lived across the park at Rosings had held Mr. Collins in her pocket for years, dictating how the clergyman—and his wife—should live their lives. "So now you may heap all your troubles onto me."

"Oh, Eliza...." Charlotte's voice was barely audible. "They think I killed him."

Elizabeth dropped the half-eaten scone onto her plate.

"*Who* does?"

"Everyone! Well, Lady Catherine."

Elizabeth felt a stab of anxiety. "Now listen, Charlotte. Though she might think it, Lady Catherine is certainly not *everyone*."

"*And* Dr. Greene. Besides, the world at large is so in the habit of going along with everything she proposes that they will follow her like sheep."

"But surely the Magistrate...."

"Oh, it will never come to that. If it did, I might have a hope of its being disproven. No, it will remain innuendo and gossip. No one will come right out and say I pushed him into the rockery. But the suspicions will follow me to my grave. My darling girls...."

The misery in Charlotte's eyes gave way to tears, and soon she was sobbing on Elizabeth's shoulder.

"My girls will be haunted by the twin spectres of not being truly sure, in their heart of hearts, that I didn't do it, and of the dubious distinction of being labelled the daughters of a *murderess*."

81

Charlotte didn't object when her friend, having sent the tea things away with Mary Ann, poured two generous glasses of Mr. Darcy's good sherry, brought as a gift.

"Now, Charlotte, your father wrote us all about it, but be assured he said nothing about any such suspicions. Tell me exactly what happened."

Charlotte took a fortifying sip of the sherry and then a few more. "It was Market Day...." By now she could tell it in her sleep. She and Mary Ann had walked into Hunsford village for the weekly provisions, while Mr. Collins had remained at home, working on his sermon for Sunday. "Everything was quite as usual. On our way back, as we passed Rosings, Mary Ann asked permission to stop and visit with her brother. Jem is under-gardener there. I consented and took one of the baskets home with me. When I arrived, I—I didn't look for Mr. Collins at first...."

Because she was happy to leave him to his own devices. In fact, she had dawdled on the way home, luxuriating in thirty minutes stolen from the day, with no household or wifely duties.

"And then I finally went round to the garden to look for him...."

She squeezed her eyes shut, but the image wouldn't go away. Hadn't gone away in a week. It haunted her day and night. Poor Mr. Collins lying face down in the garden, half in the rockery. Everything about him askew. His head against a rock. Blood around him. Undoubtedly dead.

Eliza leaned forward and took her hand. "Charlotte dear, I know it's difficult to think about, but please, just one more time, and we'll try to get to the bottom of things. Tell it as though it were happening to someone else. In a novel perhaps."

"A novel? Oh! Yes, all right. I saw him lying there...."

She stepped out of her own being and envisaged the scene in the garden. "He must have tripped on a loose stone in the pathway."

"You brave thing," Elizabeth murmured. "All alone with him."

Charlotte took a breath and pushed out the rest in a continuous flow. "And then Mary Ann came back; her brother had walked with her to carry the basket and he told Mary Ann to stay with me and he went back to Rosings for help and came back with Dr. Greene, who took charge and confirmed he had died of the blow sustained when his head hit the rock. That he must have been so absorbed in composing his sermon—or practising it— that he tripped and fell headlong into the rockery."

Charlotte paused and looked around her favourite room.

"And now I shall have to leave my beloved home." She reached for her sherry glass and drained it. Elizabeth refilled it without hesitation.

"*Do* you have plans?" her friend asked. "I know it's early days..."

"I will return home to my father's house, along with my dear girls, where we will always be welcome." But for how long? And how could she bear such ignominy? And worse, having no home of her own?

"But Charlotte, why should Lady Catherine and the doctor think *you* had anything to do with it? Do they think you pushed him into the rockery?"

"Dr. Greene gathered up some things in the garden: Mr. Collins's scattered sermon notes, his fallen writing implements, a book. He says it was because the sight of them would distress me. After the funeral, he was about to return them when..." she found her throat catching, but forced herself to go on "...he says he noticed the top corner of the book was flattened, as though it had hit something, and, and... there were some short dark hairs embedded in a crack in the spine... as though, as though...."

"As though the book had been used to hit someone—Mr. Collins—on the head."

"Exactly! And that's when Dr. Greene recalled there *had* been a bruise on the back of his head, although he hit his *forehead* on the rock. It was in his notes."

"Of course it was."

"Then Lady Catherine remarked it was very odd indeed that the book was a novel. Because Mr. Collins despised novels and looked down upon those who indulged in them—she meant me, of course, and probably you and your sisters and every other person who enjoys using their imagination. She took the opportunity to add that *her* daughter never wastes her time with novels, that Miss Anne and Mrs. Jenkinson read only improving books and essays together."

Elizabeth uttered a word which shocked Charlotte, though she wholeheartedly concurred with the sentiment.

"Is it not possible, Charlotte, that Mr. Collins was doing a little research into such sinful, degrading objects, the better to write a sermon denouncing them from the pulpit?"

Charlotte couldn't hold back a faint smile. It *was* good to have Eliza here, to have someone take her part.

"Lady Catherine then declared that Mr. Collins *must* have been hit by a novel reader; one, moreover, who had reason to be angry with him."

"That someone being you?"

"She is convinced I cannot forgive him for introducing your father to your new step-mamma, thereby bringing about his own disinheritance and losing us Longbourn."

"Ludicrous," Eliza murmured.

"Completely ignoring the fact that I love my little house, that if I killed Mr. Collins, my girls and I would be rendered homeless, that I—I had become used to him, in fact, quite fond of him, in a way."

"Oh."

"I know you find that hard to credit, and I'm sure Mr. Darcy is unsurpassed among husbands, but Mr. Collins and I have managed to rub along together tolerably well."

"Of course, Charlotte dear. I *do* understand."

"*And* disregarding the fact that if I *were* to go around murdering people, I should have chosen Lady Catherine for my victim."

Elizabeth allowed a laugh and poured more sherry for them both.

"But my dear Charlotte, can you think of any reason why the novel would be in the garden? Could someone else have left it there?"

Charlotte dropped her voice and glanced toward the door. "There is a very good reason. I put it there."

Elizabeth covered her speechlessness by taking a good measure of the sherry in her glass. "You astonish me, Charlotte," she at last managed to observe.

"You see," Charlotte now looked calmer, "he had to be reading *something*, because as we were walking into the village, Mary Ann mentioned she'd seen him go off to the garden as usual, with his book. So when I found Mr. Collins and ascertained he was quite dead, the one thing I could do for him was to protect his reputation by removing the book he *was* reading."

"Charlotte!" All manner of possibilities invaded Elizabeth's lively imagination. "*What* book?"

"A book of sermons. *Decatur's Collected Sermons for All Seasons.*"

Elizabeth admitted herself disappointed. "What's wrong with that? It sounds just like him."

"It's an American book. He bought it from the estate of a sea captain who brought it home from Boston years ago."

"But I don't see..."

"The sermons are unknown here. Mr. Collins didn't use them for inspiration. He used them. Period. Copied them in his own handwriting, changed a few of the American idioms and more revolutionary ideas, and passed them off as his own every Sunday morning."

"But... the novel...?"

"When I heard Mary Ann arriving with her brother, I dashed into my sitting room and slipped the book of sermons into the bookshelf, then snatched up the first book I laid my hands on—I had no idea what it was. I placed it on the bench, then I ran around to the front to talk to Mary Ann."

"Where is the sermon book now? I know it will sound odd, but if you take it to Dr. Greene and explain..."

"I burned it."

"Charlotte!"

"I know. But I thought it was for the best. For two days I dreaded anyone finding it. And then the morning of the funeral I burned it in my sitting room fire."

Elizabeth looked over toward the grate.

"I looked. There's not a trace of it. Not even in the ashbin outside. No one else ever saw it."

"Not even Mary Ann, when she was cleaning?"

Charlotte shook her head. "He took care no one but myself knew of its existence. Oh Eliza, what am I going to do? My poor girls..."

"Clearly, my dear Charlotte, there's only one thing *to* do. We'll have to figure out who *did* kill Mr. Collins."

Later that afternoon, Elizabeth walked over to Rosings to pay her respects and offer condolences. After suffering long discourses on the tragic event and Lady Catherine de Burgh's offended feelings (though not her suspicions), Elizabeth managed to bring the conversation around to Dr. Greene's role in the events.

"So fortunate, wasn't it, Lady Catherine, that Dr. Greene was able to get to the Parsonage so quickly."

Lady Catherine gave her a *how-dare-you-introduce-a-subject* look. Elizabeth gave her a look in return.

"Dr. Greene was here at Rosings, attending to Mrs. Jenkinson, who was suffering from a case of nerves. I am widely known for my generosity in providing professional care for all my household staff."

Household staff? *This* was how she referred to the woman who had been at her beck and call for nearly forty years, as Miss Anne's long-suffering, uncomplaining companion?

"Oh, poor Mrs. Jenkinson. Unwell, and then hearing of the sudden death of her close neighbour and spiritual advisor." Perhaps Mrs. Jenkinson could shed some light on Dr. Greene's initial reaction to being called to the Parsonage. With little ceremony she stood up.

"Going so soon, Mrs. Darcy?"

"Yes, I must. Although first I should like to pay a visit to Mrs. Jenkinson. Up in her sitting room?" She forestalled the objection she saw forming on Lady Catherine's lips. "I promised to deliver a message from Mrs. Collins."

"She is *still* unwell," Lady Catherine said, in a voice that suggested "malingerer." Still, she could scarcely forbid this act of kindness on behalf of the bereaved Mrs. Collins. A maid was called to escort Mrs. Darcy up to Mrs. Jenkinson's third floor room.

Elizabeth knocked and, bidden to enter, found the distraught lady, looking even older than her sixty-odd years, reclining on the chaise longue, a shawl around her thin shoulders. She was clearly in a state of abject misery. Elizabeth sat in a nearby chair and expressed her concern.

"Mrs. Jenkinson, I'm sorry to disturb you when I know what a terrible time you must being going through. Mrs. Collins sends her regards, and would like to know how you are faring."

Mrs. Jenkinson dabbed at her eyes with her handkerchief. "So kind," she murmured. "So thoughtful. It's been unbearably distressing."

"Yes. I'm sure it has been. Your sympathy for Mrs. Collins in her bereavement is commendable."

Mrs. Jenkinson delicately blew her nose into the sodden bit of cambric. Elizabeth offered her own handkerchief.

"I trust you are improving now," Elizabeth went on. "Lady Catherine was concerned you were unwell the day of Mr. Collins's...accident."

"So generous of her to call in Dr. Greene. My nerves were sadly shattered at the thought of poor Mr. Collins's lifeless corpse...." More sniffles.

"Oh? But surely—" A birdlike hint of unease tapped at Elizabeth's mind. "I must have misunderstood. I quite thought Dr. Greene was at Rosings *before* that terrible discovery."

"Oh yes. That's right." Mrs. Jenkinson bit her lip. "I have been in such a sad state I scarcely know what I am saying."

"You've had more than one misfortune, then?"

Mrs. Jenkinson glanced toward the closed door and leaned forward, all conspiratorial. "Dear Mrs. Darcy, you have always been so kind. *May* I confide in you? You see, I have no one..." Her lips quivered again and Elizabeth wished she had another handkerchief to offer.

"Of course, Mrs. Jenkinson." She put her hand on the old lady's and felt a stab of discomfort for playing on her trust like this.

Mrs. Jenkinson's demeanour grew more mournful by the second. "The truth is I have betrayed dear Lady Catherine's trust in me, after all these years. She gave me full charge of her daughter's well-being and amusement, and what have I done but Lead Her Astray."

"Lead Her Astray!" Elizabeth couldn't help thinking of the dead secret history of how Mr. Darcy's sister had been nearly led to ruin at the hands of Mr. Wickham, betrayed by her companion, Mrs. Younge. But she could hardly imagine Mrs. Jenkinson in the role of procuress. And besides, Miss Anne...? Still, she *was* an heiress.

"...and really, so harmless," Mrs. Jenkinson was saying. "And both Miss Anne and I are partial to them. And Mrs. Collins too. Don't you think so, Mrs. Darcy?"

"Harmless?" She'd clearly missed a crucial point.

"Oh dear. You don't agree? No, nor does Lady Catherine. She says novels are filled with dangerous ideas and vulgarity and unchaste characters."

"Oh, novels! My sisters and I read novels all the time. We thoroughly enjoy flights of fantasy, and anyone with a steady brain can easily separate fiction from reality. So you and Miss Anne are secretly addicted to novels?"

And there was one in the eye for Lady Catherine, to be sure. Though of course not so satisfactory if she were to find out.

"Oh dear...." Mrs. Jenkinson's voice quivered again.

"Ah, you think Lady Catherine suspects?"

"No, but— Oh Mrs. Darcy! Mr. Collins was adamant. He even quoted Dr. Fordyce's views on novels to me...." She fumbled about on her writing table and produced a close-written letter, evidently much read and tear-stained, and thrust it at Elizabeth, who took it with a sense of falling into a vortex. She easily found the passage, for it was underlined by the writer....

"<u>What shall we say of certain books, which we are assured (for we have not read them) are in their nature so shameful, in their tendency so pestiferous, and contain such rank treason against the royalty of Virtue, such horrible violation of all decorum, that she</u>

who can bear to peruse them must in her soul be a prostitute, let her reputation in life be what it will.'"

Good heavens. She and her sisters were familiar with the appalling and mean-spirited writings of Dr. Fordyce and his venomous contempt for all women, for hadn't her father occasionally laughed with them over the dictates of this self-appointed arbiter of female behaviour and decorum, in his *Sermons for Young Women*? But he was far more dangerous than amusing, for there were many men who took his rantings as Gospel when it came to their own wives and daughters.

How *could* Mr. Collins have used such a weapon against this weak-minded but kind-hearted lady, who was in a precarious social position dependent upon the whim of her employer? What business of his was it anyway, unless he hoped to gain approval from his patroness?

"This is monstrous," Elizabeth said when she could finally speak without sullying her companion's ears with stronger words. "Infamous!"

Mrs. Jenkinson looked up, almost with a shadow of hope in her eyes. "Oh, do you think so?"

"Do you mean to tell me Mr. Collins took it upon himself to dictate to you how you should act as companion to Miss Anne?"

"He said in light of my, my *desecrating* Miss Anne's innocent mind with such *perversions*, he had no choice but to report—oh dear—my *shameful duplicity* to Lady Catherine."

Here the good lady renewed her sobs with such force that Elizabeth hadn't the heart to push her for further details. She put her arm about her shoulder and let her cry for several more minutes.

When at last the torrent of anguish abated, Elizabeth said, in as kind-but-firm a voice as she could manage, "Well, I'm afraid you *will* have to stop enjoying them, both of you. It's a shame, because really, novels are perfectly harmless and enlivening, and Dr. Fordyce is an evil, interfering man, but you know, Lady Catherine *does* call the tune when it comes to her daughter." Though why Miss Anne, nearly forty, still had to be under the thumb of her mother was unfathomable, even when that mother was Lady Catherine de Burgh.

"I don't like to shift blame," Mrs. Jenkinson whispered, "but I'm afraid Miss Anne would read novels anyway. She adores them. In fact, though I shouldn't say this, it was *she* who introduced them to *me*."

"Life is unfair for paid dependents, I agree, but you would still get the blame, I fear."

Mrs. Jenkinson nodded.

"But I promise you, Lady Catherine will never hear it from me. And clearly, she will never hear it from Mr. Collins."

At this infelicitous observation, Mrs. Jenkinson's agonies returned tenfold.

"But that's exactly *it,* Mrs. Darcy," she howled. There was no other word for it but *howled.*

"*What*'s it?"

"He won't tell her, because, because he's *dead.*"

"Well, yes...."

Good lord. Someone who read novels *and* had reason to wish ill of Mr. Collins?

Impossible.... She took hold of the lady's frail hand and patted it gently.

"Mrs. Jenkinson, you've been here in your room, haven't you, nearly a week. Away from all the goings-on in the neighbourhood? From what's being said?"

Sniff. "Yes. I cannot bring myself to go out and about right now."

"And have you heard what's being said about Mrs. Collins?"

For the first time since Elizabeth had entered the room, she saw Mrs. Jenkinson show concern for something other than her own plight. "What could they possibly be saying about that poor bereaved lady?"

"Terrible things, I'm afraid. Lady Catherine and Dr. Greene have taken it into their heads that Mr. Collins's death was no accident."

Elizabeth stared steadily at her companion, whose complexion went from white to grey to sickly green.

"Oh!"

"Indeed. They believe Mrs. Collins cruelly and wantonly killed her husband. And I'm afraid, ridiculous though that may seem, they might convince the Magistrate of this nonsensical tale."

Miraculously, a less sickly colour rose to Mrs. Jenkinson's face, and she sat up with some semblance of strength, even a hint of determination.

"That is utter nonsense! Of course poor Mrs. Collins did nothing of the sort. As if she could. Or would."

"*We* know that, but Dr. Greene has other ideas, and when he found that book in the garden..."

"Book?"

"A novel. With one corner dented, bearing a few hairs which matched Mr. Collins's in length and colour..." It flickered through

Elizabeth's mind that she was being cruelly graphic, but she batted the thought away. "He fancies himself a Bow Street Runner and has persuaded Lady Catherine that Mrs. Collins must have had an argument with her husband and hit him on the head with the book."

"What novel?" Mrs. J's face was a study in puzzlement and horror.

"It was on the bench in the garden. Lady Caro Lamb's *Glenarvon*. Volume II."

"Oh! But I put it..." Her complexion whitened again as she nearly bit off her tongue.

"Yes? You put it in Mrs. Collins's sitting room?"

"No...." But her look said *yes*.

And now it all came out. Elizabeth listened with deepening horror as the diminutive lady's companion told her tale. How distraught she had been at the prospect of losing her position after so many years, of the unlikelihood of ever finding another. She had waited until Mrs. Collins and her maid had gone to the village, then had stolen over to the Parsonage along the footpath and confronted him in his garden. But no amount of reasoning, pleading or promising to cease this egregious habit had any effect on Mr. Collins, who maintained it was his painful duty to report all to his patroness.

Finally, as he turned away to indicate he was deaf to further entreaties, she had permitted her rage and fear to overcome her good sense, and, crying, "You horrid, horrid man!" she had swung at him with the very root of the trouble, the novel she held in her hand.

"Oh, my dear Mrs. Darcy, I fear I must have gone a little mad. He lost his balance at the edge of the rockery and fell and hit his forehead against a rock. It was clear in a moment he was quite, quite dead. But what could I do? Surely it must be taken for an accident.

"I had to get rid of the book, so I ran into the house with the thought of burning it, but then I saw I could hide it in Mrs. Collins's sitting room. I laid it on top of some other books and slipped out the side entrance, through the back gate and along the river path to Rosings."

"And Lady Catherine sent for Dr. Greene?"

"Yes. She found me practically prostrate in the conservatory. I said I had suffered a fright in the woods—a snake on the pathway—and was quite shaken up. When Dr. Greene arrived, he ordered me to bed and administered a sedative. I have been here ever since. Hiding my face."

Immeasurable relief for Charlotte's life and happiness flowed through Elizabeth's soul, tinged with anguish for this wretched lady.

"It was unintended, Mrs. Jenkinson. A moment of unbearable distress and panic—"

"Passion," Mrs. Jenkinson murmured in a tone of wonder. "I was undone by a fit of unbridled passion..."

"Well..." Elizabeth hardly knew how to respond.

"It's true, then," she continued in a disturbingly calm voice. "Reading novels *can* lead to a life of debauchery. I allowed Miss Anne to read them, encouraged her even. I would never have committed such a terrible act had my mind not been distorted and corrupted by these heinous creations, so roundly and rightly condemned by decent people. I had hoped it would be deemed an accident, but I had no idea that poor dear Mrs. Collins would be accused of the crime. When she is utterly innocent.

"Although..." Mrs. Jenkinson seemed to be fitting ideas together, "*she* reads novels too."

(Extract from the latest letter from Maria to Fanny, November 13, 1823.)

Mrs. Collins has removed with her daughters to the dower house on the Pemberley grounds, where she sees her friend Eliza every day, no doubt to discuss novels, and the girls share lessons with the Darcy children in the Pemberley schoolroom.

Mr. Darcy has busied himself with Mrs. Jenkinson too, and arranged for her to be confined to a private nursing home, where she will live out her days. Lady Catherine was beside herself with umbrage and vowed to hire a more fitting companion for her daughter. But Miss Anne, no doubt swayed by ideas garnered from her incendiary reading matter, has declared herself independent of her mother, having claimed her own inheritance (now that she has turned forty). She lives in Bath with a friend of her own choosing, reading novels. I understand she visits her old companion occasionally and brings her books. But I hear that unhappy woman now reads nothing but sermons.

By-the-by, Fanny, have you read Glenarvon? *I have all three volumes and it is, I assure you, a deliciously wicked tale. You will adore it.*

Wedding Snaps
By Jayne Barnard

Jayne Barnard writes Canadian history, mystery and geography, with occasional forays into alternate dimensions of time and/or space. Awards for short fiction range from the 1990 Saskatchewan Writers Guild Award to the 2011 Bony Pete. She's been shortlisted for both the Unhanged Arthur in Canada and the Debut Dagger in the UK. A long-time board member of Mystery Writers Ink, a founding member of Calgary Crime Writers and a member of Sisters in Crime (Toronto Chapter), Jayne also served on the board of Crime Writers of Canada. Her first book is Maddie Hatter and the Deadly Diamond.

Only Sally would dare wake Tyrone at eleven a.m. on a stifling Saturday morning after a full-moon, hot-summer-night, welfare-cheque shift. From the day her mother fled from Fruitcake #3 into Dad's basement apartment, Ty was under orders to look out for his younger cousin. Yes, even when teenage lust sent her stalking Ty's best pal. Dying of embarrassment was no excuse in Dad's book.

Neither, therefore, was a record sizzling day, an itchy brocade vest, a strangling bowtie, or a cummerbund that slid up every time Ty bent to line up a shot. Because Sally hurt her hand and needed help, he'd crawled out of bed and driven her to a dying hamlet half an hour from anywhere to photograph what she called the past-due renaissance of a good Catholic girl.

From his one glimpse of the bride, iron determination would get her over any pearly gate.

The stuffy old church was already half-full of folks perspiring into their best clothes. Having parked Sally in a back pew, he photographed their suffering for the bride's memory book. She looked like she'd enjoy that.

A nearby woman craned her neck toward the entrance, murmuring to her companion, "Do you see her?"

Not the bride already? Ty swung the camera toward the doors. Nope. Just a pack of guests unwilling to abandon the illusory coolness of the foyer.

"Maybe she couldn't face it after all," the other woman whispered back.

The main risk here, according to Sally, was a lightning strike from a vengeful god when Karlene and Rod promised to forsake all others. Maybe the bride couldn't risk it after all. Would Sally get paid if the wedding got flushed?

"She has gall enough. Karlene's the one who should have skipped this farce." Okay, not the bride. Maybe the groom had a handful of ex-wives?

The women fell silent, scanning the pews. Time to shift to the bride's side of the aisle anyway.

At least he was using his own multifunctional equipment. Sally's cameras were older than digital—hell, older than dirt. Maybe she'd abandon film after this morning's accident. Her prized close-action lens had been in her hand, unprotected, when the car door blew shut. Unlike her fingers, it wouldn't heal with a bit of tape and padding.

Ty twitched the sweaty cummerbund, grabbed his gear bag and crept to the shady side of the church. He was adjusting for the altered light when the woman nearest him whispered.

"I don't see her."

Was he hearing things? He glanced sideways.

The whisperer tucked compressed lips under her beaked nose. The next woman had rust-brown curls, these touched up with expensive highlights. The older woman beyond her had overgrown eyebrows streaked with grey.

"I don't see her," said The Beak again.

"Not yet, anyway," murmured Highlights. "Let's hope it worked."

"Karlene was sure it was done." Eyebrows fanned herself with the program.

The sun beat without mercy through the high, narrow windows, staining the musicians and the creamy walls with blazing hues. The air shimmered. The priest dripped perspiration onto his sacramental robes.

Ty snapped him mopping a shiny face with an oversized white hankie.

Three flushed men in formal wear took position near the altar. Ty snapped them from a few angles.

When the musicians launched into a processional, he tele-zoomed down the aisle and got off several shots at the approaching bride.

He grabbed the tripod and his bag, and slid into the last pew beside Sally.

"Dearly Beloved," intoned the priest, "We are gathered to celebrate...." He droned on with no pretense that the sanctity of marriage motivated the couple before him. Maybe he'd bought lightning insurance.

"Sal," Ty whispered, "people kept saying 'I don't see her.' 'HER' like it was all in capital letters."

"The groom's mistress," Sally said behind her hand.

Ty choked.

"Shh," she added sternly. "She's not here yet. I warned you there were issues."

She slid out of the pew, beckoning him outside. Under the shade of a lone elm, she slumped. "I guess I owe you some explanation, if only to keep you from asking anyone else.

"You know Karlene met Rod through my theatre group, right? She set her sights on him from the first. It took her ten years to get him here, through the breakup of both their marriages, his string of girlfriends, and finally her 'unplanned' pregnancy. If I was in her shoes, I'd have got the message a long time ago: this wedding shouldn't be happening."

"So why is it?"

"Ever try to stand in front of a tank, like that guy in China?" Sally shook her head sadly. "Rod's not that guy. Karlene's face could sink an armada whenever Missy's mentioned, but she smiles anyway, just like she has through all the other women. It's the longest-running soap opera in our community theatre group." She scratched around the edge of her sweat-stained wrist-wrap. "Karlene yearns for the role of lawful spouse and doesn't care that Rod doesn't care much for her. Though even I'm surprised she agreed he could invite his mistress to the wedding."

Tyrone leaned back against the bark, scratching his back gratefully. "Is that the only reason he's going through with it?"

"Oh, he's doing the right thing for the child. So naïve about women. Honestly. He takes them both at face value when they say they're fine with the situation. They don't care about him a quarter as much as they care about winning. Karlene gets the wedding ring and her Catholic family's approval. Missy gets his attention and approval, for being more sweet and reasonable than his new wife. Hah!"

"What's this Missy look like? If she shows up, I'll keep her out of the photos."

"Tall, skinny blonde with short, over-bleached hair."

"You said lightning might strike the church, and I didn't believe you. But Karlene is standing there in front of God and everybody, swearing eternal fidelity to a man who cheats on her, and he'll swear it back with his mistress watching. Yeesh."

Sally shrugged. "That good little Catholic bride was screwing him when they were both married to other people. She was even at his first wedding." Renaissance of a virtuous Catholic girl? Did confession really cover all those transgressions? Ty kept his mouth shut lest lightning get him, while Sally fumbled her cigarette pack out of her jacket. "More of Rod's ex-lovers are scattered around his side of the church. Maybe a few on her side too."

"He invited former mistresses as well?"

"We're all in theatre group together. Invite one, invite all. But mainly he's thumbing his nose at his new in-laws. It's like a Tennessee Williams play. These people are choking on their rage at each other. Rod's furious with Karlene's Daddy for buying Karlene's first annulment, and Karlene for trapping him with pregnancy. Karlene's mad at Rod for cheating and Daddy for pushing her into her first marriage. Daddy's pissed at Rod for the bastard grandchild and Karlene for this showy second wedding that he's paying for. God alone knows what all Mommy is mad about, but she's sweating nitroglycerine. Not a soul is happy, but Karlene is getting what she wants." She turned away. "You go back in. They'll be saying their vows in a minute. Zoom in on Rod's hands and see if you can catch him with his fingers crossed."

Clutching his camera, Tyrone made his way up the groom's side. The groom gazed with smarmy devotion into the eyes of his gloating bride. The priest, with a disbelieving sigh that echoed through the heavy air, led the eternal vows.

No lightning struck.

The bride's face shone with a triumphal glow. "I win," it blared. "All you ex-mistresses out there can go suck eggs." Maybe that's why she hadn't objected to Missy's invitation. She wanted to savour this one moment when she was centre-stage in Rod's attention.

The first notes of the recessional stirred the muggy air. Ty hurried to the entrance and caught several snaps of the approaching newlyweds. When he stepped aside, Sally was at his elbow. She still looked washed out.

"All good?" she whispered. "Let's get set up for the posed shots on the lawn. You don't need to come to the reception, but you're welcome if you want free booze."

"I'm working tonight. Once I help you pack your gear, I'm out of here."

"Lucky you. I had them last night and all morning as well. Karlene wanted a candid photomontage of herself and her sisters getting their hair and makeup done. Just try making someone look good in a green plastic sheet with her hair in goopy spikes."

She patted his arm with her good hand. "Thanks for all your help today. Really. I hate to ask for more favours, but—" she held up her splinted fingers— "could you drop by tomorrow and help me develop? Please? The sooner that's done, the sooner this will be over for me."

"Give me your films," Ty said gloomily. "Make me supper tomorrow and I'll bring your prints then."

He trudged across the parched lawn, thinking longingly of his bed. Every minute he lingered at this sulfur-and-brimstone wedding was one pared from his pre-shift nap.

Six hours later, yawning, he parked the crime scene van at his first job of the night. A beauty salon's plate glass window reflected the whirling lights of three cop cars. He dragged out his kit and trudged along to a uniform at the nearest door. "CSU."

"Second landing, second right," said the cop. "Stairs at the back."

On the second floor, a cop propped up a wall beside an open door. He held the kit while Ty slipped on latex gloves, volunteering, "Single, white female. Neighbour says she lives alone but a regular boyfriend visits. Doesn't stay over. Lots of yelling in there last night, and the boyfriend was seen leaving around 12:30."

Typical weekend domestic. Ty took back his bag and greeted the Homicide detective inside the stifling apartment.

"Hi, Bo. Cause of death yet?"

Bo nodded. "Asphyxiation. Heat screwed with rigour. Time of death was after midnight, before noon. Dust the phone first. I need a line on the boyfriend."

The corpse lay face up on the couch, one arm dangling. She had short straight hair in that peculiar orange hue of bleach damage. The long slim body wore jeans and a T-shirt. The fragile skin around the eyes was flecked with scarlet dots the size of a pin-head. A quarter-full coffee cup sat on the end table, smudged with bronze lipstick that matched the smears around the anoxic lips.

Ty slid into the routine, paying particular attention to the eyes, mouth and nose. The lips were almost un-bruised but the inside would have pressure wounds from the teeth. A magnifying glass helped him retrieve peachy-pink terry cotton fibres from her mouth and nostrils. He bagged the blue hands although the orange nails looked clean.

"Odd she didn't struggle. Smother a sleeper and they wake up in a panic."

"There's stuff in her medicine cabinet," said Bo. "She might have taken a few to wind down after the scrap. She goes under, boyfriend returns to end the fight his way."

"Tox screen it is." Ty made a note for the Medical Examiner.

After that, it was a tolerable early-summer Saturday night: bar brawls, one break and enter, and, later, a couple of women smacked around by their drunken husbands. Between yawns and stretch breaks he processed crime scene evidence.

By 5 a.m. he was printing and filing the homicide photos. He didn't bother to go over them for a good face shot. The victim's identity was on her driving licence, along with a truly terrible photo: Melissa Grant, born 1985. A lovers' squabble gone routinely wrong.

Except for her coffee. That had been laced with something. He tested a sample for the usuals and found traces of a sedative. She'd been put out and then done in. Interesting.

By six a.m. Ty was more than ready to go home. It was full light outside, hard on the eyes after a night of peering through microscopes and cameras, but he still had two hours to fill. He ran Sally's films through the lab's old developing machine while he tidied up and filled in reports. With those done, he'd be able to sleep longer that afternoon.

When the first prints popped into the slot, he glanced through them. Last night's rehearsal. Faces he now recognized, with the bride stonily smiling and the look-alike sisters uneasy. A woman smirking in the groom's family pew. The missing mistress? She looked vaguely familiar. At the dinner, her bleached-blond hair garish even by candlelight, she was caught with one hand intimately on Rod's thigh, and her bronzed lips an inch from his ear. She had gall all right, which made her wedding no-show all the more surprising. Blast Sally and her weirdo friends. Why so many pictures of the mistress, anyway? Why did she look familiar if she hadn't made the wedding?

Because...lipstick. He flipped back to one with blondie's eyes half-closed, her bronzed lips pursed as if she was blowing a kiss to someone off-camera. Melissa Grant, murder victim.

Bo found him staring at the glossy. "Lively corpse."

"My cousin took this at a wedding rehearsal Friday." Ty tapped a photo on the table. "Here's the boyfriend. The victim missed his wedding yesterday."

The detective's eyebrows lifted. "Nasty. Got his name?"

Ty gave it. "I don't have contact information, but I could get it."

"He's in her phone. You just saved ten other guys from an early Sunday wakeup call."

"I'll copy the headshots for you." He yanked Sally's second film out of the machine. If the prints weren't good, he could rerun them tonight. Right now, he'd copy the best face shot of Rod-the-groom for the Homicide Squad to show around. If just one neighbour placed Mr. Stud at the scene after midnight Friday, his honeymoon was over. Couldn't happen to a nicer guy.

A day's uninterrupted sleep restored Tyrone's equilibrium. At suppertime, he stuck his head into Sally's rundown kitchen and tossed two packets onto the table. "Here you go."

Sally dived for the prints. "Oh, you brought them. Karlene thought the police might have seized them."

"What?"

"You mean you don't know? Rod was hauled off for questioning this morning. Missy's dead!"

So much for waiting to break the news until after supper. "Why'd she call you?"

"The cops wanted rehearsal photos. She was afraid they'd confiscate mine." Sally shivered. "Rod told her he'd ended it in person with Missy after the rehearsal. Maybe she killed herself in despair."

"She didn't kill herself. She was murdered." Ty looked in vain for some sign of food preparations. His stomach rumbled, adding an edge to his voice. "If nobody saw her alive after Rod left her Friday night, he'll go down for it. I hope you got a big deposit for this job."

He lifted his eyes to see his cousin staring fixedly into the middle distance. "Earth to Sally! I said, did you get a deposit?"

"Huh?" Her face turned toward him, white and shocked. "Yeah. I got a deposit. But listen." She gulped. "I might be the last person who saw Missy alive."

"What?"

She nodded miserably. "I was waiting outside the beauty shop yesterday for the evil sisters. She was at her kitchen window. I guess she was watching for them, too."

Maybe he wasn't as awake as he'd thought. "You what? What were you doing there?"

In answer, Sally dumped the morning prints, the set he hadn't looked at, and spread them with a swipe of her hand. "There! See? The bride's family was booked at that beauty salon below her place. I was outside waiting for them, and she was at her kitchen window. About 9:30, I think."

Tyrone stared. The mix-and-match sisters were all represented, in green plastic capes, with wet hair, with suds, in rollers and under dryers. And there was Karlene, with a peachy-pink towel completely covering her rust-brown curls. Bo would go off his nut when he saw these.

"Are you absolutely certain it was her? You may have to swear in court."

Sally leaned on her elbows. "My car was parked across the street. I was leaning into the back, picking out the lenses I'd need. When I turned around, I caught a movement above the beauty shop. I looked up and there she was at the kitchen window. Same shape, same height, and kind of a halo around her head from the frizz of split ends."

There went the Crown's case. Unless... "Did Rod show up at the beauty shop?"

"Nope. He played it by the book, not seeing the bride before-hand. Pure crap. Everyone knew they lived together."

Ty leaned back. "The bitching bride was right about one thing. The cops will want these photos."

"Aw, shit. What am I going to tell her?"

"Tell her nothing. I'll run another set tonight. Now, what about supper?"

Sally blinked. "I'm sorry. I forgot to start anything. I can do it now."

"No time." Tyrone heaved a sigh. He'd pick up something on the way to work. "I'll have to report what you saw."

Sally nodded, watching him with worried eyes. He looked back at her from the door. "You're okay, right? This Melissa wasn't a friend?"

"Oh, no. I barely knew her. I'm fine." Her white face said otherwise.

"Okay. Don't talk to anyone about this until after you've seen the cops." He made himself leave. He couldn't hang around and cheer up his cousin over a photo shoot gone horribly wrong.

On his way through the precinct, he glimpsed Rod in an inter-rogation room. His hangdog expression said he had been there a while.

The desk sergeant shrugged when Ty asked. "Admits he was there Friday night but says she was fine when he left. He got married yesterday. Boffs the girlfriend one day, marries a different one the next."

He shook his head in mingled admiration and censure. Ty left a message for Homicide and spread the beauty shop photos across the lab table, to examine while he ate.

Before he'd finished his hoagie, Bo arrived. "Okay, I'm here. What's the rush?"

Ty pointed. "The bride. In the beauty shop below the scene on Saturday morning. A witness saw the victim upstairs at a window about 9:30 that same morning."

The detective glared at the table. "Whaddaya know?"

"I know 'Reasonable Doubt' on hot Rod."

"What?"

"Studly's bride and her sisters were at that beauty shop from approximately 9:30 to noon, getting their hair done for the wedding. The groom never came near the place. Now look at this close-up of the bride. What color towel is that on her head?"

Bo looked closer. "Kind of a peachy-pink?"

"Right. And what color were the fibres I picked out of the victim's nose?"

Bo's eyes narrowed. "The wife was at the girlfriend's apartment building yesterday morning, with a possible match for those fibres on her head. Sumbitch."

"Won't know for sure until I get at the towels. Let's hope that clip joint skipped laundry." Ty tapped along the top row of photos. "These are in time order. The party arriving. Tenting up, shampoos, and then a bunch of clowning around. And look who's disappearing down the hall."

"Don't say it's the wife. It's too damned easy."

"See for yourself." Ty handed over a magnifier. "This one under the dryer is the highlighted sister. There's Eyebrows. This one has the beak. But no Karlene."

"Maybe her stomach turned nervous on her. That hall could lead to the can."

Ty pointed to an earlier photo. "It also leads out to the apartment hallway."

"Sumbitch," the detective said again. They both knew Rod's lawyer could make reasonable doubt. "But did the wife know about the girlfriend?"

"Sure. It's a tacky little setup." Ty summed up the wedding

100

triangle. "What more permanent way to be rid of the rival? Check out her 'Just Married' headshot. If those aren't feathers on her whiskers, I'm a puddy tat."

"I'll have to think about this," said Bo, sweeping the photos into one hand. "Meanwhile, I guess I'll let the boyfriend go home."

"One more thing," said Ty. "I was at that wedding yesterday. When the sisters were discussing whether the mistress would dare appear, I heard one of them say 'Karlene was sure it was done.'"

"Jeez. We could get the whole lot on conspiracy to commit!" Bo hurried out, only to stick his head back in. "If I get a warrant for that shop before morning, you'll toss it with me?"

"Right." Working on other things, Ty wondered whether Karlene was capable of cold-blooded murder. And why would she snap now? It wasn't like this was Rod's first mistress. Had Melissa's inclusion at the wedding been the final straw? One thing was sure: the looming thunderstorm had broken with a vengeance.

Bo returned at 7 a.m. with a warrant, coffee, and a burst of enthusiasm. "We let the groom go," he confided on the drive through the crisp morning. "Didn't hint about another suspect. No sense him going home to tip off the missus. Jeez, these people! What idiot believes his wife and mistress don't hate each other? It's against nature."

"Did you think he was truthful?"

"So-so. The kind who makes up a convenient story and then believes it. Why'd he get married when he had a mistress? Why'd he tell his fiancée about her? And I sure don't know why she'd marry him knowing about the other woman. You see strange things in this job, huh?"

They parked and hurried across the street. The beauty salon was still closed, but a woman moved in its depths. They pounded on the door. After a long, suspicious stare, she unlocked the door. She glared at them over a basket of towels.

Bo flashed his badge and invited himself in. "You heard about the murder upstairs? Did you see or hear anything of Miss Grant on Saturday?"

"I saw her putting out the garbage when I came to work. About 8:30." That cleared Rod.

Ty asked, "Have you washed the towels from Saturday?"

The woman shook her head. "These are them. It was busy right up to closing and the girls forgot to start the washer before they left."

Ty left further questioning to Bo while he sorted the towels. The peach ones were very close in colour to his fibers. Eventually, one with greasy smears greeted his eyes. Bronze lipstick. A single, twisting, rust-brown hair was threaded through several tiny cotton loops. One for the bag.

Next, he explored the shop. Behind the main room was a smaller section with sinks. Beyond the shampoo station was a short hall, with a washroom on one side, ending at an office/storeroom. A second door led into the apartment building's hallway, across from the rear stairs. He set his stopwatch and walked quickly up to the second floor, touched the timer again when he got to the victim's door. Twenty-seven seconds. He checked his time again going down and bumped into Bo on the last step.

"Easy, huh?" the detective asked rhetorically. "The owner says the bride was gone twice, for about fifteen minutes around 10:15 and about the same again an hour later. The second time, someone banged on the bathroom door and she answered."

"Transit time, fifty-four seconds," said Ty. "Did anyone else leave?"

"Everyone went to the bathroom at least once, but she's the one with the motive. We get the slightest trace and she's going down."

Ty displayed the towel in its evidence bag. Bo crowed.

They searched the apartment again. While the detective pawed through garbage hoping for a container that might have held a sedative, Ty tried to think of anything Karlene might have touched. Surely she could not have worn gloves while the victim was awake. Maybe a coffee cup? He dusted mugs and the kitchen taps but found only Melissa's old prints. He pushed aside a skimpy curtain.

From the kitchen window, the cop car was just visible, probably about where Sally had parked on Saturday. She must have seen Melissa at this very window. If the mistress had offered Sally a coffee while she waited, would Karlene have been scared off? But she couldn't have yelled to Sally from this window. It was painted shut, right over the latch.

The apartment told no new tales. By the time he loaded his gear back into Bo's car, it was nearly nine-thirty. Just about when Sally last saw Melissa on Saturday morning. He looked up. The windows gazed back blankly, gleaming in the eastern sun. Sally could not have seen anyone there, much less identified them.

"Bo, what do you see in those upstairs windows?"

"Nothing with the sun on 'em. Why?" Ty explained Sally's statement. Bo shrugged. "If the window was open, no glare."

"It doesn't open. It's painted shut. Sally lied."

102

"Now why would she do a thing like that?"

"I have no idea." But Ty did. "We" are all in the same theatre group. "We" the ex-mistresses? When she told him about the window she'd just learned, from his big mouth, that Rod was Suspect #1. She had alibi'd him in the next breath.

"I'll talk to her," said Bo. "Get clear just what she saw."

Ty glanced up at the blank window again, feeling queasy. "I'll go with you."

Sally, in pajamas, opened the door to them. "Is this the guy to take my statement?" she asked, yawning. "C'mon in. I'll put on some coffee." She led the way to the kitchen, so seemingly normal Tyrone's half-formed fear receded.

"So," he said, "How'd you get this wedding gig?"

"Rod's idea," said Sally. She fitted the coffee filter and awkwardly filled it, her wrapped hand tipping dark-brown grit across the counter "He wanted me there. For support."

Rod's idea. Ty's stomach turned. "How long were you involved with Rod?"

"Gosh, it must be nine years at least." Sally turned on the water.

He raised his voice to be heard over it. "Since the early days of the Rod and Karlene saga?"

"About that. We had to break it off when he was divorcing his first wife. So I wouldn't be dragged through court with him."

Gad. She was one of the many exes in the church. "And after that? Did you get back together with him?"

"I was always there for him, and he for me."

Translated: he'd call her up between his mistresses, because she was a sure score. And, like with her high school obsession, Sally had stayed stuck on Rod all these years.

"So you were friends with benefits until when?"

"Right up until the brood-cow got herself pregnant." Sally's voice could have curdled milk. "I thought we could just be discreet, but he didn't want to lie to her about still seeing me. He's honourable that way."

Ty swallowed the impulse to gag. Rod had been clearing the deck before the wedding. But he'd have been back, eventually. Or on to someone else.

Sally took the initiative. "You going to arrest Karlene?" she asked Bo.

"What for?"

Her eyes widened. "For murder! She had the opportunity. And she sure as heck had a motive."

"She sure did," Bo agreed. "But first, let's clear up what you saw when you were unloading your car. Do you mind if I tape this?"

Ty watched the tape being set up, listened to the standard identifiers. Sally's face and voice were without guile. He never would have guessed she'd lied if he hadn't seen those windows. In his head, Dad bellowed. *Shut her up, distract her, stop her making a false statement on the record.*

"Was the window open or closed?" Bo asked.

Sally's brow furrowed. "Open."

"And you could see her well enough to be sure who it was?"

Ty sunk his teeth into his lower lip.

Sally nodded. "Sure. That hair was really bright."

Bo nodded too, encouraging her. "How did you know that was the kitchen window?"

"I guessed because of those skimpy curtains."

Ty swallowed hard. Sally had always been a convincing liar in high school. But two new lies in a row, without the slightest hesitation. She had walked right into Bo's trap. Discredited herself with every word.

The detective's expression didn't change. "You can't see them from down on the street. Not in that light. When were you in the victim's apartment?"

"Why are you asking that?" Sally demanded. "Why aren't you out arresting Karlene? We all know she did it."

"What exactly did she do?"

"She killed Melissa. She doped her first and she went back later and killed her."

An invisible boot thudded into Tyrone's stomach. "How did you know about the doping?"

"I heard the evil sisters at rehearsal," said Sally sulkily. "They got roofies from some guy and were going to dope Melissa so she'd miss the wedding." Her eyes lit with the same triumphal gleam Melissa had worn at rehearsal, the same Karlene had beamed at the wedding. "So now you're going to pick her up, right?"

After this performance, Ty wouldn't pick up a dog on Sally's say-so. But if the bride didn't do it, and the groom didn't do it, then who?

"Isn't her hair on the murder towel enough?" Sally asked, with a fine show of innocent inquiry.

104

No More Waiting
By Helen Nelson

Helen Nelson is a life-long reader and storyteller. She has previously published stories in The Whole She-Bang, The Whole She-Bang 2 *and* Nefarious North. *She is a past-president of the Toronto Chapter of Sisters in Crime. She will co-chair Bouchercon 2017, which will be held in Toronto. A recently retired IT consultant, she is looking forward to a life of crime (reading and writing).*

Alice will be there. Waiting. It's been twenty-five years, well, closer to twenty-seven, all things considered. But she'll be waiting. There has never been anyone else for either of us, not since we were fifteen years old.

Early this morning, I flew to Saskatoon—just a few hours east to west. Twenty-five years ago, I would have taken a bus the whole way.

Now I am on a bus; it's taken more time than the flight. I've dozed a lot, waking every few minutes when we stop in each town along the way. Five minutes here, five minutes there, ten miles out of your way here, twenty miles out of your way there. With a car it wouldn't take much more than an hour. Maybe an hour and a half, I wouldn't want to get caught speeding.

No more napping now; my town should only be a few minutes away. Town is an overstatement for the string of nine houses and the hotel lined up along Railway Avenue. The tracks are gone. The grain elevators, gone. Five people left, every one of them a pensioner. Not that there were all that many folks back then, maybe thirty and a couple more houses. The empty houses are burning down, one by one.

A song eats at the edge of my consciousness. Something about yellow ribbons and oak trees. And a bus. Never mind. It will come. The song is there because Alice and I will be together soon, by our tree. It's an old apple tree. The apples from that tree have always been small and bitter. They're barely fit for the birds to eat. In the fall the ground is strewn with apples that have been pecked at and discarded. It's spring, no apples now. Too late for any blossoms. Maybe ragged remnants.

We met the first day of school in Grade 10. I had turned fifteen in January. Alice would turn fifteen a few weeks later. Me, the son of a small-time farmer and big-time boozer. She was the daughter of the new vice principal. I was a bit wild; already on the list of usual suspects for the local cops. She was naïve and innocent and drop dead gorgeous. A few weeks into September, I asked Alice to the first school dance. She declined. Broke my heart. But I still went, stag. She went with a group of girls. I asked her to dance. She agreed. Oh, I could dance then; we both had the moves. Danced every dance together. For the rest of high school we were never apart for long. I knew we'd be forever. And though her dad made it clear he didn't approve of her hanging out with one of the school's bad boys, he held back from putting his foot down.

We had our ups and downs. For me getting to school meant taking the bus from twenty-five miles away. Alice walked. She lived only a few blocks from the school. Neither of us was old enough to drive. I would "borrow" dad's car sometimes but opportunities for that were rare. Older friends, or, on rare occasions my dad, might offer a lift.

Oh we used to fight too. At first over the way I dressed for school events. Or didn't. Jeans, tees and running shoes were my style. Always with holes. I didn't want the dress pants Alice thought I should wear sometimes. Didn't have them. Couldn't afford them. End of story. I won those early rounds, though she would raise it again.

Got my driver's licence the day I turned sixteen. Written test in the morning, road test in the afternoon. Everyone did that. A driver's licence spelled freedom. A way out of the middle of nowhere, to the mall, the food court, the school events, an occasional movie. Off the school bus. And out from under the control of parents. The next day I got myself a beater that would get me in and out of town. And a part-time job in the food court, flipping burgers. With that first pay cheque I caved and got the dress pants Alice wanted me to wear, and a shirt. We went to a movie and didn't have to walk or catch a ride with someone else. A bit of parking, a bit of kissing. She wouldn't share the bottle I had laid my hands on, so after I dropped her off I found a couple of friends to socialize with. And that became the pattern most Friday and Saturday nights. As time went on there was more than a little kissing. Not enough more, but that too would soon change.

106

The bus stops. Again. Finally.

"Hey you, off you go," says the bus driver.

"Wait, I thought you went into town! This is still a couple miles away."

"Yup. Two miles to be exact. No point going in to town. There's only five of them left and they ain't going anywhere, any of them." With a chuckle the bus driver adds, "Most of them have one foot in the cemetery anyway."

I groan. It means six miles to walk. Two to town. Will the old hotel still be open? If it is, maybe I can get a drink before walking the last four miles. A drink is a welcome prospect. It has been a long time since I had a real drink.

I grab my pack, hop off the bus and start to walk. The bus drives away behind me, but I don't look back. Walking will be a good change; bus butt is killing me anyway.

That song is flitting in and out again. I can hear the first line as clear as anything. Especially the tune. The first note is an "F." How can I know that and not be able to place the damn song? Why yellow ribbons? Alice always wore blue.

Blue. That was from a song too. One her grandmother used to sing to her.

I had asked her about the blue clothes on her sixteenth birthday. She had a beautiful new blue dress for that. And a party. Sixteen kids, sixteen candles, sixteen roses from me, aah and when her parent's backs were turned sixteen kisses, passionate kisses, lots of tongue. And oh, that blue dress.

"Why always blue?"

"Well, for the song," she said.

I must have had a blank look on my face. "My grandmother used to sing it to me—you know it, 'Alice Blue Gown.'" No change in that blank look. So, in her sweet, pure voice she sang the first lines of "Alice Blue Gown."

Shortly before Alice's grandmother died, she made Alice a dress to match the song. Alice treasured that dress and wore it till the seams were almost splitting. It was a reminder of her grandmother. After that, she always wore something blue. Other colours too, but always something blue.

We used to sit for hours under our tree. We'd meet after school, drive out to the farm. And there we would sit, playfully tossing apples, talking and dreaming, kissing and touching. And on a warm fall day, shortly after Alice's sixteenth birthday we made love for the first time. Under that tree, planted by my mother, who knew how long ago. I always felt close to my mother there. It had been my spot and it became our spot, then and always.

I was no longer quite the bad boy I had been when we met; she wasn't quite the good girl she had been. When we fought those days, it wasn't about how I dressed. I had learned how to clean up. And did it, just often enough to please Alice. No, we fought about drinking, my drinking. Alice would take the occasional sip. But she had huge objections to my boozing style which boiled down to: drink till the bottle was gone, find another bottle, repeat. Any time was party time. Alice thought I was following in my father's footsteps. I maintained I was just a kid who wanted to have some fun.

She was probably right. But it wasn't the big problem she thought it was, at least not then. My dad was a lot of fun. He wasn't a mean drunk or a maudlin drunk or even a particularly loud drunk. He was just a frequent drunk; he pretty much never stopped. It's hard to believe he even noticed when mom decided she had enough and took off for parts unknown, leaving the two of us to fend for ourselves. I was about six or so when that happened.

Yes, I did get up to a few youthful stunts when I was well and truly gone. Burning dog shit on a few door steps. Badly placed firecrackers, pushed over tool sheds. If those crazy little two-seater cars had been around back then, me and my drinking buddies would likely have tipped a few. No fights, nobody hurt, just thoughtless kid stuff that my pals and I found outrageously funny.

Our fights had a pattern. We would fight, she would threaten to leave; I would clean up my act for a few weeks and then would slowly get back to my old ways, till a new fight erupted. She shed a lot of tears over my drinking and other antics, but she never did leave. Never. She only came close once.

The hotel is still open. There's a small neon sign that tries to say "open". The middle stroke of the "e" is missing. Open but it looks deserted.

Not quite deserted. There's one old guy at the bar. For a second I think it might be my father. That would be a stroke of luck, and might even result in a ride. But no, it isn't. Probably just someone who lives in one of the few remaining houses. There's the bartender too. He's even older than the customer. Probably just runs the place to get his booze wholesale and have the occasional drinking buddy.

On the spur of the moment I decide I'd like to stay here tonight. Head back to the farm and my dad, tomorrow. Begin life as a farmer, tomorrow. See Alice, tomorrow.

"Can I get a room?"

"A room?" The bartender looks doubtful.

"Yes, it's a hotel, right?"

"Well, yes, but nobody took a room in about twenty years. They ain't even made up or cleaned since the wife passed," says the bartender.

I sigh and order a scotch.

"Nah, none of that fancy stuff here. You got your rye, vodka, rum and your gin for the ladies. Or beer. You can have beer."

"Well, beer then." He doesn't say what kind; he probably doesn't have more than one kind anyway.

The bartender places a beer and a glass in front of me. Fancy that, a glass. I doubt the old man can see well enough to clean the glass properly. I sip the beer from the bottle.

I realize the old man running the bar is the same old guy as twenty-seven years ago. The guy was already older than dirt back then.

"Not from round these parts, so where you from son?" says the bartender. Imagine that, pushing fifty and in this place I'm still young enough to be called son.

"I grew up around here. Been down east for about twenty-five years."

"Oh, where'd you grow up?" asks the guy at the bar.

I gesture in a vaguely westerly direction and say, "Oh a few miles out that way." I look down at my beer and hope I'm giving off the vibe that I'm not in the mood to talk.

The bartender and his customer seem to get the message. They stop trying to talk to me. They go back to talking about... well, I don't know. I'm not paying attention. So whatever old farmers and bartenders talk about.

I finish the beer and the bartender asks if I'd like another. I know I shouldn't, but have one anyway.

About half way through the beer, the bartender turns on the television. News time. More stuff in the Middle East, some sort of political scandal, fire burns down half a town, freight train derailment, murderer gets parole, hot rock group coming to the city, some Hollywood couple break up or get married or something. I ask the bartender to turn off the television.

109

"News is just depressing, and the rest is just noise."

The bartender refuses. "The television is what we have around here. The customers like it and I do too."

"What customers? You only got the one other than me, and he looks like he's about to leave."

"My hotel, my bar, my television. It's staying on," says the bartender.

Well that's that. I give some thought to popping the old guy in the nose. I've learned to fight while I've been away, had to. To protect myself. But it doesn't seem worth it, an old guy like that, and anyway, I've never been a violent man. So I down the remaining beer, turn down the offer of another, pay the tab and leave.

Four miles to walk to the farm, most of it uphill. Years ago I would have shortened it by cutting through the fields, but I don't know who owns those fields these days or what kind of trouble I could get into for trespassing. Don't want trouble; I just want to get back to my Alice.

Our serious differences began during the last year of high school. For her whole life, Alice assumed she would finish high school and go to university. And her family assumed that too. Not what I had in mind. University wasn't for me. To be honest, I didn't really know what I wanted. Get a job, make a few dollars, help dad on the farm. Settle down with Alice in a few years. They were all vague ideas; but none of them involved university or heading to the city, and none of them involved any kind of separation from Alice.

Alice loved me. Knew it then. Know it now. But she was as determined that we would go live in the city. She wanted me to go to the university. "Study agriculture," she would say. But if I didn't want to go to university, at least I should come with her to the city while she went to school. We didn't break up, but we fought about it almost every time we got together.

Alice's family was relieved and glad that she was so determined to continue with her plans for university. And I think they hoped that she would end up going off to the city alone. My dad thought I was being a stubborn fool.

"What difference does it make where you get a job? Let her do her thing and when she's done, you can both come back here. This place isn't all that big, I can handle it just fine on my own—have for years anyway what with you flipping them burgers and all." But then he'd pour us another drink and we'd move on to other subjects.

110

Several times when she was in my arms I almost gave in and agreed to go with her. But each time stubborn pride intervened and I just couldn't do it.

In the end, after a tearful summer, Alice followed her dream to the city. I found a job in a local feed lot and stayed on with my dad.

Now I wonder what difference it might have made in our lives if I had given in to Alice and gone with her.

That song again. I stop dead in my tracks. Prison. The yellow ribbons and bus guy was coming home after being in prison. "Well, I'll be damned."

As I walk toward the farm and our tree, I think about my history, the twenty-seven years away. Everything I learned. Yes, how to fight, how to defend myself, but also the university courses I took and aced, the degree I worked toward and achieved. The years of sobriety. So here I am, cleaned up, educated and sober and on my way back to her. Alice's dream come true, after all these years.

Twenty-seven years. A long time. Over a year waiting for the trial, then life, with no chance of parole for twenty-five years. I was a model prisoner, avoiding fights, taking classes, helping other prisoners, doing the work assigned, and, after the first few years, sobering up and avoiding the drugs and alcohol trap. Well some alcohol, but after a while, vodka made from kitchen scraps didn't really appeal. I never admitted to the crime, so in some ways I was surprised that I got parole at all, even though in the end it took almost twenty-six years of jail before I finally got out. But there it is: I'll be on parole now for the rest of my life. It should be okay, all I want to do is farm and spend the rest of my days with Alice.

During the first two years Alice was in university, I visited her in the city once a month and she came home and visited me once a month. We had Christmas, and reading week and the whole summer between her first and second year.

When Alice was away, I worked and drank. No trouble with the police any more. Mostly I sat at home and drank with my dad. Night after night. We had each other for drinking buddies, there was no need to risk driving home from the hotel after hoisting a few.

By the time Alice came home for the summer after her second year, I was missing a lot of days at work. And toward the end of August, I got fired for missing a full week for no reason other than that I was simply too hung over to handle the job. Or life.

I also missed that week with Alice; we had gone back to fighting about my drinking.

I got another job. She went back to school in September leaving an unresolved tension between us. I made the first scheduled trip to the city a couple weeks later. It was like old times. I didn't drink. She relaxed with me again. We made love, had fun, talked about the future. She would get her teaching degree and come home and work. I would slowly take over more and more on the farm while working a day job. I'd stay sober. Then? Well, maybe....

On my way home, I stopped in a bar, had at least six beer, got stopped by the cops and charged with drunk driving.

Two weeks later Alice didn't show up. She wasn't around when I called. I left messages on her answering machine, she didn't reply. I figured her parents told her about my drunk driving charge and she was pissed off at me.

By mid-October, I decided to go see Alice in the city. Unannounced, I arrived at her place. When I knocked on the door of her apartment, she opened the door with the safety latch on. At first she didn't want to let me in, but when she realized I was sober, she relented. There were no welcoming hug or kisses; she told me we were done.

"I can't take a lifetime of your drinking. I'm not going to."

I promised to change. She pointed to my history of failed promises, including the promise I had failed on as soon as I was out of her sight last time I visited. I told her I hadn't had a drink since my arrest; she reminded me that it was a condition of my bail.

Was there someone else? She hesitated. And confessed.

Yes, there had been. No there wasn't. She had started to see someone else and quickly knew the guy wasn't for her. But that also helped her see that I wasn't for her either. It had been a hard realization. She had thought about coming home to tell me, but she hadn't been able to screw up her courage yet. No, she would not have waited much longer. It wouldn't have been fair to me. She knew that. But it wasn't easy to break up with someone who she had been with for more than five years. Her first lover, her only lover. But she needed time to be free, she didn't want to be hooked up with anyone. She wanted to explore herself. To get to know herself again. To find out what she wanted from her life. I would no longer be part of her picture. "Not now. Not ever."

She cried. I can still see her standing there in her blue dress— her Alice Blue Gown—crying.

It was two weeks before she was missed. Her parents hadn't been able to reach her and reported her missing when she hadn't phoned or come home by late October.

There were reports in newspapers, on television, radio. But there had been no trace of her. Alice was gone.

Eventually the spotlight turned on me. And evidence came to light, evidence that pointed at me. I had been seen in the city that night, the last night anyone saw her or talked to her. And I had never mentioned that trip to anyone. In fact I told people I had been drinking with my dad that night. Dad even backed me up—but everyone knew he wouldn't know one night from another. I had also told people I had talked to her on the phone several times in those last couple weeks. There were no records of any phone calls on her phone or ours to back up my claim. There were fibers, blood and hair in my car. But of course there would be, I was still driving the car I had driven since I bought it back in Grade Ten. The blood in the trunk was her blood. Her hair. I said I didn't know. After all, she was in that car a lot. I said it must have come from camping.

She had told her friends that she was planning to end it with me the next time she saw me. She had told her family.

By late the following fall, I was on trial for her murder. No body. No weapon. Circumstantial evidence only. But the jury saw it the same way the prosecution did. And the judge sentenced me to life. Twenty-five years with no chance of parole.

Through every day of those years I proclaimed my innocence.

I have arrived. It is late afternoon; I'll go see dad shortly. Give the old man the bottle I brought along for him, though I won't be sharing it with him. But first Alice. I sit beneath our tree. I sing, "Alice Blue Gown," but the voice I hear is Alice's from that long ago day when she first sang it to me.

I have never confessed, never told anybody where her body was. And I never will. They would take her from me. At least she's still here, where I put her twenty-seven years ago, under our tree. Waiting, for me. Right beside where I helped my Dad put my Mom all those years ago.

Where There's a Will
By Elizabeth Hosang

Elizabeth is a computer engineer who wants to be a writer when she grows up. She has been published in a number of mystery anthologies. Her interests include poisons, art fraud, and convincing her mini schnauzer that squirrels in the yard do not constitute an emergency. A fan of a well-told story in any genre, she especially enjoys mystery, urban fantasy and science fiction. She continues to hone her craft, enjoying the freedom to use adjectives, adverbs and pronouns, unlike when writing code, but still needs to practise not writing run-on sentences.

"I thought we'd be done with these stupid get-togethers now that the old girl's dead." Rachel stabbed an olive with her toothpick and swirled it around her martini glass.

"Hush, dear. Don't speak ill of the dead." Her mother Maureen tipped up her highball glass before realizing that it was empty. "Jeffry, would you be an angel and freshen my drink?"

She waved her glass in the direction of the young man staring out the window at the late autumn sky.

"Yes, Jeffry, get Mommy another drink. Now that Grandma's dead she doesn't have to sneak around to get tanked."

Jeffry frowned at his sister, but took the glass from his mother's outstretched hand. "Can't we be civilized for one afternoon? We're here to fulfill Grandma Alice's final wishes. All we have to do is have one last Thanksgiving dinner together, listen to some recorded message from her, and go our separate ways. Once the estate passes probate we never have to see each other again."

He handed the refilled glass to his mother, then looked at his watch. "Sara will be down shortly. I'm afraid she still finds the journey rather tiring."

Rachel snorted into her glass. "Lucky thing Edward is always available to help her freshen up."

"Rachel!" Maureen turned so sharply she splashed some of her drink onto her skirt. Jeffry looked as if he'd been slapped.

"Come on. Every year we come out here for Thanksgiving, Grandma Alice forces us to play along with one of those stupid murder mystery weekends, and Sara and Eddie sneak off to 'get firewood' or 'fetch a bottle from the wine cellar.' After five years you'd think they'd come up with a better cover story. Sara's never lifted anything heavier than her cellphone and Eddie couldn't pick a good wine in a French vineyard."

Maureen frowned at her daughter and glanced at her watch. "Jeffry, see if you can get the television working. The lawyer said he'd be beaming his message to us at two o'clock."

"Streaming, Mother. It's called streaming."

"Excuse me." An older woman in a maid's uniform stood in the doorway to the great room. "The turkey is in the oven. Everything is covered, so it should be ready for you to eat at six this afternoon. You just need to take it out. The table in the dining room has been set. Will there be anything else before I go?"

"No, thank you, Adeline. I can't imagine what my mother was thinking when she insisted that you go back to the mainland instead of being here to serve."

The woman in the maid's uniform smiled. "Unfortunately, the lawyer insists that I go."

"Very well. Be here promptly on Tuesday morning." Maureen dismissed the other woman with a wave of her hand.

"Pity she didn't leave her apron, Mother," Rachel said. "I don't think I've ever seen you in one."

"So sorry about that." Sara sailed into the room, her fashionably thin arm smoothing her artful blond highlights into place. "I loved Grandma Alice dearly, but I am so glad the next family get-together won't have to be way out here in the middle of Lake Ontario."

"Well said." The assembled family turned to the patio doors as Edward stepped through them, smoothing his wavy brown hair into place above his well-chiselled features.

"I see you didn't bring any wood with you," Rachel said.

Edward smirked.

"And just in time for the announcement of who gets the money," Rachel continued.

Everyone settled in as Jeffry turned on his laptop and connected it to a large-screen television. He brought up the video software and the sound of a ringing telephone filled the room. After a moment the screen showed a middle-aged man with an expensive haircut, seated in a high-backed leather chair.

"Good afternoon. As I mentioned at the formal reading of the will, one of the stipulations of Alice Warner's estate was that her heirs spend one final long Thanksgiving weekend together in her family's home on Belle Isle. Only those who arrived Friday afternoon for supper and remain until Tuesday morning will inherit. Anyone who does not meet these conditions will have their share divided equally among the rest."

He slipped on a pair of frameless reading glasses and opened a manila folder on the desk in front of him.

"Now, there are some additional conditions. Miss Alice wanted to explain them herself. There is a recording in the sideboard drawer, inside a sealed envelope containing some papers. I myself have not viewed the recording, nor am I familiar with the contents of the envelope. My client sealed the envelope herself, as should be evidenced by her initials across the opening. I have delivered the envelope, unopened, and placed it in the house as per her instructions. If you wish to retain my services to interpret the contents of the envelope, you may contact me during business hours next week. Happy Thanksgiving."

"Well that was a lot of weasel words, even from a lawyer," Rachel said. "I wonder what it is he's pretending he knows nothing about."

Edward moved to the sideboard and opened the first drawer he came to. "Bingo." He pulled out a nine by twelve inch envelope and ripped it open. "Let's see what hoops the old bat wants us to leap through this time." He dumped a silver thumb drive into his hand. "Here Jeffry, see what you can do with this." He tossed it to his older brother, who grabbed for it and missed.

Jeffry made a noise of disgust and bent down to retrieve the small metal rectangle, ignoring the snickers of his siblings.

"Don't tell me the old witch expects us to play one of her murder mysteries when she isn't here," Rachel said.

"How would she know if we did?" Sara replied.

After some fumbling Jeffry got the thumb drive inserted into his computer and a video began to play. Grandma Alice appeared on the large television screen, her familiar dusty rose shawl wrapped around her shoulders and her half-moon reading glasses perched on her nose. She must have recorded the video with a camera on someone's laptop computer, because the camera's viewpoint was looking up her nose. Her double chin bulged out as she cleared her throat, giving the family members a clear image of the whiskers under her chin and at the corners of her mouth.

"Ew. All that money and she couldn't get a facial once in a while?" Rachel asked. Maureen snickered.

"Welcome everyone. I'm sure you've all had a few drinks, and you've unpacked or napped or whatever your excuse is this time Edward. Now that I'm gone I'm sure you're all chomping at the bit to hear how much money I'm leaving you. Why else would you be here? Certainly not because you miss me. You've all made it very clear how much you hated visiting, and how much you hated acting as a family. After growing up in comfort thanks to your grandfather and me, was it really so much to ask that you spend one weekend a year indulging the whims of a lonely old woman? Yes, it was silly to dress up and play parlour games. But was it any worse than going out in public in a short skirt with no underwear, Rachel? Or dressing like a horny teenager, Maureen? A weekend murder mystery may not be as exciting as fiddling the books, Jeffry, or adultery, Edward. But it was my fun, and your refusal to play along just goes to show what a bunch of ill-mannered, greedy cretins you are.

"So, this weekend, I get one last chance to make you play a little game. Only this time it's not going to be just a game. You see, I can finally do what I really wanted. I don't know if any of you remember, but my favourite book has always been *And Then There Were None*. That's the one with the party of murderers who kill each other off. This weekend, you're going to play it for real. You see, I've decided that I'm going to make you work for your inheritance. At the end of the weekend, my money will be divided equally between whoever is left alive. There is a time-lock safe in my bedroom. Tuesday morning the safe will open. Inside is an envelope with the banking information for the account in the Cayman Islands with your inheritance. There is also an envelope with enough cash to purchase a one-way ticket to the country of your choosing, along with a list of countries that do not have extradition treaties with Canada. I've included this for those of you, Maureen, who are not familiar with anything outside of the country club. What I suggest is this: whoever is alive Tuesday morning should be standing at the docks with their luggage. When Adeline returns you can take the boat, head to the mainland, and be on your way before the police arrive. Unfortunately, I cannot control the weather and trap you on the island with a storm. So, to make sure that you play the game right, the phone to the mainland has been disabled, which will disable your internet connections, and cellphone jammers have been installed all across the island. These measures should take effect after you've been in contact with my lawyer.

"If for some reason you decided not to kill each other, a separate set of instructions will be opened by my attorney. If all five of you are still alive Tuesday morning, all the money in the Cayman account will instead be donated to the Humane Society, and you'll

117

have to fend for yourselves from now on. I realize that will be a challenge for some of you, Rachel, who don't even have the skills to marry for money, despite repeated attempts to do so. I've also seen the way you look at each other. I think it would take a lot less than the threat of poverty for there to be a death or two before Tuesday. For the sake of those of you who aren't sure how to commit a murder, I hope you remember something from one of our previous Thanksgiving weekends. Good luck. And good bye."

A shocked silence filled the room as the video stopped playing. "Well, Mother. I hope you're enjoying Hell," Maureen said at last.

At her words everyone pulled out their cellphones, and Jeffry started clicking away on his computer.

"Anyone have a signal?" Rachel asked.

Grunts and head shakes confirmed that they were indeed cut off electronically.

"How could you let her do this!" Sara demanded, turning to her husband.

"Me?" Jeffry replied, slamming his laptop closed and shoving it away from himself. "I'm not her lawyer! I'm an accountant!"

"Why weren't you her lawyer? You couldn't have studied something useful at that stupid school Daddy sent you to?" Rachel demanded, glaring at her brother.

"Me? Remind me what you studied? Shopping?" Jeffry glared back at his sister before stomping over to the sideboard and pouring himself a drink.

"Enough!" Maureen stood up, wobbling once before reaching her full height. "This is ridiculous. We aren't going to kill each other. The old bat was clearly out of her mind. We'll just take this video to our lawyers and have the whole will overturned. Right, Jeffry? Jeffry? Are you listening to me?"

Her oldest son nodded before resuming his seat in the desk chair and downing his drink in one gulp. "You can't enter into a binding contract for an illegal act. My lawyer should have no problems convincing the court to disregard the will once we present this."

"As long as you don't mind waiting for your inheritance." Edward looked around the room as he took another sip from his highball glass. "With no will, we should get our money in, oh, say, five or six years? And that's assuming we don't fight each other in court. If anyone gets greedy the proceedings could drag out even longer."

His head tilted as he looked up from his drink and stared at

Maureen. "Tell me, Mother, how much of Daddy's money do you have left? Enough to buy the loyalty of that ski instructor in Calgary who's been keeping you company during the winter?"

"Shut up, Edward," Rachel said.

"Ooh, what's that little sister? Gonna claim you're just here to honour Grandma's memory?"

"And you need the money so you can keep your bookies from breaking your legs. We've all been coming here for years and putting up with the old lady so we'd get our share when she died. Well, she's dead now, so we just have to get through this weekend, not kill each other, and not fight each other over the will in court. We don't even have to pretend to get along with each other. Supper will be ready in a few hours. So if you'll excuse me, I'm going up to my room to watch television until it's time to eat." Rachel picked up her glass and strode out of the room, her heels clicking on the parquet floor.

"More like so she can get high," Sara muttered. She turned to her husband. "So you're sure that if we show this to the lawyer, all of Miss Alice's money will be split up between us?"

"Not 'us,' Sara," Jeffry said. "Just the blood relatives."

"Sorry, dear," Maureen said. "You'll have to settle for half of Jeffry's share." She walked over to the sideboard and refilled her own glass. "I think Rachel has the right idea. I'll see you all at supper."

The three people remaining in the study looked back and forth at each other, the awkward silence stretching between them.

Finally, Sara could bear it no longer. "Well, I suppose someone should check on the food."

She walked out of the room, leaving the brothers to stare at each other. After a few more moments Edward stepped out of the study through the French doors into the grey autumn evening, leaving Jeffry sitting at the desk, playing with a metal letter opener in the shape of a dagger.

Twenty minutes later Edward strode out to the gazebo that stood on a small cliff overlooking the choppy waters of Lake Ontario. The woman waiting there stood with her back to him, a grey scarf wrapped around her head to protect her hair. The roar of wind and waves muffled his footsteps on the gravel path, but as he stepped up onto the gazebo the wooden floorboards creaked, causing the woman to turn.

"You wanted to see me, Mother?"

She smiled, reaching up to brush at the lapel of his jacket. "Edward, dear. I just wanted a chance to speak to you away from your brother and sister."

"And that's why you left a note in my room?"

"Well, yes. I know the other two are jealous of our special relationship. A mother shouldn't have favourites, but it's hard not to love your youngest child just a little bit more."

"Enough to make up for the loss of your other two children?"

"Now, Edward. You can't think of it that way. Think of it as ensuring the family legacy isn't diluted. After all, Jeffry would have to share his with that dear little Sara."

"Dear? You never liked her, Mother."

"No, but you do." She sighed and looked up at him, her expression just a little pouty. "But really, dear, don't you think you could find someone else? Especially after splitting the money two ways."

"Two ways, mother? I don't think so."

"All right, if you insist on keeping Sara around, you can split your share with her."

"Actually, mother." Edward swung his fist up and made contact with Maureen's jaw, knocking her into the railing. Her eyes rolled back into her head as she slumped to the floor.

Smirking in satisfaction he bent down and reached under her, preparing to lift her in his arms. Unfortunately her dead weight was heavier than he'd expected, and he staggered as he tried to straighten up. He grunted, then cried out as a painful spasm ripped through his back. As his body jerked he dropped his mother's torso, then lost his balance. He toppled over, landing on top of the unconscious woman with one arm pinned beneath her legs.

After a brief struggle he finally managed a sitting position, but was appalled to see that his mother was now lying on her face with her bottom sticking up in the air. Rising to his feet, he flipped her over and grabbed her ankles before dragging her across the gazebo floor and down the three steps to the ground. The dragging action caused her dress to ride up until it caught under her armpits, exposing red thong underwear and a matching lace bra.

With a shudder Edward dropped her legs and pulled the dress down to cover her hips.

Finally he grabbed Maureen under her armpits and dragged her over to the edge of the bluff. After a few manoeuvers resembling a k-turn he got her lined up parallel to the cliff.

He stopped to catch his breath, his hands leaning on his legs then, took a deep breath, placed his foot against her back, and pushed.

It took several tries before his efforts were rewarded and she rolled off the edge of the bluff. He gasped a few more times before standing up straight.

"As I was saying, Mother, I don't want to share the money with anybody."

He turned away from the bluff, one hand on the small of his back where the strained muscle was screaming in pain, and stumbled toward the house.

As he crossed the front yard he thought he saw movement on the great veranda that surrounded the three-storey brick mansion. He hesitated, wondering which of them had followed him outside. The only man left on the island was his big brother. That jerk hadn't had the guts to stand up to him since they were kids. Edward had taken everything Jeffry had ever had that was worth wanting, including the blond bimbo he'd married.

Edward made an effort to straighten his posture and strode forward, confident he could handle whatever feeble attempt the other man made.

Sure enough, Jeffry stepped out from behind a large scrub oak on the path. Edward smiled to himself, remembering all the times he'd made the other man suffer, right up until the moment his brother raised the rifle and fired.

Jeffry shut the door behind himself and leaned against it, his breath coming fast and hard. He was torn between throwing up and shrieking with joy. At last he'd gotten the better of his brother. He pushed himself off the door, dropped the rifle on the floor, staggered forward another step, and then dashed for the powder room just off the hallway.

After the vomiting stopped, he rinsed his mouth out, then splashed water on himself. The face reflected back at him in the mirror was pale, but a wicked light shone in his eyes. He started to laugh, softly at first, then louder, as he remembered the shocked expression on his brother's face. Finally the cackling subsided, and he strode out into the hallway, wondering what to do next. Or rather, who to do next. He walked down the hallway toward the study. Surely he had earned himself a drink. He strode across the parquet floor, his victory filling his thoughts, until the moment a great weight crashed down on him, and all thought fled.

"Yes!" On the third floor Rachel looked over the railing at the sprawled body of her older brother. She'd always hated the way her father had gloated over Jeffry. Jeffry didn't need to be bailed out of jail. Jeffry managed to stay in college without their father making a huge donation to the school. Jeffry managed to hold down a real job. Well, Jeffry's big brain turned out to be a perfect target for that ugly marble monkey statue Grandma Alice liked so much. Rachel spat down at her brother for good measure and headed back to her room, humming to herself. As she reached her door she paused, one hand on the knob. She wasn't sure where her mother was, but that could wait for the moment. She released the doorknob and continued down the hall toward her grandmother's room. Most of the outrageously fancy jewelry was in a safe, but even Grandma Alice's small pieces had been exquisite. The rings would need a little cleaning and resizing to fit her hands, but she could try on the earrings now. She was still humming as she reached for the handle on the large oak door. It refused to turn at first, but it didn't occur to Rachel that it might be locked. She grabbed the knob with both hands and tried to jiggle it. She was so engrossed in her task that she failed to notice the footsteps behind her, or the raised frying pan until after it made violent contact with her skull, causing her head to bounce off the door.

Sara was still holding the cast iron pan when she reached the bottom of the long stairway, but it slipped from her hand as she stepped onto the ground floor. She'd been waiting inside Rachel's room, but the coke-fiend had decided to wander off down the hallway. She thought she'd feel better after killing her sister-in-law, but swinging the pan seemed to have exhausted the anger she'd been storing all these years. In a daze, Sara made her way to the study and poured herself a Scotch. As the amber liquid splashed into the glass she shuddered, remembering that it was Edward's drink of choice. Five years she'd been sleeping with that pig while being married to his wuss of a brother, waiting for the day one of them was worth something. She'd grown to hate everything about them both, including their favourite drinks, but Scotch was the strongest alcohol she could stand, and she needed a stiff one. She raised the glass to her lips. Small white chunks of ground-up pills swirled at the bottom of the bottle.

At 6 p.m. the clock in the dining room chimed, summoning the household to the evening meal. The melody sounded through the empty room, echoing down the empty hallways. The light glinted off the sparkling stemware, and polished silver utensils lay between gleaming bone china plates. Finally the last ringing of the chimes faded into nothingness.

A faint shuffling intruded on the silence, growing slowly louder, approaching from the hallway that led to the back of the house. From another doorway the scent of seaweed wafted into the room. Groans and moans from all directions grew louder and louder, disrupting the pristine order of the empty dining room.

At last a figure appeared, leaning heavily against the doorframe. Edward winced and reached down to tighten the tattered edge of his designer shirt, which had been ripped away and wrapped around his left thigh. Blood seeped through it on the outside of his leg.

The door from the kitchen opened and Jeffry staggered in, a tea towel wrapped around a large chunk of something and pressed to his shoulder. Jeffry stopped at the sight of his brother, then dragged a chair back from the table, dropping into the seat.

Edward glowered, hopped forward to the nearest chair, dragged it away from the table and sat heavily. Through the now-empty doorway Rachel lurched, catching herself on the sideboard, one hand clamped to the back of her head. It took her several tries to navigate to a chair, but she finally sat at the head of the table.

A gasp from the hallway to the front door caused the two men to turn their heads in that direction, while Rachel leaned forward and rested her head in her hands. The gasp was followed by Sara's exclamation. "Oh, dear, Mom, what happened to you?"

"Give it up, you little bitch." Maureen stomped into the room, water dripping from her hair and clothes. Sara followed, her eyes red-rimmed and her face pale. Edward reeled back in his chair as if he'd been shot again. His mother strode around the table and slapped him. "Did you forget about the lap pool? I swam five miles every day, trying to keep my figure thanks to your bastard father and his damn pre-nup clause about divorcing me if I gained too much weight. I can't believe you thought you could drown me."

"To be fair he probably thought you were unconscious."

"Shut up Sara. What the hell happened to the rest of you?"

"Someone dropped a block of marble on me."

"I can't believe I missed your big fat head," Rachel ground out.

"If his skull is as thick as yours, it wouldn't have mattered," Sara said.

"Maybe if you didn't starve yourself to stay thin you'd be able to put some muscle into that swing," Rachel fired back.

"Lucky for me Jeffry's a bad shot," Edward said.

"And you?" Maureen asked, facing her daughter-in-law. "How come you aren't broken or bleeding?"

Sara smiled. "I wasn't stupid enough to go out in the open. By the way, Maureen, if you're going to spike the drinks with a tranquilizer, make sure you grind it up small enough that there aren't any chunks left over to warn your victim."

"Guess all that binging and purging finally came in handy," Maureen retorted.

The sorry party stared around the table at each other, the angry glares broken only by wincing or re-positioning of bandages, the silence broken only by the dripping of water coming from Maureen's clothing. "Well, aren't we a sad group," Maureen said. "Apparently we aren't as good at murder as my mother thought."

"So now what?" Rachel looked up at them through a tangle of hair that had fallen over her face.

"I call a truce," Jeffry said. "No one dies, and we all go to the Caymans together to claim the money before the lawyer can get his hands on it." There were a few grunts of assent around the room. "Can we at least eat before we try to kill each other again?"

"I'm going to get out of these wet clothes first," Maureen said. "Then we can eat. Everybody serves themselves, and everybody eats some of everything, to make sure there's no funny business."

"I guess I'd better turn the oven back on," Sara said.

"Rachel should go with you to watch," Edward said.

"Edward and I will stay here and keep an eye on each other," Jeffry said.

"Why is the oven off?" Rachel asked, shoving her chair back as she stood shakily.

"I thought it was a gas stove," Sara said. "I was going to shove your head in it."

"Idiot," Rachel said, following her through the door to the kitchen.

A stunned silence filled the squad room as the homicide detectives finished watching the video of Miss Alice instructing her family to kill each other. After a moment the captain cleared his throat. "Is this a joke?"

"Apparently not. We talked to the lawyer. The old lady could be pretty cruel."

"And they actually tried to kill each other?"

"It looks like it. The coroner says that some of the bodies show signs of trauma that were inflicted before death. Broken collarbone, bullet wound to the thigh, concussion. The Scotch in the study had been laced with prescription medication."

"So which one of them actually succeeded in killing the others?"

"None of them." The detective flipped through a file folder. "The coroner says it was botulism. Apparently the turkey and the stuffing weren't cooked properly. It took all weekend before it killed some of them, but the entire party succumbed to food poisoning. It was one of the most gruesome crime scenes the reporting officers have ever seen.

The captain shook his head sadly. "So after all that, the turkey did it."

The Finest Quality
By Andre Ramshaw

Walter Perchkin was, if nothing else, a man with an eye for a bargain. That and he had extremely bad feet. It's why he was shuffling painfully between the aisles of haphazard castoffs at the Goodwill Charity Emporium on a drizzly Wednesday morning. He flicked mechanically through hangers and hangers of shapeless jeans and fashion-rewind chinos before shambling over to the footwear rack where he scored a perfect pair of oxfords, in just his size.

Perchkin bounced up to the front counter, his inner tightwad tickled with the savings to be gleaned from a pair of $15 shoes, but stopped short to poke through a box of fresh arrivals. Sweat-stained dress shirts? Check. Puffy ski jackets, deflated? Check. Over-washed tees with tired corporate logos? Check. Uncle Mort's funeral suit, 1979? Check.

The poorly shod, parsimonious Perchkin was on the verge of giving up the hunt when he saw The Coat. He threw aside tees, tweeds, ties and tracksuits in an eruption of dejected duds that drew tut-tuts from stout ladies in red pinneys and nametags that said "Community First." Lifting the trench coat from the sartorial slag-heap he'd created, Perchkin stood to admire the exquisite piece of outerwear, its buttery soft material and black-trimmed collar setting it apart. Another score! It was becoming quite a day for bargains, Perchkin reflected as he tossed the shoes onto the counter, holding out the coat with the wistful gaze of a lost lover.

"I'll take this as well," he told the young female cashier, whose red pinney was just a little brighter than the rest.

"It's just come in, sir. It hasn't been dry-cleaned yet."

Perchkin beamed. "That's fine, young lady. I'll take it as it is. This is a McNeers, and I haven't seen one of these since they went bust thirty years ago."

The reference to a long-lost department store clearly eluded the cashier, who bundled shoes and coat into a thin grey plastic bag and held it out to Perchkin with an indifferent shrug.

Back at his basement flat, where rising damp and lowered expectations met halfway, Perchkin laid out his purchases on the fold-out sofa bed. He put the shoes on and set to work inspecting the coat. It had been well-made and well-maintained, and Perchkin noted a nametag sewn into the detachable winter lining: ART MCRANEY. Rummaging through the pockets, Perchkin discovered a zippered pouch within an inner pocket. A touch of added security. This wasn't just a coat, after all, it was a McNeers. Perchkin unzipped the hidden pocket and gingerly probed its depths. His hand withdrew holding two items: a receipt and a glossy photograph.

Perchkin sat on the edge of the bed to examine his discoveries. He swept two days' worth of unread News-Heralds onto three days of unswept parquet flooring. He placed photo and receipt beside each other with elaborate care and reached over to his night-table, from which he extracted a large magnifying glass.

An avid bargain hunter, Perchkin also fostered an interest in life's little intrigues, which were extremely limited for a basement-dwelling bachelor and waterworks night watchman. So he savoured them where he could get them.

He pored over the photograph first. A small colour snapshot of two men standing at the edge of a deep-blue evergreen-fringed mountain lake. One was cradling a massive fish and wearing a great gash of a grin. The other was standing just off centre, looking at the man with the fish as if from miles away, a toothless smile pulling at the corners of his mouth. On the back was written: "Art and Doug McRaney, brothers fishing trip, British Columbia, 2007."

The receipt was from a fishing lodge, the same year, and included a name, Doug McRaney, and a local telephone number.

Perchkin considered his options. He could alert the Goodwill shop and return the photo (boring), or he could have the photo framed and return it to the brother in person (intriguing). There was no doubt in Perchkin's mind. Here was a chance to do a family a good turn, and have a little adventure in the bargain.

He shrugged on the coat, carefully dropped the photograph and receipt back into the pocket from which they came, appraised himself in the reflection of his kitchenette toaster, and slipped out into the street.

A few minutes later, having bought a tasteful 5x7 black frame from the Dollar Store—naturally—Perchkin sat at a food court table sipping a decaf coffee and penning a small note to the "McRaney family," within which he explained how he came upon the photograph and expressing his profound hope that the McRaney clan would appreciate his small gesture of kindness.

With only a few hours to go until the start of his night shift at the water plant, Perchkin had to work fast if he was going to complete his mission.

He fished the lodge receipt from his pocket, bustled to a payphone, punched in the number listed and waited. He'd have to assume it was Doug's number. A brittle "Hello," answered the third ring.

"Is that Doug McRaney?"

The voice at the other end was wary.

"Who wants to know?"

"Oh, you don't know me," Perchkin began, his inflection rising with nervous excitement, "but I have something—a photo—that belongs to you and your brother Art."

"Who is this?"

"My name is Walter. Can we meet down at Portview Park at four this afternoon, at the bandstand? I apologize for being so mysterious but I have a little surprise for you, and I've only got a short time until I start work. Can you make it?"

"Listen, what the hell is this? How did you get my number?"

Perchkin checked his wristwatch. "Look I have to get ready. I'll see you down there, all right?"

McRaney's voice remained edgy. "Wait, I need to know more." But the line was already dead.

Doug McRaney arrived fifteen minutes ahead of the rendezvous time. He paced the empty bandstand, rubbing his hands to keep off the late-autumn chill.

At precisely two minutes to four, Perchkin bounded across the park's manicured lawns toward the Victorian bandstand that floated in the evening mist like a stricken tugboat.

He allowed himself a quick smile at the cloak-and-dagger thrill of it all, casting an admiring glance at his Bogart trench and new shoes.

McRaney pivoted on his heels as he heard Perchkin's footsteps on the bandstand's creaking wooden stairs.

"What the hell's going on? That's my brother's jacket. How did you get that?"

Perchkin rocked backwards, concussed by the belligerence of the stout man standing across from him, his eyes ablaze.

"Sir, I beg your pardon," Perchkin stammered. "I didn't mean to alarm you."

Doug's eyes burned through Perchkin as he spoke. "What is this all about? I don't have time to play games."

Perchkin cleared his throat and managed a smile, but it was as weak as his knees. A thread of cold sweat crept up his neckline.

"I have something for you."

He reached into his left inside pocket. "What.... No!"

It was all Perchkin managed to croak out before he was shot. He crumpled into a heap on the damp-slicked slats of the bandstand stage, his hand still clamped on the framed photograph.

"Hey you! What's going on down there?"

McRaney thrust the pistol into his waistband and ran across the greensward and away from the angry voice that carried through the trees. The spongy, damp grass felt like cement as he plowed his way toward his car parked on Queen Street. Seconds later, he exploded through a grove of cedars onto the busy thoroughfare, his face clouded by panic and terror.

He didn't hear the clang-clang of the night tram, nor the screams of dog-walkers; he didn't remember the delicious drift into unconsciousness.

When he awoke two days later, two detectives were leaning over him with clipboards and that insistent manner they cultivate. The one that says, 'Bud, you got trouble. And we ain't leaving till we hear all about it.' McRaney thought at first they were priests. He had a confession straining inside him like a redlining V-8 on its last quart of oil.

"Officers, forgive me, for I have sinned."

"So McRaney spilled." Detective Constable Grinson riffled through his notebook as Detective Inspector Trelawney looked on expectantly. "We took a statement at his hospital bedside. He's got a broken leg and a concussion but he's lucid and gonna make a full recovery. He thought poor old Perchkin was trying to blackmail him."

"Over what?"

DC Grinson flipped through more memo pages. "Well, like I said, McRaney spilled. His brother Art died two years ago—drowned on a fishing trip out in B.C. Only it wasn't an accident, he now admits. He and Art had feuded over a soured business deal and Doug lashed out while they were on the boat. Neither of them was wearing a lifejacket and both of 'em were pretty lit up on booze at the time. Witnesses later said they saw Doug trying to help Art by reaching out with a bargepole, but Doug says it was a crock—he was trying to push Art away. When the local Mounties and coroner got through with the case, there was nothing left but some lingering bad blood and a death by misadventure verdict. Art was two times the drink-drive limit and a poor swimmer. Well, I guess two years of guilt and jitters put old Doug on permanent edge, so he took no chances when Perchkin invited him to a mysterious meeting involving the dearly departed. He seems relieved to have the burden lifted. Claims he thought Perchkin was going for a gun and he fired in self-defence."

DI Trelawney rapped out a tattoo on his desk. "Must have a helluva guilty conscience to admit to murder and attempted murder all in the same day."

Grinson jabbed at his open notebook. "Like I said, and I'm no shrink. I think the dam just broke when he saw old Perchkin appear out of the mist in bro's favourite trench coat. It was like he seen Jacob Farley's ghost or something."

"Jacob Marley," said the inspector.

"What?"

"The character from Dickens who comes back to haunt Scrooge is Marley, not Farley."

"Whatever. You get my point."

"I do, Constable. I do, indeed."

The Inspector's tattoo became a two-handed jitterbug. He was either very excited or on the verge of losing it, the junior officer mused.

"Excellent work, Constable."

Grinson sighed in relief.

"And how is our victim, Mr. Perchkin?"

"Gonna be fine, sir. The surgeons say his arm took the brunt of the impact. His golf game'll never be the same, but hey...."

Trelawney nodded. "Damned lucky, too, that it was only a twenty-two."

Grinson snapped his notebook shut. "Just one odd thing, sir."

"Go on, Columbo," the inspector said.

"It seems like Perchkin was not only wearing Art McRaney's favourite jacket, he was also sporting his favourite oxfords. The victim's wife must've had a big clear-out and got rid of most of hubby's wardrobe. Anyway, those shoes are a bit odd. They've got special orthotic inserts for fallen arches. They wouldn't work for most men."

"Well, well," the inspector replied. "So our victim and our accidental hero, the hapless Mr. Perchkin, shared something in common with the plodding policeman."

"Too right, sir. Chalk one up for the flatfoot."

Two weeks later, back at his flat, the chastened intrigue-chaser Perchkin placed buffed oxfords and the trench coat, now professionally laundered, its bullet hole neatly patched over, into a cardboard box. He placed the box under his left arm, the right still tender and bandaged, and walked briskly out his front door.

A few minutes later he was back at the Goodwill Charity Emporium, studiously shunning the racks of rejects. He stood at the counter while a Red Pinney counted out change for a pensioner who grumbled about Goodwill's rising prices and sickly stock.

"Sally Ann's the place to go," the pensioner told Perchkin with a conspiratorial wink.

Perchkin returned the gesture with a smile as thin as the Mona Lisa on downers.

He turned his attention to the clerk. "Madam," he said, "I wish to donate these goods."

She flipped open the lid on the cardboard box and hoisted the shoes. She turned them over with a desultory glance and plopped them onto to the counter. She flashed Perchkin what might have been a grin of appreciation.

"Good quality," she remarked.

"Mmmmm," said Perchkin.

Her dainty hands returned to the box and a flash of recognition lit her kindly face as she withdrew The Coat.

"My goodness!" she declared, holding it at arm's length, much as Perchkin himself had done only a few weeks earlier.

"Now this is quality—a McNeers, no less. Why, I haven't seen one of these in a good twenty or thirty years."

Perchkin fleshed out his grin.

"Indeed, madam, and I hope never to see one again!"

With that, Perchkin flitted out the store, jaywalked across four lanes of traffic, and crossed the Rubicon. Or, in his case, The Gap. It was time for a *new* wardrobe.

Willard's Way
By H. MacDonald-Archer

H. MacDonald-Archer draws on almost forty years of experience as an editor, reporter and feature writer. As a journalist, she worked on a number of Thomson newspapers, The Ottawa Journal *and* The Canadian Press *before landing at* The Toronto Star *for 29 years. She is a member of the Toronto Chapter of Sisters in Crime, as well as Sisters in Crime International.*

No one wanted to talk about my mother's disappearance. Even those closest to her—my grandma, great-uncle and father—were reluctant to answer when I questioned them. More oddly, they were reluctant to share even the smallest details of her life, which of course made me hunger all the more for details of what she was like before I came along.

I know her story now, of course. I know why she disappeared—and when. I know what she was wearing the day she vanished, the events surrounding her disappearance and the frantic activity that took place before and after it happened.

What I realize, fifty-six years later, is that I probably knew the key to her disappearance all along. I just didn't listen; I didn't want to. I wasn't aware, as a child, of the illusions and lies adults weave for their survival.

I barely knew my grandma, Clara Bridges, or her much younger brother, Willard Semple, when I went to live with them. Clara was always Clara, never Grandma or Granny, and Willard was just Willard, never Will. And my mother? Liza Meunier was, for many years, a creature frozen in time, captured in my mind as a distressed figure on the worst day of her life.

I've spent my entire life, except my first seven years, in this Maine farmhouse.

I graduated from Bowdoin College with a liberal arts degree and went away just long enough to qualify as a teacher. I came home and taught at area schools until I retired last year—a mistake, surely. I should have just kept teaching, stayed busy.

Perhaps if I had, I wouldn't know what I know now—that the

truth, instead of setting you free, can change everything and make your life a lie.

My mother vanished one weekend when I was seven. I have a fuzzy memory of her driving us from our home in the Eastern Townships of Quebec to visit my American grandmother. It was July, the air thick with humidity, the smell of pine trees and my own fear. I remember all the windows down in the car, my mother's fair hair blowing about her face. She cried as she drove. We made many stops during that trip, my mother seeking out phone booths and stopping to make tearful calls. She grew sadder as we neared her childhood home, an old wood-frame house with windows that seemed to rattle in the slightest breeze. An old grey barn, falling in on itself even then, sat behind the house. I only managed to have it demolished recently. There's still an odd collection of rusty machinery at the edge of the property, all of it found in the barn's rubble.

We arrived very late after all those stops and phone calls. I recall relief at finally being out of that car and away from the tears. Clara was completely surprised to see her daughter, which made me think none of those calls along the road were made to her. But she was delighted to see me, swooping me off my feet into a gigantic hug so my toes dangled halfway down her calves. She smelled like soap and clean air and rubbing alcohol. She smelled like home.

After my mother and Clara put me to bed, they sat talking for hours. I struggled to hear their voices as they rose and fell, reaching me in foggy snatches through the old furnace grate set in the floor of my little room above the kitchen. I knew Uncle Willard was in his favourite spot on the verandah, rocking gently in his big old chair. A fan, the cord plugged in through the living room window, blew gently at his back on low speed. Always on low speed.

I fell asleep, despite my attempts to remain awake and know what was going on. My grandma's gentle voice continued for hours in a tone that seemed to advise, mollify, then urge silence. My mother's voice was raised, her sobs heart-breaking. It seemed, I concluded, she was leaving my father, but I couldn't understand why. At least, I thought, lying there, she wasn't leaving me. That would be disastrous.

She was gone by the time I woke up. There was no trace of her. Her car was gone; her large brown purse was gone. The green scarf she'd used to keep the hair off her face, and which she'd dropped on the hall table when we arrived, was gone.

My grandma and uncle had long finished their breakfast by the time I came down the back stairs, but they sat with me silently at the kitchen table and watched as I struggled to eat a piece of toast.

"Where's my mom?" I asked. They shook their heads. "Did she go home?" More silence. "Will she be back for me? Is she leaving my dad?" At this, my grandma swooped me up and sat me on her knee, sobbing on my neck.

"She's gone for a while," was all I was told. She dried her tears on my nightgown. Willard, his hands wrapped around his coffee mug, sat quietly. "Just for a while," he said in his low, flat monotone. "Things and people that go, are always still with us in our hearts." His voice hummed, like a machine.

It was weeks before I knew for sure my mother was not coming back, that I would not be returning to Quebec to live with my long-distance, truck-driving father. From then on, I only saw him occasionally. He'd turn up with presents on birthdays or just before Christmas, saying little to my grandma, but hugging me close, telling me how much he missed me.

As I got older, I realized he was angry with Clara, angry and confused, and that he blamed her for my mother's disappearance. They argued loudly once, my father's voice raging over hers, his constant rapid-fire questioning drowning out her tearful denials.

I was there a year when my grandma adopted me formally and changed my surname from Meunier to Semple, my grandma's maiden name. I don't know how she got my father to agree to that, but I became Ailie Semple.

Clara worked well into her seventies as a nurse at a local seniors' home. This was probably because of my arrival and the need to support me, but she never said and I never asked. Every morning, even in my last year of high school, she made my breakfast, got me into her pickup truck, dropped me off at school, a mile away, and went to work.

In time, I settled in and got to know Clara and her much younger brother, Willard, who was—to a child—a most unusual man. I realized, as I grew up, that he had many disabilities that probably weren't fully understood at the time. But it wasn't the disabilities I saw as a child. I saw a pure spirit and his desire to protect me.

"Willard's a special person, Ailie," Clara told me. "Understand that. He's a man with a special soul. You may think he doesn't know things, but he does. He knows so much more than we realize. Everyone's head works differently. Willard's brain is special."

And that was all fine by me. He made the best grilled-cheese sandwiches, corn chowder and Indian pudding I've ever tasted—then or since—and he was kind and gentle.

Willard was a kindred spirit until the day he died last year at the age of ninety-five. I cared for him until the end, just as he looked out for me during those difficult days after my mother vanished.

I know now I could have saved myself a lot of sorrow and pain if I'd just listened to him through the years as he made his flat pronouncements and odd statements. It's not that I didn't pay attention. I just didn't understand what he was trying to say.

No one, except for Clara and me, gave much thought to Willard. And quite often, even Clara struggled to understand what he was talking about. Wherever we went—church, shopping, or events in town—people chose to turn away from him or pretend he wasn't there.

The disabled—as I've come to learn as a teacher—are invisible to so many. They are often feared and frequently misunderstood. It's a fact of life.

Willard was a figure of fun—short, round and powerfully built. He wore dungarees and T-shirts all day, every day. He wasn't a great conversationalist and he spent a lot of time gazing off into the distance, his blue eyes searching for something that seemed just beyond his reach. He was a master of non sequiturs and surprised people with statements like, "Change comes from the heart, not the trees."

Whether he was speaking about winds of change or something else, I never knew, but it was one of his favourite expressions.

It didn't matter. He was our cook and housekeeper, my constant companion and the brother Clara protected fiercely. Willard was meticulous in everything he did. He rarely got angry and if he did, it showed only in the puckering of his lower lip. He never laughed and he never raised his voice. He spoke only in a monotone, his voice never rising or falling, his words formed slowly and carefully into concise sentences. He rarely made eye contact and his way of comforting me would be to lay a hand on my wrist if I was crying. "Hush," was all he'd ever say to my distress. But it was enough.

Willard claimed to hear "special noises." They didn't come from inside his head—"I'm not one of those," he'd say proudly—but from things through the air. This fascinated me and I struggled to hear things in the air, as well. I couldn't. Willard swore if a good enough wind blew, if the furnace was humming in the winter or a fan whirring during the summer heat, the noises would start. Sometimes, he said, it came in the form of a lovely tune drifting about his ears. Other times it was soft voices, murmuring and whispering, like hearing a conversation through a closed door.

Summertime was best for the noises, he said. That first summer he made us a little living room on the front porch with two rocking chairs and lots of cushions, a round table that was big enough to hold the fan, two cold drinks and a big bowl of potato chips.

One hot August day, a month after my mother disappeared, we sat companionably on the front porch with the old fan cooling our faces. He turned to me with a blissful expression on his face. "Hear that, Ailie? Hear it? It's Frank Sinatra! He's singing 'Fly Me to the Moon!'"

I heard nothing, of course, but didn't tell Willard that. Instead, I asked him, "What did my mother look like when she was younger?"

He turned to me. "An angel. Smart. Change. Gone. Sometimes it's time for change."

Emboldened, I asked, "Where? And why?"

"I will find out for you. Frank might know." And he smiled, the beatific face of a cherub.

The noises came to him anywhere. One warm fall day, a year or two after I'd arrived, the three of us went to a local diner just outside Topsham. Money was scarce, but it was Willard's birthday. The waitress placed us at a table near a window that had an air conditioner, whirring and ticking, trying to keep out the unexpected heat wave. All through his chicken à la king and mashed potatoes, Willard ate, eyes closed, head nodding in time as though agreeing to something someone was saying. "You're right, you're right," he said, leaning in closer to the AC, which blew his fuzzy hair back.

"Willard!" Clara hissed. "Stop that, please."

"It's Paul Harvey," he seemed offended. "I'm just agreeing with him."

When he informed us the AC had just started playing Perry Como's song, "Catch a Falling Star," Clara snatched up the bill, took me by the hand and said brightly, "Time to go."

My mother became a faint memory. I had trouble remembering her face by the time I finished high school. I couldn't remember what her voice sounded like. What I could remember vividly was her beautiful long blond hair, held by that green scarf, blowing in the wind as we sped south on that hot July day. I remember how the sun glinted off the flying strands before they dragged across her tear-stained face. I remember the tears.

My life hasn't been full; it hasn't been empty.

Clara died during my last semester at university. I didn't think I'd be able to finish my year, but I did.

My father remarried eight years after my mother's disappearance. She'd been declared dead, but I never gave up hope. His new wife, Emilie, had three little boys, but I never met them. My father continued to stop by and visit me from time to time on his driving route through Maine. He died suddenly of a heart attack at the age of fifty-six. That happens to truckers.

I retired last year, two years early. It was just after that I discovered what had happened to my mother. In the aftermath of that discovery I became exhausted, depressed and felt betrayed. I just didn't see it coming. But I should have. All the signs were there.

Willard died in March, and by the first of June I just decided it was time to make a few changes. I handed in my resignation, got my pension sorted and made plans to tear down the barn and plant the rose garden I'd always dreamed of growing along the front path.

In early July, I cleared out the back yard, had it landscaped and hired my neighbour, Seth Goodman, to build a gardening shed and a gazebo. I had some of the lawn turned into flagstone patio and put out tubs of flowers and planted small trees and shrubs. What a sight it was. I sat there, long into the warm evenings, candles lit, listening to the woodland rustlings and wondered why.

And then, in late September, I finally had that old barn cleared away. I left that job for last. I made sure Seth—a man with three kids all about to go into university in the next year or two—was there to help. I warned him beforehand what he might find and paid him handsomely to do the job. He suggested I bring in the pastor from our Unitarian church—"for support, like." And the day before the scheduled demolition, he said, "Maybe you should have the sheriff on hand, and perhaps a police officer or two."

I didn't want that, but I agreed in the end.

We gathered just a little after 8 a.m. one Friday morning. We found my mother by mid-afternoon. Seth and Pastor Bill were hauling old boards, boxes and rusty machinery from the caved-in debris when I stepped in. "Right there," I said. "She should be right there." I pointed to the spot where an old Acme Harvester dump rake had been sitting for decades.

"Are you sure?" Pastor Bill asked. I nodded.

Seth and Bill picked up shovels, while the police officer—I can't even remember his name—stood back with a camera and watched. Seth and Bill began the laborious job of sifting dirt away from what I believed to be my mother's final resting place. The sheriff, Chuck Moyers, asked if I had any gardening tools and I fetched a couple of trowels from my new shed. He got down on his knees, like an archeologist, and scraped at the ground. But it was Seth who found the first bone, a fragile bit of white that may have belonged to a foot.

"Time for the coroner," Moyers said, getting to his feet. He handed me the trowel.

Four hours later, my mother's bones lay exposed. Her hands were folded over her chest. There were still remnants of her beautiful blond hair, now dirty and dark. Her gingham shirt, which had been a green and white—the collar always worn up—was now black from the earth. Her once-beige moccasins lay beneath her feet. Her brown purse peeped out from the top of her spine. For one silly moment, I thought how uncomfortable that must been all these years.

Maybe I was white as a ghost, I don't know, but there was a sudden scramble to get me away from the barn, find me a chair and a glass of water.

"You were right," the sheriff said, his hand squeezing my shoulder.

"No, he was right. He was always right. I just didn't listen."

I told the whole story that evening at the kitchen table, the pastor, sheriff, a homicide detective and Seth listening. Seth's wife, Hannah, had brought in a lasagna and was hovering over us, making pots of coffee and fussing with a tin of homemade oatmeal cookies she insisted we share.

"When did you know for sure?" the young homicide detective asked, his notebook open. He had introduced himself as Clayt Evans when he arrived, a little more than an hour after we found my mother's remains.

"He told me as he lay dying," I said.

"I don't mean to offend you," the young man said, "but I understand your uncle didn't really converse much with anyone. He had a disability, didn't he? Did he confess?"

"Not in so many words," I said. "He was autistic. There was some schizophrenia, too, but he was able to manage on medications."

"Go on."

"I was able to put it all together at the end. It was like joining the dots." I paused to take a long gulp of coffee. How could I tell them that long-dead personalities like Frank Sinatra, Perry Como and Paul Harvey had acted as spiritual conduits for my poor uncle Willard, who was the real culprit?

I drank more coffee and stared at the table. The detective didn't rush me. I took deep breaths and remembered a day when I was thirteen.

Willard had come in from the barn and I remarked that it wasn't a safe place to be, what with the roof hanging halfway to the floor. He said nothing, but later he remarked, "Angels keep us safe in bad places."

I looked up at Evans and told him, "He often said my mother was close by, always watching over me. But lots of people say that about the dead, don't they? So, of course, I began to wonder if she really *was* dead."

Willard always added, "Perry says so, too. Catch a falling star." But I left out that fact as I talked to the sheriff.

"But he said other things, too, over the years," I told the sheriff. "Once my grandma suggested having the barn brought down and cleared away and Willard had been most upset. He never made eye contact with anyone, and that night he sat at this table, staring at the table cloth, fists pounding slowly on the table, saying over and over, 'The barn has seen so much, it knows so much. So much history.' So my grandma gave up on the idea." I shrugged.

"Did she know? Did she know what he'd done?"

"She must have. Of course, she did. Did she help him? I don't know. And that suggestion to tear down the barn must have been a taunt. As much as she wanted to protect her brother, Willard had killed her own daughter. What an awful dilemma this must have been for her."

"And she never told you, or intimated any knowledge of what he'd done?"

"No."

"What did he tell you, exactly?"

"He didn't make a deathbed confession, if that's what you're wondering. He said things over the last few days he was still able to communicate. I don't even know if he knew I was sitting beside him. He just muttered and muttered. I wrote it all down, put it together and to me, at least, it makes sense."

"Tell us, Ailie," the pastor said.

I went back fifty-six years, to 1955, to the night my mother and I arrived. "I assume my mother had fled a somewhat abusive marriage and decided to come home to stay with my grandma. I only remember my grandma consoling her, comforting her.

"But I think Willard must have overheard their conversation, too, that night. He had a habit of sitting out on the verandah long into the night. He wasn't much of a sleeper even then, less so as he got older."

Hannah reached over my shoulder with the coffee pot and poured me another cup. "Do you have any brandy to put in there?" she asked.

"Thank you, maybe later," I waved a hand.

"I think he heard things that upset him greatly. I think he became alarmed at the situation—his niece leaving her husband, arriving home with her young child, wanting things to change."

"Did he tell you that, ever?"

"No. Not until he was dying. It came out in bits and pieces, as everything did with Willard. He was lucid on and off for three days near the end. Apart from coming down to make meals, I stayed with him, sleeping in a chair. A nurse from the community services would come in the morning and evening and help me clean him up and change him. But in between he'd ramble.... 'Liza was a slut, she wanted him kicked out of his own house, she had no right.' And so on."

"This was never said in one sentence? Like an admission?" the detective asked.

"No. It wasn't a confession, as I've said. He referred to things like 'wringing a neck'—his exact words—and then 'buried by the rake'."

I got up and turned to the old dresser that stood inside the door, pulled open a drawer and drew out a spiral notebook of mine. "It's all in here, in order. And the dates are there, too."

"You realized he was talking about murdering your mother?"

"Of course! What else could it be? And no, I didn't hasten his end in revenge. He was full of cancer. And he'd always been so kind to me, so caring—as much as he could be."

"You must feel betrayed, Ailie," Pastor Bill said, touching my hand.

"I did. I do. I feel like my life here has all been a lie."

"Why did you wait five months to search for her? And under the rake?" the detective asked, one eyebrow raised.

"I needed time. I had a lot of things to sort out in my head. I kept hoping I was imagining things, I guess. And why under the Acme rake? He kept using the word. 'Rake, raked.'"

Evans watched me for a moment and then began flipping through the pages and reading aloud. "March 23, the raker, evil; March 24, said I should be in a home; March 25, Clara is tired, kept the secret."

"Just ramblings." I looked at him. "But I'm guessing that night we got here my mother suggested we stay with Clara, that she could help with the house, and that perhaps it was time for Willard to go to a home—to give my grandma a break. Maybe I'm imagining that last part. And then I think there was a fight. I think Willard might have been angry with my mother for arriving unexpectedly and making suggestions. I think he snapped, killed my mother and buried her."

"What about her car? Could Willard drive?"

"No, not that I ever knew. I think somewhere, not too far away in a bush, there's a burned-out or rusting vehicle. What's another old car sitting in the bush in Maine? No one seems to notice.

"My grandma was fit and strong. She loved her daughter, but she also loved her brother and had sworn to her own mother she'd care for Willard. My mother came home and upset the balance."

"What did they tell your father?" Evans asked.

"They let on that she'd just up and disappeared. He never believed it. Never."

The silence that followed was deafening. The kitchen clock ticked, fresh coffee dripped into the pot, the chair on the verandah outside squeaked as it rocked against a table in the rising wind.

"I'm so, so sorry Miss Semple," the sheriff said. He reached across the table to pat my hand. The detective closed the notebook.

"The van is coming to remove the remains," he said slowly. "You can go ahead and plan a funeral. We won't be taking any action. But we will be closing the existing missing person's case. I'm sorry it ended this way."

"I am, too. I'm so very sorry. I didn't want it to end this way."

During the first few weeks after I retired, I blamed myself for the situation. What should I do? I told myself I should have ignored Willard's mad, death-bed ramblings, pretended he was talking nonsense and that Paul, Perry and Frank were just feeding him a load of crap for all those years.

I told myself if I'd kept teaching, tutoring, volunteering, perhaps I wouldn't be in this predicament, feeling alone, my emotions savaged. The barn would still be standing (sort of), there'd be no roses, no gazebo, no patio.

And then I realized it wasn't my fault—any of it. How does a child stop a murder? What could I have done?

The cloud of bereavement, which had hung over me for years, began lifting and I began planning. I looked beyond the five acres of farm, beyond Cumberland County. And then I realized that the renovations I'd done to the house over the years—not to mention the new shed, patio and gardens—had added value to the property.

The For Sale sign went up the day after I laid my mother's cremated remains beside Clara's. The house sold quickly, to my great relief.

I said my goodbyes to former colleagues and friends at a nice dinner they held in the church hall. It was a surprise event and I was impressed at the turnout and tears. I hardly knew what to say. I've known them all of my life, save for seven years. I'll miss them, to be sure. But everything to do with my past is tainted, is lies.

The day after that farewell dinner I took all my savings, the money from the house sale and left Cumberland County.

I don't plan to go back anytime soon.

I'm back teaching, for now, and I love it. The children call me Mademoiselle Meunier. My French was always pretty good as it was my first language, after all. It was all I spoke with my father. The little village, where I now live and teach, is so different from anything I've ever known. I never dreamed I could feel so at home and happy in a place like Provence.

But best of all? There's this man I've met....

142

Avenging Desdemona
By Ed Piwowarczyk

Ed Piwowarczyk is a veteran journalist, having worked as a copy editor for the National Post *and* Toronto Sun, *and as an editor and reporter for* The Sault Star. *A lifelong fan of crime fiction and a long-time member of the Toronto chapter of Sisters in Crime, he is also a film buff and plays in a Toronto pub trivia league. His short fiction has been published in* World Enough and Crime *and* 13 O'Clock. *He lives in Toronto with his wife Rosemary McCracken, author of the Pat Tierney mystery series.*

"Put out the light, and then put out the light..."

It won't be long, Otis Thompson thought. She'll be dead soon.

Otis stared at the Royal Alexandra Theatre stage, transfixed by a British touring company's production of *Othello*.

Beside him, Denise squeezed his hand.

Such cynical times we live in, he thought. The audience believes the Moor of Venice is a fool, duped by his malicious subordinate, Iago, into killing his loving, faithful wife, Desdemona.

But Otis understood Othello's pain, the sense of betrayal that fuelled his jealousy. He had almost brought his own world down with his rage over Tess, before he'd met Denise.

"Kill me tomorrow, let me live tonight!" Desdemona pleaded on stage.

"It is too late," the Moor replied.

Otis's eyes were closed, but he could picture Othello's hands tightening around Desdemona's neck.

It hadn't been too late for the unfaithful Tess; she was still alive. And it hadn't been too late for him, either. He had found happiness when he married Denise.

"'Twill out, 'twill out. I hold my peace, sir? No!"

He opened his eyes. On the stage, Emilia, Iago's wife and Desdemona's faithful servant, was denouncing her husband, who had schemed to plant a handkerchief, Othello's gift to Desdemona, on the Moor's chief lieutenant, Cassio.

Dread welled up inside Otis as Othello realized the horrible mistake he'd made in believing Desdemona had been unfaithful. Before stabbing himself, the Moor declared he wanted to be remembered

143

as one who loved wisely if not too well.

Otis was relieved when Iago was led away, and the curtain came down.

"What is it, honey? Where have you been since we left the theatre?"

Otis glanced up from his menu to see the worried look on Denise's face.

"It's nothing, really."

"C'mon then." She flashed him a grin. "Lighten up. Who's bigger than Tiny Thompson?"

Otis smiled. Tiny Thompson had been his nickname since he was a linebacker at college in Mississippi. His quickness and ferocity in chasing down quarterbacks had drawn the attention of pro scouts. They were willing to overlook some ill-advised roughing calls and game ejections, but, because he stood barely six feet tall, he was passed over as being too small.

He decided to try his luck at football in Canada, and was soon a star in Toronto. Then his public profile, along with the hard work he put into his business studies during the off-season, landed him a job with a Bay Street investment firm, where he quickly moved up the corporate ladder.

He found the racial acceptance that had eluded him in Mississippi. He had friends at work and in the community. There were parties, ball games, hunting trips in the fall.

Hunting was one of the few things that he and Denise disagreed about. She told him she hated anything to do with guns. Did he *have* to keep that shotgun in the house? She finally relented when he agreed to lock it away in his den.

Still, as he approached fifty, with a good job, beautiful wife, and a nice home in Moore Park, he thought life hadn't turned out so bad for the poor black kid from Mississippi.

Yes, life was good.

But he had nearly lost it all. While he was working his way up in the investment firm, he had been bewitched by Tess, the raven-haired beauty from a wealthy Rosedale family. Nearly ten years younger than he, she was spoiled, and had been hell-bent on shocking her family by marrying a black man. But he hadn't been able to see it.

She complained about his long hours at the office. Bored, she tried to occupy herself with expensive home renovations. He

144

agreed, hoping to satisfy her and hold their marriage together.

For a while, it did. Tess couldn't wait to show him the architect's drawings, or the designer's suggestions about paint and furniture. When construction on an addition started, she became preoccupied, no longer caring about what he thought or how late he worked.

One day he arrived home early. He felt a migraine coming on. The right side of his head pounded. Nauseous, he climbed the stairs to their bedroom.

He heard moans on the other side of the door. Sounds of pleasure, not pain.

Flinging the door open, he found Tess naked with Dave, their carpenter. He imploded. He wrestled Tess onto her back, both hands squeezing her throat. Dave tried to pull him off as she struggled beneath him. He lifted one hand from Tess to shove Dave away. As his grip on Tess tightened, from the corner of his eye he saw a flash of brass—a bedside lamp. Then blackness enveloped him.

The following weeks were a blur of police interviews, divorce papers and gossip in financial circles. Otis agreed to a generous divorce settlement, and the police investigation was dropped.

"Hey, big boy. You there?"

Otis snapped out of his reverie.

"It's the play, isn't it?"

He nodded sheepishly.

"Damn it! Why did we go?"

"It was a gift from Roger and Erica."

"They should have known better." She paused. "Sorry. Make that *Roger* should have known better. Erica goes along with whatever he says. After the business with Tess, he should have known it would upset you."

"Aren't you being too harsh? Roger probably picked it because it got all those rave reviews in England."

"You're too trusting sometimes. If you were Othello, Roger Kane would be Iago."

Otis smiled at Denise's analogy as she returned to studying the menu. If life imitated art, her woman's intuition might be right.

Roger was thirty-five, and there was no doubting his ambition, Otis thought. He hadn't been able to hide his disappointment at being passed over for promotion at the firm in favour of Steve Adams.

After Otis had introduced Roger to Denise at an office party a few months before, she told him, "He's a creep. He was sucking up tonight to everyone he thought was important."

But Roger's wife, Erica, was another matter. At twenty-nine, the auburn-haired Erica was only a few months older than Denise. The two women hit it off at the party. They belonged to the same fitness club, shared an interest in art and went out together whenever he and Roger worked late.

Otis didn't believe Roger was quite the "creep" Denise thought him to be, but he silently agreed with her that choosing *Othello* showed Roger lacked sensitivity. Roger knew how much the publicity about Tess's affair had hurt him, and that the strangulation scene would hit too close to home.

After the split with Tess, he took court-ordered anger management sessions. Immersion in work kept his pain and loneliness at bay.

One night, he ducked into an all-night coffee shop near his office building for a jolt of caffeine and something to eat. That's when he saw a woman in her late twenties huddled over documents in a booth.

He slid into the booth across the aisle, placed his order and studied her. She periodically ran her fingers through her short blond hair, occasionally biting her full lower lip as she pored over papers.

Sensing him watching her, she glanced up, gave him a cursory look with green eyes that said, "Not interested." When she got up to pay her tab, he admired her trim figure and shapely legs. She left the coffee shop without taking any further notice of him.

Captivated, Otis returned the next few nights looking for her.

It was another week before she was back in the same booth. Otis summoned up the nerve to ask if he could join her. Just coffee and a chat, he said. She hesitated, then gestured to the seat across from her. His first "date" with Denise.

In the beginning, their evenings out consisted of dinner, a movie, or small talk at a bar. Later, their discussions became more personal.

Denise had been a teenage bride. After divorcing her abusive husband, she left the small town she'd grown up in and found a job as a clerk for a legal firm near Otis's office. Since the end of her marriage, she had developed a sixth sense about men. She hated constantly being hit on—at the office, on the street, at bars—and warded off advances with an ice-queen demeanor. But her intuition told her that Otis was a decent guy.

Otis admired her for summoning the courage to divorce her

spouse when he became abusive. When he shared how he'd almost killed Tess, she embraced him.

After he and Denise married, there were whispers that it was a mistake—she was too young for him, he was too old for her; she was white, he was black. But they were happy, so what others thought or said didn't matter.

"Otis, you ready to order?"

Denise brought him back to the bustle of the restaurant.

"What? Oh." He snapped the menu shut. "I can't decide. I'll have whatever you're having."

I know why you did it.

Roger leaned back in the leather armchair in his living room, sipped his single malt scotch, then cradled the glass in his hands. He closed his eyes, remembering his meeting with Denise a few weeks after the office party.

He should have known something was up. She had been cool to him at the party, so why had she called him at the office and asked him to meet her at a nearby diner?

"I know why you did it, Roger."

"I don't know what you mean, Denise."

"*Othello.* You knew it would upset him. You were getting even for his passing you over for promotion. You can't stand that the job went to Steve Adams."

Damn right I can't. "What makes you think—"

"Don't try to bullshit me. I know your type. Hitting on me at the office party told me all about you."

Roger said nothing.

"I didn't tell Otis. Or Erica. I don't want to hurt them. But if you try to pull a stunt like the *Othello* tickets again, I will."

Roger laughed. "That's it? I have a few drinks at a party, I make an innocent pass. Do you think Otis or Erica care?"

"Maybe, maybe not." Denise smiled. "But Erica might not understand your walks on the wild side."

Roger froze.

"You like to make excursions to where hookers hang out."

"That's preposterous."

"Is it? One night, I drove downtown to pick up Otis. When I was almost there, he reached me on my cell to say he'd be another couple of hours. I was about to go back, when I saw you come out of an underground parking lot. My intuition told me the direction you were heading in wasn't for home. I had some time to kill, so I followed you to that street."

"You can't prove it."

"No? I didn't want to risk being spotted by you, so I left. But the next day I hired a private investigator. He got shots of you negotiating for the services of some pretty young things."

Roger shifted in his seat. "You're bluffing."

"Want to try me?" Denise leaned forward. "That *Othello* performance was agony for Otis, and I wanted to make you squirm. But how? Proof of your 'excursions' were just what I needed."

"How do I know this 'proof' exists?"

Denise dug into her shoulder bag and slid him a sealed envelope. "They're copies. Just for you."

Roger turned the envelope over in his hands without opening it and swallowed hard. "What do you want?"

"Not money."

"Then what?"

"The pictures are locked away, unmarked, on a disc in a safety deposit box. They'll stay there unless you cause Otis any more trouble. Do you understand?"

He glared at her but nodded.

"Good. I can't say it's been nice talking to you, but thanks for the coffee."

Roger snapped out of his reverie, took another sip from his glass.

I know why you did it.

He seethed. *Yes, Denise, I want to hurt Otis. I hate kowtowing to a washed-up jock. I hate obeying his orders. I hate sucking up to Otis and the rest of them. How do they reward me? They give my promotion to a nobody like Steve Adams.*

He gulped down the rest of his scotch. *Now you bitch, you're threatening me.* He slammed his glass down on a side table. *No!*

Denise wasn't bluffing about the photographs. If she ever released them, his world would fall apart. Something had to be done.

Then it hit him. What better solution to his problem than revisiting *Othello*?

Roger laughed as he poured himself another drink.

"Here's to the happy couple."

Otis clinked glasses with Roger, acknowledging the toast. They sat in a pub around the corner from their office. After a hectic day,

Otis had welcomed the invitation for a post-work drink.

"Thanks again for those tickets, Roger. Great seats. But..." Otis hesitated. "Don't think we're ungrateful, but Denise has a bone to pick with you about the play."

"But it's a big hit. Erica and I loved it. It's going to New York and—"

"That's what I told her, but she didn't think it was an appropriate choice after what happened with Tess."

"Tess? What's she—" Roger stopped. "Oh, I get it. I'm sorry, Denise is right. It never occurred to me. I'm sorry."

"Forget it, Roger."

They sat silently, savoring their single malts.

"Hey, I really *did* enjoy it," Otis said. "I can see why it's touring. The cast is pretty good. Especially the guy playing Othello. I could really feel for him."

"Maybe Denise was thinking about what you'd do if you ever found her in a position like Tess."

Otis began to rise from his chair. "How dare you suggest—"

"Whoa!" Roger threw up his hands. "I'm not suggesting anything."

Otis slowly sat back down. He tried to keep his voice even. "Are you saying Denise is having an affair?"

"No, but...."

"But what?"

"Denise and Steve Adams seemed to be cozying up to each other at the office party."

"That's it?"

"They just seemed kind of chummy. It's probably nothing. Forget I mentioned it."

Otis leaned across the table. "I *am* going to forget it, Roger. And I suggest *you* do, too. If I ever hear this...*fantasy* again, I don't know what I'll do. You understand?"

Otis got up and walked out of the pub.

The woman seated across from Otis in the food court wasn't what he expected a private investigator to look like. Cathy Doyle wore a loose-fitting grey jogging suit.

"Yeah, no trench coat or fedora," she said with a smile. "Dressed like this, I could be a mom out to pick up her kids. You need to keep a low profile in surveillance."

Doyle had been watching Denise for the past two weeks, just in case Roger was right.

The investigator briefed him on Denise's activities—tennis, the fitness club, shopping, watercolour classes.

Nothing amiss there. "Did she meet anyone?"

"She went to the movies a couple of times with Erica Kane, then they went back to your place."

"Yes, Roger and I often work late. Denise told me she likes to have Erica over for coffee and cards. Anyone else?"

"She had lunch with Steve Adams at Alfredo's, that Italian restaurant near your office. I was a few tables away, so I couldn't hear what they were saying."

Please don't let what happened with Tess happen again.

"It looked pretty innocent to me," Doyle went on. "Call it woman's intuition, but I don't think there's anything going on between them."

She gave him a reassuring smile. "From what I can tell, Mr. Thompson, your wife's a model citizen."

In bed, Otis tried to read a book. Beside him, Denise finished her magazine, and shifted to turn off the night table lamp.

"Your lunch with Steve Adams last week. What was that about?"

Denise rolled over to face him. "What?"

"You heard me."

"Who told you? Someone from the office?"

Otis said nothing.

"I should have known we'd be seen there," Denise said. "It was supposed to be a secret."

She paused. "You don't think Steve and I..." She started to laugh.

"I don't see what's so funny."

"That you'd think there's something going on." She nudged him gently with her elbow. "C'mon, there's no reason to be jealous. The 'secret' was the birthday party I've been planning for you. Your fiftieth is coming up. I wanted some ideas about where to have a party. I talked to Erica, but I wanted another opinion." She sighed. "But now you know. Satisfied?"

Otis nodded, and forced himself to smile.

"Just promise to act surprised, okay?"

She kissed him, then snapped off the light.

It sounded reasonable, Otis thought, but his suspicions still gnawed at him.

When he finally fell asleep, he dreamed he was back in the old house, and as he climbed the stairs to the bedroom, he heard Tess with Dave.

But as he opened the door and Tess turned toward him, he realized it wasn't Tess—it was Denise.

The white tennis outfit, the short blond hair, the shapely legs—there was no mistaking Denise stepping out of the Thompson house, Roger thought as he watched the scene unfold on the widescreen TV. It was Erica's book club night, the perfect time to watch this DVD alone.

The DVD wasn't Hollywood quality, Roger thought, but it didn't have to be to fool an audience of one—Otis Thompson.

He watched it with a satisfied smile. There was no mistaking that the woman who placed her tennis gear in her car, and then roared off, was Denise.

When he'd shot the segment with his camcorder, he waited under the tree across the street from the Thompson house, standing well back so she wouldn't see him. It meant shooting at a distance, but that was exactly what he needed.

Denise, the car, the Thompson house—there had to be no doubt in Otis's mind that Denise was the star of this production.

But Denise soon gave way to an actress, someone of roughly the same age and with the same build. Dye her hair, dress her in matching clothes and sunglasses, and voilà! No one would know it wasn't Denise.

Finding "Denise" and her co-star—someone who vaguely resembled Adams when he put on sunglasses—had been surprisingly easy once Roger waved cash under a talent agency manager's nose.

If "Denise" and "Adams" had wondered about the production—no script, no lines to memorize, no crew—they said nothing.

Roger booked a patio table at a busy downtown restaurant at lunch time. His instructions were simple: Keep your sunglasses on, kiss when you sit down, hold hands, lean close to each other a few times when you eat, and embrace when you leave.

He sat a few tables away with his camcorder, close enough to see them but far enough away not to hear them. He wanted the camcorder microphone to pick up only ambient sound—the din of passing traffic, the clatter of the busboys clearing tables, the incomprehensible babble of conversation at the tables around him.

The finale, of course, was at a sleazy motel.

"Denise" and "Adams," still wearing sunglasses, embrace outside the motel room door. "Adams" fiddles with the lock as "Denise" leans into him, her arms around his waist. They kiss before stepping into the room. The door slams shut.

Perfect! Roger hit the Eject button on the DVD player. *Just the thing for Otis.*

For Your Eyes Only was scrawled on the envelope on Otis's office desk.

From Roger, Otis thought. Since that evening at the pub, their relationship had been strained.

A DVD with a note wrapped around it was in the envelope. He would find what was on the disc painful, so he should watch it alone, the note read.

He considered throwing out the disc, but he had to see what was on it.

His secretary wheeled in the TV and DVD player that were used for presentations. He told her to hold all calls and not to disturb him. Then he locked his office door.

He pushed Play, and his nightmare came to life on the TV screen.

When the disc had finished, he stared numbly at the screen. Then anger began to percolate inside him, and he had his secretary summon Roger.

As Roger closed the door behind him, Otis yanked him forward by his tie and held up the disc. "Is this from you?"

Roger gasped and coughed when Otis released the tie. He nodded. "Otis, I know how much this must hurt."

"You can't *possibly* know."

"I was only trying—"

"I don't want to hear it. Just tell me when this was shot."

Roger hesitated. "The day before yesterday."

It fit, Otis thought. Adams had taken some time off work just when he'd called off his surveillance of Denise.

Otis tossed the disc to Roger. "Take it with you. I've seen plenty."

"Otis, if there's anything I can do..."

"You've done quite enough." Otis closed his eyes. "Please leave."

Roger quietly closed the door behind him.

How could she? Otis's head began to pound. He felt nauseous.

Put out the light, then put out the light...

The words ran through Otis's mind as he stood outside the bedroom, listening to the moans of pleasure.

He burst into the bedroom. then zeroed in on the writhing forms under the bed covers.

"Denise!" The figures froze.

Denise's head peeked out from the covers. "Otis? Oh shit!"

He lunged at Denise as she scrambled naked from the bed. A figure draped in a bedsheet dashed out the door.

"Go! Go!" Denise urged.

Otis grabbed Denise around the waist and swung her onto the carpet. She tried to kick free as he pulled himself on top of her. His hands curled around her neck; the more she thrashed, the harder he squeezed. Her body went limp.

He didn't know how long it was before he released his grip on her. He staggered to his feet.

There were sirens in the distance.

The pounding in his head started up again.

I've got to make it stop!

He remembered the shotgun in his den.

"'Put out the light, then put out the light,'" he whispered as he closed the bedroom door behind him.

Roger lay naked on the bed, his hands cuffed to the rails of the brass headboard, his ankles secured by leather straps to the bedposts. He was looking forward to this night with Erica.

"Why don't we try something different tonight?" she had said at breakfast that morning. "There's a motel, really out of the way, where we could..."

What she was suggesting was startling. He'd married Erica because of her cool, aloof beauty. And because of her well-to-do family. They had sex regularly, but he sought kinkier thrills elsewhere. This new Erica was a welcome surprise.

"It's the middle of the week, so we should have the place pretty much to ourselves," she'd said. "Rent the unit farthest from the motel office, and park in front of it. Make yourself comfortable until I get there."

"Where will you be?"

"Picking up a few 'toys' to make the night special."

She'd arrived wearing a shoulder-length blond wig and dark glasses.

"What's with the get-up?"

"It's all part of the game. You strip and lie on the bed." She'd rummaged in her bag to dig out the restraints. "Now let's get you settled."

He closed his eyes and smiled. No more Otis. No more Denise. The papers had been full of stories about the murder-suicide. Otis's death meant a major reorganization at the firm. He would be moving up.

"I know you did it!"

His eyes snapped open. Erica was sitting naked astride him, clutching a chef's knife in her right hand.

"What are you talking about?" Roger squirmed; the handcuffs and straps remained tight.

"You killed Denise."

Roger pulled at his bonds. "Otis killed her!"

"You goaded him into it. With that disc."

"What disc?"

Erica slashed his shoulder. Roger screamed as the blood began to ooze from his wound.

"The one I found mixed up with our home videos," Erica said.

Roger cursed inwardly. *Why didn't I trash it?*

"Then I remembered the tickets for *Othello*. So this was your little production."

"Denise was having an affair with Adams." Roger tried to keep his voice steady. "That's why Otis flipped."

Another slash, another scream.

"Denise *was* having an affair, but it was with *me!*"

Roger's eyes widened in surprise.

"The first time we met, I felt...something...between us. She was the best lover I ever had."

Erica paused. "What we had was special, but Denise cared for Otis. She wanted *both* of us."

She wiped a tear from her cheek.

"I was with her when Otis burst in. Denise told me to get out. She knew I wouldn't be able to stop him. I've felt so ashamed. I should have stayed, tried to save her."

Her eyes hardened as she stared down at Roger. "When I saw that disc, I knew I couldn't blame Otis. You're the one who took Denise from me."

Roger thrashed in vain. "Whatever you're thinking of, it will never work."

"No?" Erica smiled. "You arrived alone. No one knows I'm here."

"Someone will see you."

"I parked on a side road, and walked here," she replied. "And if someone saw me, they saw a blonde with dark glasses."

"The police. They'll suspect you."

"A dutiful wife from a Rosedale family? I doubt it. Tomorrow morning, I'll call them and say you didn't come home. Naturally, I'm worried. You often work late, but you always call."

"What happens when they find me?"

"I will be stunned and distraught. And I'll have no idea what you were doing out here."

Panic swept over Roger as he tugged at his bonds. "It will never work."

"I don't care." Erica clasped the knife with both hands, and raised it over her head.

"How does that line from the play go? Something about the light? Well, it's lights out for you Roger."

"Please!"

"For Otis." Erica plunged the knife into his right shoulder.

"Don't!"

"For Denise." The knife came down again, piercing his left shoulder.

Roger began to whimper. Erica took a deep breath, brought the knife back over her head and poised it above his heart. "For me."

He squeezed his eyes shut and sobbed. He remembered the line from *Othello*.

Put out the light, and then put out the light...

Then all was darkness.

A Terminal Affair
By Lynne Murphy

Lynne Murphy is a founding member of the Toronto Chapter of Sisters in Crime. She is a retired journalist. Her short stories have been included in several anthologies including The Whole She-Bang. *She lives in Toronto.*

"I wouldn't want her to suffer."

Was I dreaming? It was my husband's voice, coming from the bedroom next door. But it couldn't be Bud, because why would he be home in the middle of the afternoon, on a weekday? And who on earth could he be talking to? I shook my head which reminded me of my migraine and the pain pill I had taken.

"She won't suffer, darling. We'll think of something painless. Something that looks natural."

Well, at least now I knew who he was talking to. That voice belonged to my former executive assistant, Pamela. Why was she calling him "darling"?

"You're sure she's gone for the afternoon?" Pamela asked.

"It's Wednesday. Every Wednesday she has lunch with her friends and then they play bridge all afternoon. You saw for yourself, her car is gone. Honey, I wish we didn't have to—to get rid of her. I mean, we've been married for thirty-five years."

"And that's why we have to get rid of her. She'd get half the business. Maybe more than half because her parents started the first funeral home. She's going to say she sacrificed herself to raise the kids and all that bullshit and we'd be lucky if you came out of a divorce with your shirt. And then there's the life insurance you've got on her."

That was when I woke up. I mean, really woke up. They were talking about killing me. *Me!*

"You'll be going sailing this summer. You could get her out on the boat—"

"She hates sailing. She never goes out on the boat with me."

"Swimming then...."

"She's a very strong swimmer. Nobody would believe it."

"Then hire a hit man. For God's sake, Harrison. Use a little imagination. Do I have to do it myself?"

I could have told her imagination wasn't my husband's strong suit. He was a wonderful salesman. Why Bud could sell a ten-thousand dollar casket to a bereaved wife faster than you could say "knife." But I was the one who provided the vision, running the three funeral homes we owned.

"I can't think about it right now," Bud said. I always called him Bud. Harrison was the name he used after we got rich. "I want you too much. Come here you sexy little thing."

The unmistakable noises started. Remembering Bud's performances with me, I figured that I had about three minutes to get out of the house. I picked up my shoes and purse from beside the couch and tiptoed down the stairs and out the back door. I stopped to put my shoes on, then I hurried past the pool, out the gate at the back of the garden and down the lane to the little park at the end of our street. I sat down on a bench, where I couldn't be seen easily, to think about what I had heard. My migraine was still lurking at the back of my head, like an animal waiting to pounce if I did anything too quickly.

The migraine was the reason I was home instead of playing bridge. The headache had struck while I was driving to my friend Amy's house. I had managed to park the car at my regular service station and asked the owner to call me a taxi. There was no way I could drive home. Fred had agreed to deliver my car later when he had someone free. At home, I called my hostess to apologize, took a pill and lay down on the sewing room couch. I chose the sewing room because it gets less light in the afternoons. And then I had awakened to hear Bud and Pamela planning to murder me.

I had known for years that Bud had girlfriends. He wasn't very imaginative there, either. Never ventured too far from his own patch. A pretty new receptionist at the golf club, someone from our accounting firm. But Pamela was obviously a cat of a different stripe.

I thought about Pamela. Smart and capable. We had recently promoted her to manager of one of our out-of-town funeral homes. Divorced, fortyish, no children. Not pretty but striking. Big boobs. Bud was a pushover for big boobs. Once upon a time, mine had been a major attraction. But that was years ago.

So what could I do about this? Go to the police? Bud played golf with the chief, Arnie Olafson. I could imagine the conversation. "Marge is getting kind of overwrought these days. Her time of life, you know. And of course, she has a bit of a drinking problem." They would likely be remembering the incident at the Miller girl's funeral. Well, several recent incidents.

Pamela was quite right; I would fight for my business. I was the one who had brought it from the single funeral home, started by my parents in our small city, to a thriving chain of three. Bud had played golf and sailed with the locals but I had done the work.

At this point I realized the headache was going to come back if I kept obsessing. An hour had passed since I left the house. Bud and Pamela would surely be gone by now. I would go home and take another pain pill and try to sleep. Then I would be better able to cope.

When Bud came home, I still hadn't decided what I was going to do. I hadn't even started dinner. And I had abstained from my before-dinner martinis because I needed to keep a clear head. When Bud walked in, I was sitting in the living room with the drapes drawn. I took a good look at Bud, a little overweight but still handsome. All his own hair. Still able to attract women with his easygoing charm.

"What's going on, Marge?" Bud asked. "How come it's so dark in here?" He turned on one of the lamps and then he looked hard at me. "What's the matter? You look terrible."

I had no idea what I was going to say until I said it.

"I didn't go to bridge today, Bud."

He got very still except for his eyes. They kept moving back and forth, looking anywhere but at me.

"How come?" he said, finally.

"I went to the doctor. Not Dr. Christie. A specialist. I haven't mentioned it but I've been having some problems. Women's problems."

That was a good touch. Bud turns green at the mention of the word "uterus."

"What did he say?"

"She, Bud. It was a woman specialist. She says I have a terminal illness. There isn't anything they can do."

Bud swallowed. "How long?" he asked, hoarsely.

"Maybe six months," I said. And then I added. "Don't worry, Bud. She said they won't let me suffer."

"Oh, my God. My God."

"I think I'll go upstairs and lie down now. I'm going to take a sleeping pill. Can you get your own supper?"

"I don't need much. I had a big lunch with some sales reps from Toronto. Marge, isn't there anything they can do?"

"The specialist says there's nothing. She offered to talk to you if you'd like to come to her office with me."

I figured I was quite safe in suggesting this and I was right.

"You know I'm no good at things like that. What about telling people? The kids?"

"I want to wait a while. I'd kind of like them to enjoy the summer." I thought that was a noble touch. Our kids both live in other provinces so I didn't have to worry about putting on an act for them. "For now it's just you and me that know, okay?"

"Okay."

Bud waited an hour to make sure that I was asleep. Then he tiptoed upstairs, opened the door and whispered, "Marge?" I kept breathing regularly and heavily, like someone who has gone off with the help of a pill. He went back downstairs and I got out of bed and opened the door just a crack. I could hear him on his cellphone.

"Pamela? You won't believe this. Marge saw the doctor today. She's got something. Something terminal." He sounded relieved. He really hadn't wanted to kill me.

There was a pause then he said, "Six months, maybe. She says there's no hope."

He listened again and then his voice got quite cross. "No, dammit, we're not going to hurry things up." How dare she suggest that, I thought, when I might only have six months left. The vicious bitch. Then I remembered that I wasn't really ill. "She's my kids' mother and she's entitled to all the time she's got left." There was another pause and then he said, "That's okay, honey. I understand. I want to be with you all the time too. But six months isn't that long to wait. Maybe we should cool it for a bit. I'll call you tomorrow."

At that point I thought I had better scurry back to bed.

Of course, there was a flaw in my plan, as anyone could see. What was going to happen when six months had passed? Seven months, eight months and I was still alive and doing well? All I had done was buy myself some time to think of a way to deal with the murderous pair.

I would have to separate them. In all the years of girlfriends, Bud had never thought of anything like this. Pamela was different. So I would have to get him away from her. Once she was out of the picture I would tell Bud the doctor had made a mistake in the diagnosis, mixed up the charts. Then I would file for divorce. And he would be lucky to come away with the clothes he stood up in.

I started going in to the office every day, keeping an eye on things. I cut back on the martinis too and since I was picking at my food like someone with a poor appetite, I was losing weight and

159

looking better. Meanwhile, Bud was being very attentive. He and Pamela must have cooled it because he was home for dinner most nights and his golf dates with the boys were genuine. But I would have to get things moving.

"Bud," I said, one early June evening, "I think this year we better have the employee barbecue at the beginning of the summer, rather than the end. I may not be feeling like it come August."

"I didn't think you'd want to do it this year. Won't it be too hard on you?"

"Bud, it's a family tradition. I'll get caterers for everything. It's important to me to do it this one last time. How about in two weeks? That will give people time to make plans."

The Sunday I chose, in June, was a glorious day, sunny and hot. We had turned up the pool heater so the kids who came with their parents could swim if they wanted. Our guests started arriving mid-afternoon and there was a crowd. We leave a skeleton staff at the funeral homes for these events. Pamela brought a male friend. That is what is called "a beard," the date you bring along so people won't know who you're really sleeping with. I had to admire her technique.

I had been searching for someone to supplant Pamela in Bud's affections and had settled on our new neighbour, Barbara, a nice-looking woman in her thirties. She had brought her little boy to the party with her. That was good—Bud likes kids.

My next move was to single out Pamela. Considering that she had been plotting my death a few weeks before, I thought she might be a bit hesitant about talking to me but not a bit of it.

"Great party, Marge," she said. "Then she took a second look at me. "You've lost some weight."

"It's this new diet I'm on."

"You look very well." She sounded surprised.

"We must have lunch sometime soon. I'd like to talk to you. I don't see enough of you now that you're at the other location." Then I moved on. Let her wonder what I was thinking about. I circulated, in my best hostess fashion, until Bud and I were side by side.

"It's going well," I said.

"You always do a great job. Sure you're not getting overtired?"

"I'm fine. Have you talked to our new neighbour, Barbara? She's the pretty dark-haired woman in the red bathing suit."

Bud turned around to take a look.

"So that's Barbara. Gee, she is pretty nice-looking, isn't she? That her kid with her?"

160

"Yes. She's a single mother. I guess I'd better move around, see everybody's having a good time."

Later I saw Bud in the pool with Barbara and her son, helping the boy learn to float on his back. Pamela was laughing a bit too much and snuggling up to her date, not something people usually did at these family parties.

I gave Pamela a few days to stew. Then on Thursday evening I phoned her and asked if she was free for lunch the next day. We went to the nicest restaurant in town, where they know me, and we got the quiet table I wanted. Pamela ordered the special, poached salmon, but I said all I wanted was a salad. I just picked at it.

"My appetite hasn't been very good lately," I said when I saw her watching me.

"You look fine," she said. There was a pause. "You said you wanted to talk to me about something?"

"It's Bud. I don't usually talk about our private lives but I felt I *could* ask you, Pamela, because I've known you for a while. We worked together so well."

"Oh, yes?"

"I have reason to believe Bud is having an affair."

Pamela had a forkful of poached salmon near her mouth. She had very sharp white teeth. Her hand shook and the salmon dropped on to her silk-clad bosom.

"Oh dear, you've spilled on your lovely blouse. Better get it to the cleaners as soon as you can so it doesn't stain."

She didn't even glance down. "You said something about an affair?" Her voice had gone flat.

"You haven't heard any gossip? I'm almost sure it's our new neighbour, Barbara. Maybe you met her at the barbecue Sunday? I probably shouldn't tell you this but he's been sending her text messages—well, of an explicit nature. I'm very upset."

She put down her fork.

"I'm sorry, Marge, but I'm not feeling well. My stomach was a little funny this morning and now—I think I may be getting flu. I don't know anything about Mr. Foster and anybody."

She had turned an interesting shade of purple.

"I'm so sorry. I hope it wasn't the salmon."

She pushed back her chair and hurried out of the restaurant. I waved the waiter over and ordered a martini. I thought I deserved it.

At about eight o'clock that evening, a police car drew up in front of the house. The police chief, Arnie Olafson, got out, followed by a young man in uniform, who I recognized as the Clancy boy. They came up the walk, marching in step. I could see them straightening their backs before the chief rang the bell.

"Marge," Arnie said, when I opened the door. "I'm afraid I have bad news. Is there anyone here with you?"

"No, Bud isn't home yet. What's wrong?"

"I'm afraid we have bad news," he said again. "Could we go inside?"

I led the way into the living room and asked them to sit down but they remained standing.

"I better just tell you straight up," Arnie said. He was perspiring heavily. "Bud was attacked in his office this evening."

"Bud is in hospital?"

He hesitated. "God, Marge, I'm sorry. He succumbed to his injuries before anyone got there."

"Someone killed Bud?"

"Stabbed him right through the eye with a paper knife," the Clancy boy blurted out. Arnie glared at him—there was going to be trouble when they got back to headquarters—then turned back to me.

"There was nothing we could do. We have someone in custody. A woman. There doesn't seem to be much doubt about what happened. Your cleaner heard her screaming at Bud and then the sound of a scuffle. He called us but we were too late."

"Bud is dead. My goodness."

I could tell from the look on Arnie's face that this wasn't an adequate response.

"Well," I said, and then I found the right words, "I hope he didn't suffer."

Family Traditions
By Susan Daly

"Hey, Terri, we're getting low on chips in here!"

Terri sighed and ripped open a bag of pretzels and another of beer nuts and dumped them into big plastic bowls. Football Day in America.... A time-honoured tradition in the Taggart household and millions of others from sea to shining sea. Which meant, once again, an assortment of loud, hungry, thirsty men in her family room, keeping out from under the feet of their grateful wives who were home making their own turkey dinners.

Family room. That was the label on the plan of the suburban house when they'd bought it eight years ago, but that only worked if everyone in the family wanted to watch Leo's choice of football, basketball, baseball or hockey.

Certainly the 1976 American Family.

Thanksgiving Parade Extravaganza was not one of Leo's choices. She and Kim would have to watch it on the little black and white TV in the breakfast nook.

What corporate idiot had made the decision to broadcast the parade at the same time as one of the football "classic" games? For that matter, what idiot decided football was more important than family togetherness?

A roar of approval and cheerful profanity indicated the right team had done the right thing.

Kim wandered into the kitchen and scrunched up her nose at the image on the screen. "When are you going to get the living room TV fixed?" she demanded.

It was a rhetorical question. "Here, take these out to the family room, please."

Kim scowled at the concept of being helpful, but took the bowls.

Terri didn't know why she should field the blame for something Leo had promised and then relentlessly neglected to do. Maybe she should have reminded him again.

Kim returned with her coat on. "I'm going over to Genna's house to watch the roller derby."

Oh. "I thought we were going to watch the parade together. We always—"

"Get real, Mom. I'm fourteen. Anyway, who wants to see it in black and white?"

And another family tradition bites the dust.

"All right. Go. Have fun." She could hardly blame her. "Just be back before five, when Grandma and Grandpa get here."

"Sure." Kim grabbed a bag of chips and was gone.

Fine. She would darn well watch it herself. As long as she was stuck in the kitchen, heating up these damn sausage rolls and making more nachos and basting the turkey and scrubbing the carrots, she might as well tap into the fantasy that somewhere in this blessed land, happy families took their children to watch parades.

If one person continued it all alone, did that still count as a family tradition?

Man, it was getting hot in here. She peeled off her sweater. No one was likely to come in and see her in her sleeveless shell.

"Where would you like me to put these?"

Terri looked up from the carrots to see one of the guys, someone new, holding a stack of bowls and dirty plates. He didn't look like Leo's usual type of buddy. Younger, thinner, longer hair.

She casually reached for her sweater and pulled it on before he could have a chance to notice her arms. "Just put them down on the table for now, thanks. I'll wash them later."

"Hot in here," he said, sliding open the patio door in the breakfast nook to access the massive supply of beer keeping cold outside. He held up a bottle to her, questioning, as though it were the most natural thing in the world to offer her a beer.

Which was more than Leo had ever done in his life.

"Sure, thanks, why not?"

He took out a second bottle and shut the door.

God, it was good. She knocked back a third of it. Why hadn't she thought to open one herself? The guys would never miss it from their hoard.

"How can you drag yourself away from the game?" she asked as she wiped the sweat off her forehead.

"Half time. There was a general stampede for the bathroom, plus some channel-changing to see what other sports they're missing." He suddenly gave her a grin and held out his hand. "Sorry... Denny Waite."

She shook his hand. Nice. Like she was someone in her own right. "Terri." she said. It would sound pretentious to say Terri Taggart.

164

"Thanks for having us all here. It must be a lot of work."

She shrugged. What was the point of saying it came with the territory? She glanced at the label on her beer. "Golden, huh? You must be the Canadian Leo mentioned. You work at the plant with him, right?"

"Yeah," he said, leaning back against the counter. "Trying to balance a job with university. Post-grad."

Canadian and well-educated. Maybe that explained why he brought the dishes in and introduced himself and offered her a beer.

"You must miss not being home for Thanksgiving." She took another swig, wishing she could invite him for dinner. Yeah, that would go over big with Leo.

"Not exactly. I'll be heading back to Toronto for Christmas."

"Toronto? Hey, you might be interested in the parade on TV. The American Family Thanksgiving Day Parade, but it's not really. They got a Canadian parade in there too."

"Yeah?" He turned to look at the TV with interest. "Must be the Eaton's Santa Claus parade. When I was a kid, my grandmother used to take us to see it. Me and my cousins."

Terri reached across the counter and turned up the volume. Great! Someone to watch the parade with. The tradition lived.

Denny actually preferred it here in the kitchen, as a break from watching a bunch of refrigerators with legs charging into each other and the armchair quarterbacks yelling profane advice.

"They keep showing a bunch of different parades from different cities," Terri explained. "There—that's Toronto."

The screen showed two anchors, a broad-shouldered talk show host in overcoat and scarf, and a cute little blonde half his age, cocooned in a white fur coat and a matching hat.

"Well Andrea, it may not be snowing here in Canada, but it sure is cold. I hope you're warm enough in that coat."

"Yes, I'm nice and toasty. You know, Rick, these Canadians sure know how to dress for their cold weather." Under her inane voiceover, the camera panned the building across the street from the telecast setup, to focus on the line of people standing on the roof of a building. An assortment of parents and kids.

"Look at that, Rick. I love to see a family outing like that. Mom and Dad and the kids. That's what makes America great, the strength of the American family and its traditions."

He let himself be amused by the woman's confused geography.

165

"So, Denny, this is where you got to." Leo loomed in the kitchen doorway. "Making time with my wife, huh?" He said it with a laugh, but without humour, as he opened the door to the general beer stockpile.

Why had he accepted Leo's invitation? He didn't particularly like the guy, but it was a chance to socialize on a day when the plant was closed and everyone else in this country was gorging themselves with football and turkey.

"Just getting a beer," Denny said, and drained the one he had. He took another and turned to offer a second to Terri, but she gave her head a small shake.

"Canadian beer," Leo said with a snort. "You drinking that sissy stuff?"

"Actually," Denny couldn't help saying, "the domestic beer in Canada is stronger than American beer. They just water it down for export to the States."

"Is that a fact?" Leo's polite interest didn't deceive him. Yeah, he really shouldn't have come.

Leo walked over to the counter and took the half-empty bottle from his wife.

"You don't drink beer," he informed her.

"I like it sometimes." There was a defensive note in Terri's voice. "It's a furnace in here, slaving over a hot stove for your friends and then for your family."

"It that so? If you've been working so hard, why isn't everything ready and out there?" He poured the remaining contents down the sink. "It's half-time, and the guys are getting hungry."

They'd been stuffing their faces all day.

"I'll take them." Denny picked up the tray of sausage rolls and nachos and other manly snacks.

Leo scowled at his wife and picked up a case of beer to take back to the family room. Denny caught Terri's look that said, *don't come back in the kitchen. Please.*

Peace. Blessed peace for maybe an hour, between the departure of the guys and her in-laws' arrival. With luck, time enough to clean up the disaster area she knew the family room would be.

Terri took another of Denny's beers—*ah...that's good*—and left the door open to cool down the room and let out the smoke that had choked up the house.

She leaned against the door frame and allowed herself the

166

luxury of indulging in her favourite fantasy. Her own private tradition. How she could rid herself of Leo.

Leave him? She'd worked out a dozen complex scenarios that would let her get away from him. (Something safe, so he couldn't track her down.) Change her identity. Find a job (as what?) to support herself. Fake her own death.

But there were so many specifics to cope with, and she'd have to desert her family too, or he'd find her through her parents and sisters. And of course there was Kim. Nothing could be done at all until Kim was grown and living on her own.

She took another pull of her beer and sighed. Even her fantasies refused to come out right.

No, the better option was killing Leo. She'd indulged in plenty of those daydreams too.

Again, the devil was in the details. She hadn't a hope in hell of overpowering him. A gun? Too hard to obtain; too obvious.

Poison? Better, especially if it was natural, like mould or ptomaine. She'd allowed herself many pleasant hours coming up with possibilities there.

Arrange an accident? Too uncertain. Falls were tricky and he might only be maimed.

She'd even gone so far as to do a little research into what kind of a blow to the head would do the trick. Precisely where on the back of the skull. *Columbo* episodes helped, along with some pop medical books at the library.

Everyday kitchen objects offered themselves as blunt instruments. She knew of at least five.

This was all very well, but it was nothing more than imaginative plotting to help her through the worst times. Because the opportunity would certainly never arise. Let alone her will to actually carry it out.

She drained the beer and straightened away from the doorframe. Enough of this harmless fun. Time to get back to—

"You don't complain to outsiders." She turned to see Leo, yet another beer in his hand. "Understand?"

"Complain?" She walked over to the kitchen counter and idly picked up the paring knife and a potato. For support. "I said it was hot and I'd been working hard all day."

"When I have my friends over, you don't need to bitch about it. And you don't need to start drinking, either. You're thirsty, there's soda."

She put down the knife and potato with regret, then turned to face him.

"I'll drink beer if I want." The second one was making her brave. And stupid. "It wasn't even yours. It was your friend Denny's. He offered it—"

"Yeah, what was he doing in the kitchen with you? Helping out? That's the last time I invite him over here. Because either he's got the hots for you, or he's a goddamn faggot, and no way is he coming back into my house."

"He was watching something on the TV with me. And that's another thing." *No. Bad idea.* Hassling Leo was another indulgence best left to her imagination. "When are you going to get that living room TV fixed? Kim's never home any more. She's always over at Genna's, watching TV there."

He was silent for a few moments, his eyes narrowing, his breath almost a hiss. Then he spoke in a dangerously quiet voice. "You wanna quit nagging me about that?"

"Oh yeah? Funny how when *you* keep ignoring your promises, *I* get accused of nagging."

It was almost comical to see his mouth drop open at her nerve. "What...did...you...say...?"

Shit, couldn't she just shut up? The last marks hadn't faded yet. Besides the bruises and cut lip, her neck had been stiff for weeks. She'd almost forgotten what it was like to move her head without pain. But she was on a roll.

"I'll quit 'nagging' when you get off your butt and actually do it."

The first backhanded smack across her face was always the worst. Stars and pain and panic swirled in her consciousness. The second came on top of the first, from the other side. Leo's old one-two attack.

Another Taggart family tradition. Leo beating the shit out of his wife.

"You ready to shut up now, or do I have to get rough with you?"

The last thread of self-preservation instinct snapped.

"And just what the hell do you call that? A love tap? That *was* rough, Leo. It was more than rough."

"I'll show you rough, you little cunt." His voice dropped and his eyes got real mean. Meaner than she'd ever seen them. Terri's stomach clenched with terror. She'd done it now.

Leo's next hit wasn't open-handed. It was a fist to the jaw. Lights flashed inside her head and all around her and the pain was unbearable and she knew she was going to die.

Oh hell, let it happen.

She squeezed her eyes shut and braced for another blow, hoping it would knock her out, and maybe then Leo would quit.

The blow didn't come. At the sound of another person in the room, someone yelling "Hey!" she opened her eyes and saw Denny had yanked Leo away from her. Leo landed his next punch into Denny's gut. It sent him sprawling back against the table in the breakfast nook.

Leo's rage was terrible, and with a volley of profanity he lunged at the smaller man. Terri knew he would kill them both, but she didn't dare raise a hand to help Denny. Poor guy. He'd meant well.

It could go on his gravestone.

But Denny turned out to be stronger than he looked, and he rolled to one side. When Leo crashed into the table, Denny pulled him up and landed a punch to the jaw and then to the stomach and Leo staggered backwards and fell against the counter with a sickening sound and slid to the floor.

He lay still. Unconscious.

"Shit," Denny remarked, wiping the blood from his mouth as the two of them stood looking down at the motionless pile of muscle and fat.

Denny knelt down and checked his wrist, his chest. "He's breathing. Heart's still beating." Leo emitted a faint moan, but didn't stir.

"You shouldn't have done that." Terri reached for the phone. "He's going to be real mad when he comes to."

"He was already real mad. I thought he was going to kill you."

"Yeah, so did I. Now he'll kill you, too. What'd you come back for, anyway?"

"I left my backpack. I figured I'd just slip in the back door and grab it."

"You should leave. I gotta call an ambulance, and they'll probably call the police."

She dialled 911 and said there'd been an accident. Her husband had fallen and hit his head. Yes, he was unconscious. Yes, he was still breathing.

She answered a few more questions, then snapped, "Look, quit wasting time and send an ambulance, will you?"

"Does he do this often?" Denny asked when they finally let her go.

"Not...too often." He knew she was lying. "Oh darn, his parents are coming for supper tonight." She realized with twist of amusement she'd have to cancel supper. So much for that family tradition.

"Look, Terri, I've got to stay. You know that. Is there someone you can call? A friend? Parents?"

"No. No one." Her family lived half a continent away and she didn't seem to have many friends any more. "Please, Denny, just go. If his parents find you here...."

"I'm not leaving you alone. If he comes to before the ambulance and police get here...."

He didn't elaborate, but she got his point.

But it wouldn't matter when Leo came to. If it was before the police arrived, she was dead meat. If after they left, well, she'd be just as dead.

"Anyway," Denny said, "the police will need to talk to me. You told the dispatcher he fell, but clearly there was a fight. I have the injuries to prove it. We both do."

She looked down at her husband again. Hell, it was like her fantasies coming true.

Except Leo wasn't dead.

Damn him. He'd hit the back of his head on the edge of the counter. He *should* be dead.

The pain in her head and neck became overwhelming, and she felt nauseous. "I feel terrible," she said, putting her hand to the back of her neck. Denny swore quietly and dragged a chair over for her to sit on.

"You should lie down. Hell, the beating he gave you...."

"No, I can't leave him alone like this." Okay, that made sense. "But if you could just get me some painkillers?" She looked around the kitchen, the movement threatening to knock her head off. "Um, up in the bathroom? There's some triple strength in the medicine cabinet." She winced with the effort of speaking.

"Of course. Just take it easy, don't move."

"I won't."

She could hear his laboured progress on the stairs. Poor guy. He'd been beat up pretty bad too. But probably not repeatedly over months and years.

As quickly as her pain would let her, she found the granite mortar and pestle set she'd got as a shower present from Leo's sister. Oversized and too heavy to be practical, it had remained a decorative object for fifteen years.

Until now.

Mercifully, the pills were kicking in by the time the ambulance men arrived. As expected, they called the police. And naturally, the police would have to be told the whole story. Most of it.

It would be hard on Denny, of course. A nice guy; he had certainly saved her life. And he'd been so sweet about getting her the painkillers.

No way he'd get home for Christmas this year.

At best he'd get off with a self-defence plea. At worst a couple of years for manslaughter. Harsh, but nothing like the prison she'd endured for the past fifteen years.

She gazed out the front window from the family room at the flashing red lights from the police cars.

Family traditions. Some of them just had to die out.

Annie's Secret
By Valerie Hauch

The library was Valerie Hauch's favourite place as a child as soon as she discovered the joys of reading. In Grade 8 she decided to become a reporter and eventually made her living for forty years as a reporter and editor at Canadian newspapers. The last sixteen were spent at The Toronto Star. *Now living in Muskoka, Ontario, her retirement goal is to keep writing and reading.*

The whispers were harsh, like a small dog's clipped, growly barks when he's just giving warning. But they came from a man. She could tell that much. What was a man doing in the girls' washroom?

"Don't say anything. You'll be sorry.... Shut up.... Shut up." Annie's ears picked up the ugly words and she strained to hear more.

There was whimpering coming from a bathroom stall farther down from where she sat, hunched on her heels on a toilet seat. Guttural sounds, groans. Gurgling, like someone trying to speak. It made Annie stiffen. Her thumbs turned white, pressing down on the book she held while her ears almost twitched with the effort of honing in on the sounds. Who was there? She couldn't tell from her perch. But it didn't sound good.

All of the stalls in the girls' bathroom at the swimming pool had doors that stayed almost closed when empty. The way the doors were hung created a one-quarter gap. It was perfect for someone who wanted to hide. As someone who hid a lot would know. If you didn't see any feet below, you couldn't tell someone was inside one of the dozen stalls until you pushed the door open.

Annie had been perched on her seat and alone in the washroom, when she'd heard someone push into a stall down from her. She'd been galloping through the pages of *The Ship That Flew* and wishing that she could find such a boat that fit into your pocket and could magically grow and fly wherever you wanted to go.

At that moment anywhere else would have been good.

The whimpering had stopped. She heard rustling and suddenly a door banged open and someone with heavy footsteps rushed past her stall. Annie moved her head to the side so she could just barely see through the crack of space created by the partially closed door.

His bald head tilted forward in a way that reminded her of the top end of a hand mixer, Mr. Goodwin, the Phys-Ed teacher, churned past, toward the sinks. She heard the water blast out for a few seconds. Then the sound of heavy footsteps and she saw another glimpse of Mr. Goodwin as he quickly went toward the space that linked the bathroom with the change area. Then there was the whoosh of the outer door that opened onto the foyer and street. She held her breath.

Was someone else coming out? There'd been someone else in the stall with him. Was that person too scared to come out? Annie could understand that. Mr. Goodwin was a bully who yelled at everyone in gym class, especially picking on the kids who weren't athletic. She felt sorry for whoever had been in that stall with him. She was also too afraid to look.

Annie put her legs down and tried to stand up in the stall but almost fell. Noodle legs. She knew the feeling when she sat this way too long. She waited a moment and felt stronger as blood flowed, fear ebbed. The clock was ticking. She had to get ready for everyone coming back from swim class. That meant having a quick shower so she would be wet, like the other girls.

Annie had discovered long ago that the teachers only kept track of who joined the short, supervised walk from school to the swimming pool for lessons, once a week. Once the students changed into their bathing suits, no one watched to see who actually went *into* the pool. The chaperoning teachers went somewhere and talked. The lifeguards only counted and kept track of the students in the water. Annie would change into her suit and wait in the toilet cubicle, with a towel-wrapped book, till everyone went into the pool, shower before they came back at the end of class and then emerge and get dressed. She liked the water but hated the rigid swim lessons and the harsh-voiced male instructors clad in skin-tight swim briefs that were embarrassing to look at. Being twelve, she and the other Grade 8 girls could get out of swim lessons once a month because of their periods, but that was it.

Annie didn't have any real friends at school so no one kept track of her. There were times when the shield of invisibility that went with being the mousiest, quietest person in class, who spoke only on the rare occasion a teacher called upon her, had its advantages. She didn't whisper to others, complied with all tasks and managed to get by with passing grades even in her worst subject, math. She was a ghost. Only in English did Annie materialize and come alive. She excelled in grammar and thrived in composition, the natural result of an addiction to the written word. Books were the drug that made life bearable. The only time her classmates noticed the thin girl with the awkwardly cut hair and the eyes that constantly scanned the ground was when the English teacher, Miss Macdonald, read her work aloud. Like last week.

"An excellent composition, class," said Miss Macdonald. "Listen to this—this is the sort of imaginative writing I'm looking for. Annie, you're a wonderful writer."

Annie's ears sucked those words of praise out of the air like a vacuum and tucked them away in an inner compartment, every nuance, syllable and inflection captured, for savouring later when she was alone.

But at the time, as heads swivelled to look at her, Annie turned beet red and slunk down into her seat as Miss Macdonald read her story about how a young girl, separated from her parents during a hurricane, manages to find them, moments before they die from injuries. The girl's left alone and vulnerable, mourning for what might have been.

Miss Macdonald was the only teacher who actually *saw* her. Perhaps she should tell her what had happened in the washroom. Annie knew it was something bad. But how could she explain being there? And she didn't know who else was in the cubicle with him. If she told Miss Macdonald, she might call Annie's mother. Her mouth went dry at the thought even as she stepped into the shower. No, she couldn't tell anyone.

Still dripping, she went back into her cubicle and this time locked the door. Still not a sound from the other cubicle. She opened her book but couldn't make sense of the words. The girls would be traipsing in from swim class any minute now and the shower and change room would turn into a noisy cauldron of high-pitched chatter, shouts and giggles. Annie would wait a few minutes, then emerge unnoticed from the cubicle and change.

She heard a couple of girls approaching, laughing about something in swim class and left as they entered. Within seconds she was changing into her clothes.

Suddenly there was a scream from the bathroom. Annie and other girls in the change room looked up as a couple of teachers came running. Suddenly, the noise volume coming from the bathroom was pitched high and hysterical. Annie ran to the doorway and saw teachers gathered at one cubicle. Other girls were standing nearby crying, some covering their faces with their hands. A couple of girls broke away and ran toward the change room.

"I can't believe it...they, they said Rita's dead," whispered one to the other as they brushed past Annie.

Annie felt blood rush to her head. She swayed for a moment, trying to grasp what she'd heard. Then she walked slowly over to the two girls, who were now sitting on a bench.

"Did you say Rita's dead?" she managed to ask. Rita was one of her classmates, a nice girl, well-liked. She'd been noticeably quieter lately but everyone knew her parents were divorcing.

"Yes," one of the girls said. "Somebody opened that cubicle and she was just sitting there...her eyes were open...and she was...she was dead. Oh my God, I can't believe it."

Annie couldn't either. She moved away without saying anything, gathered her books and bag and left the pool in a daze.

On the plodding walk home, her mind started to work. What should she do? Should she tell someone what she saw and heard? Could she have done something? She felt terrible.

When she got home, the drapes were drawn, the TV droning. The depressing lives of the characters of *As The World Turns* were unfolding. Mother sat slumped in a well-worn chair, nodding off while her hand curled around a precariously tipped sherry glass. Annie tiptoed down to her desk in the basement, where she spent most of her time when her dad wasn't around. It didn't do to wake Mother.

She sat in her chair and her mind drifted. She thought about how some of the other girls in her class would often chatter about the after-school snacks their moms would have waiting for them. Annie would listen and she'd get this feeling inside, a yearning so strong she'd have to deliberately shut it down and box it away in her mind. She didn't care so much about the homemade brownies or cookies, although of course that would be nice. Rather she thought of the soft hands that would serve them, the gentle caress that would surely accompany them. Those girls could tell their moms about what had happened today at the pool, she thought, opening her math exercise book and trying to work.

She didn't hear the slippered footsteps approach. But the crack of a wooden spoon on the back of her head made her turn in a hurry. "Set the table, stupid."

Mother was up.

The next day at school, there was an assembly in the gym. The principal, Sister Mary Angelica, faced the students and grim-faced

175

teachers and told them that she had some very sad news. Their classmate, Rita Jones, was dead—she had been murdered. If anyone knew anything about what had happened—anything at all—they should tell their teacher, talk to their parents or come to the office. Sister Mary Angelica led some prayers for the soul of Rita and then the students turned and filed out of the gym. Mr. Goodwin was one of the teachers lined up at the back, and Annie stole a look sideways as she walked by. She heard him chatting with another teacher about the "terrible tragedy." He looked solemn, but not sad.

A pall hung over the school for weeks and even the most badly behaved kids were somber and restrained. There were whisperings among the older students that Rita had been sexually assaulted before being murdered. The principal again appealed for anyone who knew anything to come forward because the police were looking for information.

Annie's stomach had been tied up in knots ever since that terrible day. She often had stomach aches but this was the worst yet. She knew she had to say something—but who could she tell? Would anyone believe her? She knew there'd be hell to pay at home for skipping out on swimming, but that was nothing new. This was more important. Rita had died and Mr. Goodwin had something to do with it.

That week in English class, Miss Macdonald said the homework assignment was to pick a topic and write a composition. It could be pets and you could write about your dog or cat. Or family and you could tell a story about a favourite aunt. Anything you wanted, she said, but it had to be true, not made up.

Annie went home and sat at her basement desk. She picked up her pen and her story spilled onto the paper, page after page. By the end she felt purged, but she knew it was honest and true.

Her topic was secrets. She told her biggest one. This time Miss Macdonald didn't have her read it aloud but she asked her to stay after class.

"Annie?" Miss Macdonald said, when everyone had left the room.

"Yes, Miss Macdonald," whispered Annie, her eyes looking down at the floor. Annie wished she could drop through it.

"Oh Annie," said Miss Macdonald and her voice faltered. Annie looked up and saw tears in Miss Macdonald's eyes. "You did the right thing in writing this."

She put her hand on Annie's shoulder. It was a gentle touch of comfort. And it broke the dam. The story of what Annie saw and heard that terrible day now came rushing out. This time it was a tumultuous river of spoken words.

The secret was out.

Reputation is Everything
By Elizabeth Hosang

"Doctor Edgars, have you seen Doctor Lopez?" Gwen Peterson asked the short man with the gleaming bald patch, who was piling a paper plate with cheese cubes from the buffet table.

"She was over by the burial masks." Edgars gestured in the general direction with a half-eaten, brie-smeared cracker. "I must say, Doctor Peterson, I was surprised to see her name on that article you submitted to the journal. Given the scandal around her paper on Mayan trade routes, I don't know why any reputable faculty of archaeology would associate with her."

Gwen stepped back to avoid the shower of cracker crumbs spewing from her colleague's mouth. "Because the attack on her work was a hatchet job by a man with a grudge." She was getting tired of this discussion. "Doctor Lopez successfully defended herself against all of the accusations in a juried forum. The facts on which she based her theories have been validated, and the supposed flaws in her arguments are baseless. She is a brilliant analyst and researcher, and I look forward to collaborating with her further."

"Whatever. It's your reputation." The little man turned back to the buffet table. Gwen shook her head and walked in the direction he had indicated. As she made her way through the room she scanned for Maria's black hair. Being five foot nine and wearing heels gave Gwen an advantage—most of the wealthy donors attending the gala at the museum were petite, elderly types. Normally Maria wore bright colours and patterns, which would make her stand out despite her five-foot-two height. However, tonight was a "meet the money" event, meaning Maria would be in formal mode, wearing something understated, with her hair tied back into an elegant chignon.

Gwen smiled and nodded to people she recognized. It was a black-tie gala, granting the museum's best patrons an up-close viewing of some of the most spectacular pieces in the collection. Unfortunately, the organizer of the gala was big on pandering, and the items were not behind glass. The velvet ropes created a discrete distance, and docents stood by each display to answer questions and discourage touching, but the students and retiree volunteers were hard-pressed to scold the wealthy patrons. Yet another strike against a man she already had reason to dislike.

Speak of the devil. Cory Davidson was standing side-on to her, his face a mask of contempt. The person he was berating was hidden from Gwen by a group of older men. She stepped sideways to get a clear view and her heart sank. Maria. As Gwen started toward them, the two turned and headed to an exit, the crowd parting before Maria's angry stride. Just great, Gwen thought. The last thing she needed was for Maria to have a public fight with Davidson.

Twenty minutes later Gwen was chatting with Dorothy Rogers, the chair of the museum's fundraising committee, when Maria joined her. "Doctor Lopez. What a pleasure to see you. I was just telling Doctor Peterson that the evening is turning out to be a great success. I realize that you've had your differences with Doctor Davidson, but you must admit, he certainly knows how to pack them in."

"Oh, he's good at getting attention."

Gwen glared at Maria, who avoided eye contact and took a mouthful of her drink. Gwen looked back at Mrs. Rogers, who was smiling indulgently. "Now, dear, you don't get to be chairwoman of as many committees as I do without learning how to use people to your advantage. And if they think they're the one using you, and it makes them happy, so much the better."

Maria gave a tight little smile as the older woman continued. "I must say, Doctor Lopez, I can't fault your taste. He certainly is charming. Too bad he's got the ego to go with it. I take it you broke up with him?"

"How did you know?" Gwen asked. Maria had told Gwen about her brief liaison as soon as Doctor Davidson's attack had come to light, but very few others knew. This was one reason why Maria was having so much trouble defending herself.

"I've met my fair share of Doctor Davidsons. That dreadful editorial he wrote attacking your paper was clearly born of wounded pride. I wouldn't worry about him. I just know you and Doctor Peterson are going to do good things together. And now if you ladies will excuse me," she handed her empty glass off to a circulating waiter and snagged a new one. "I need to pay my respects to Mrs. Ewing."

With that she drifted off into the crowd.

"Well?" Gwen asked.

"I'd rather not talk about it here."

"That bad?"

"Worse. He says he's managed to get himself assigned as a

reviewer of the paper we just submitted. He intends to make sure it never sees publication." Maria looked like she wanted to strangle someone.

Gwen choked back a string of vulgarities. "Look, don't worry about it. The best defence is a good offence, and I'm ready to be offensive. Now put on your best "meet the money" smile. Here comes the dean with a woman wearing the gaudiest diamond ring I've ever seen."

They spent the next hour making small talk with people of varying ages and taste in jewelry. They discussed their field work and explained the artefacts on display, some of which Gwen had unearthed on her last dig. They had worked out their repartee before the gala, but on several occasions Gwen had to prompt Maria when it was her turn to speak up. The younger archaeologist kept looking at her watch and glancing around the room.

The latest group of donors finally moved to the buffet table, leaving the two women alone for the moment. Maria looked at her watch again. "Everything okay?" Gwen asked.

"No. There were supposed to be speeches. The Creep was to go first. Welcome to our esteemed patrons, we couldn't do this without you, we hope you continue to donate to us in future. But they're late starting. And even Mrs. Rogers is looking stressed."

Gwen glanced at her own watch. "Well, one way or another the museum closes at eleven, so hang in there. Want to make a bet on how many more times we give our spiel?" She took a deep breath and smiled as another group of little old ladies and men headed toward them.

Finally, Gwen excused herself and headed into the hallway leading away from the reception to the bathrooms. Her feet hurt and she was starting a stress headache. A scream from behind startled Gwen as she reached the bathroom door. It had come from the direction of the kitchen. She ran toward the sound of hysterical sobbing. A female server was standing at the door to a deep closet. The back half was full of stacks of dining room chairs. In front of the chairs a man was curled up, his knees pulled up under his chin and head down over his legs. As Gwen stared he fell out of the closet and his head flopped sideways. The sightless eyes of Cory Davidson stared up at her.

"How long can it take to make a statement?" The elderly woman looked around, but no one replied to her. The police had been interrogating the museum guests individually. Gwen shifted from one foot to another and wished the reception had been a sit-down dinner. At least then there would have been chairs. Maria had been called into the small room for interrogation half an hour before. Other guests were being interviewed and released, but Maria had not re-emerged.

To one side of the room Gwen saw Doctor Edgars emerging from the interrogation area. She headed to intercept him before he left. "Doctor Edgars?"

He glanced at her, then hurriedly looked away and scurried out of the reception room. Gwen sighed. Of course he'd told the police about Maria's history with the victim. She twisted a paper napkin in her fingers and checked her watch again.

Finally she saw Maria re-enter the reception room. She was wearing a white plastic jump-suit. Her shoulders slumped, and her head hung down. She wasn't even looking around. Gwen hurried over. "Maria?"

"Oh. Hi."

"What's wrong?" Gwen pulled the other woman away from the remaining guests. To her shock she saw tears in Maria's eyes.

"My dress had blood on the skirt. I don't know how. I never went anywhere near him. And my skirt had just been dry-cleaned."

"Well then, how?" Gwen started

"I don't know!" The tears started streaming down Maria's cheeks.

"Do you need a lawyer?"

Maria nodded.

"Do you know one?"

Maria nodded again. "One of my cousins. I've already called and left a message."

"Can you leave?"

Maria nodded. "They have my contact information."

Gwen looked at her friend sympathetically. "Let me drive you home."

"My car..."

"Will be fine in the parking lot overnight. You shouldn't be driving. Come on." Gwen put an arm around the younger woman and led her toward the exit.

Two days later Gwen was staring blankly at her computer screen. A knock on her door brought her attention back to her office.

She looked up to see Doctor Edgars in the doorway. "I heard the police are looking at Doctor Lopez as a person of interest in Cory Davidson's murder. Looks like you had a close call."

"Excuse me?"

"You've still got time to withdraw the paper and remove her name."

Gwen stood so she could glare down at her colleague. "Doctor Lopez co-wrote that paper. It is good work, and I will not be omitting her from anything."

"You can't be serious! She's going to be convicted for murder! You know how bad that will look?"

"No. Tell me." The little man jumped and whirled around. Maria was standing in the office doorway.

Edgars cleared his throat. "Doctor Lopez." He beat a hasty retreat out of the office and down the hall.

"Ignore him." Gwen rounded her desk and pulled the younger woman to the visitor's chair. Gwen closed the office door and resumed her seat behind the desk. "So how's it going?"

"Badly. The blood on my skirt was a match to Cory. My lawyer is having a hard time lying to me about everything being fine." Maria sat down and put her purse on her lap. She fiddled with a beaded worry doll that dangled from the zipper. "I've just come from the bank. I had to cash in some bonds to pay his retainer."

"I'm sorry to hear it." Gwen twisted a pen in her fingers and tried to think of something to say.

Maria took a deep breath, glanced up, then down at her hands again. "I guess letting him goad me into a fight in front of a room full of witnesses was a bad idea. I just, I mean, it was just supposed to be casual, you know? A one-time hook-up at a conference. How was I supposed to know he'd take it so badly?"

Gwen nodded. "They need to wear a sign: Danger, Crazy Person."

Maria smiled a little, then it faded. "I don't even think he was really that into me. He's just mad that I didn't turn into one of his starry-eyed fans, so instead I'm his target."

"Not the only one," Gwen said. At that Maria looked up. "He's got a long history of attacking other academics. Almost every article he has attacked in the past three years has been validated. And in each case at least one of the paper's authors had a personal relationship with him prior to the attack."

"You've been looking into him."

Gwen shrugged. "You know what they say about the best

182

defence being a good offence."

Maria looked back down at her hands again. "So that's what you meant."

"Pardon?"

"At the museum. You said not to worry about him." Maria tried to look up and meet Gwen's eyes, but her glance only came up as far as the surface of the desk.

Gwen felt a cold chill run down her spine. "You thought it was me."

Maria tried to smile, but it didn't work. She looked around the office, then back down at her hands. Tears pooled in her eyes, and she blinked them away. Finally she shrugged. "You do have a reputation for tackling problems head-on."

Gwen looked down at her own hands. "And I was there when the body was found." An awkward silence filled the space between them, stretching painfully across the desk. It was finally broken by a sob from Maria.

"I'm so sorry Gwen. You've been so good to me. You barely knew me and you offered me a job when I lost my grant. And then the asshole who nearly destroyed my life threatened to destroy my second chance and I was so angry!"

Gwen looked up in alarm. "What did you do?"

"I told him, I actually said I'd kill him. In front of witnesses! And then two hours later he's found dead not ten feet from where I threatened him, and now I'm going to go to jail, and the man's dead and he's still screwing up my life!" She grabbed a tissue from the box Gwen offered her and wiped her nose. "I didn't really think you'd killed him. I just don't know what to think."

"It's okay," Gwen said. "I think we're even. Although for the record, if I was going to kill him it wouldn't have been at a big gala with lots of people. I'd have lured him someplace quiet and out of the way and made it look like a mugging gone wrong."

"Or mummified him."

"Or dumped him in the ocean, or fed him to the lions at the zoo, so he was never seen again. But I wouldn't have killed him on the spur of the moment." She paused. "At least, I assume it was spur of the moment, given how stupidly the body was hidden."

Maria nodded. "It looks like it. Apparently the murder weapon was taken from one of the displays."

Gwen frowned. "What was it?"

"A stone knife."

"What knife?"

183

Maria shrugged. "The detective didn't say. Just that it was an old knife with a stone blade."

Gwen leaned back, staring sightlessly at the wall opposite her. "What's wrong?"

"There was a knife on display, but it didn't have a stone blade." She logged onto her computer and brought up her email. She scrolled through until she found a message from the victim. "Here's the inventory list we agreed on for the exhibit. The mask, urns, a stingray spine, some stone figures and a ceremonial dagger, but no stone knife." Gwen frowned. "Do you think the detective would meet with me?"

The next afternoon at the police station, Gwen and Maria were shown into a small meeting room by Detective Ivan Knutson. "So, ladies. I understand you want to talk to me about the death of Doctor Davidson." He gestured to two chairs.

Gwen put on her "meet the money" smile. "Thank you for seeing us, Detective. I don't know if you were aware, but I was part of the committee that selected the items for the gala exhibit." The detective nodded. "Doctor Lopez told me that the murder weapon was a knife with a stone blade. I was wondering if I could see a picture of it."

"Why?" Knutson said.

Gwen pulled a folded piece of paper from her purse. "I've got the final list of exhibits. There wasn't supposed to be a knife with a stone blade."

Knutson pulled out a smart phone. He tapped on it, then turned it to face Gwen. The screen showed a stone-bladed, bloodstained knife next to a ruler on a table. Gwen pulled out her own cellphone and tapped the screen. Finally she turned her phone around to display the same knife, without the bloodstains. "If that knife is the same one as in this picture, then it's something I recovered on my last dig. But it wasn't on display during the gala. It's an ordinary household knife, interesting to archaeologists, but not to the museum donors. There was a ceremonial dagger from a later era on display in another part of the exhibit, but no stone knife."

The detective looked back and forth between the photos. "Are you sure? Maybe someone put it out anyway?"

Gwen shook her head. "I don't think so. Doctor Davidson wanted to impress the donors, and it wasn't very impressive-looking."

"But did you see it during the evening?"

"No. It would've been on the far side of the room, with the items from the later period, and I was standing by the items from my own excavation."

"So why are you bringing this up?"

"It would mean that whoever stabbed Doctor Davidson had access to the storage room where the murder weapon was kept, and brought it with themselves on purpose," Gwen said.

Knutson shook his head. "There was an empty display stand by the door to the hall. It had a card describing a knife. We were working under the assumption that the killer," here he looked at Maria, "grabbed the knife off the display as he or she followed the victim into the hallway."

"But if it was premeditated, then the killer could've stabbed Doctor—I mean the victim—with the stone knife and then taken the dagger later when everyone was distracted. And Maria wasn't the only person there who had reason to hate the victim. He's destroyed more than one reputation. She was just the one seen arguing with him. Which might be why the killer chose to frame her by smearing blood on her dress."

Knutson appeared unconvinced, but he turned his phone around and began tapping on it before holding it out again. "We got pictures from any guests with a camera that night. You think you can find a picture with the dagger in the background?"

Gwen nodded and reached for the phone. She spent the next five minutes scrolling through the pictures. A few times she zoomed in on a something before frowning and swiping. Finally she held up the phone. "That's the display where the dagger should be, but the zoom-in feature on your phone is limited. Is this the empty display you found?" Knutson nodded. "Do you have a larger screen?"

Knutson took his phone back and tapped on it for a moment, then muttered something that sounded like "...ing autocorrect." Finally he looked up. "I've sent the picture off to the techies. If you don't mind waiting a few minutes, they should be able to print something larger for us."

The two women nodded. A moment later the detective's phone made a ping, and he brought up a new picture. "Here. Which knife is that?"

Gwen took the phone, tapping and swiping. "It's the dagger. And the tag is wrong. It describes the stone knife, not the dagger." She tapped again. "And the meta-data on the photo shows it was taken about five minutes before Davidson was found. Maria was with me for over an hour until just before he was found, and then right up until we were separated by the police for questioning. She couldn't have done it."

Knutson took the phone back and stared at it. "So who has access to the storage area where the knife was kept? The museum staff, obviously. Anyone else?"

"The docents," the two women said at the same time.

Knutson finally smiled, just a little. "Okay. Docents it is. Now what's a docent?"

"The volunteers who help out at the museum. They give guided tours, and several were there that night," Maria said.

"Would they have been working in the kitchen?"

"No. The caterers were hired for the occasion, although the company they use has worked at the museum before." Maria looked at Gwen. "Did you work with them to set up for the reception?"

Gwen shook her head. "I dealt with the gala by email. I didn't want to have anything more to do with Doctor Davidson than I had to." Knutson turned his hawk-like gaze on Gwen and she recoiled. "It wasn't me. I didn't need to kill him. I've been looking for leverage on him ever since we submitted our paper for publication. I was afraid he'd come after Maria again, so I'd been doing research. I have a list of papers he'd attempted to discredit, and proof that he was wrong in each case. I also had information on his personal relationships with the authors of the papers he'd attacked. They were all either former girlfriends or women he'd harassed who had refused to sleep with him. If he attacked us I was ready for him."

Knutson took his phone back and tapped at it before handing it to Gwen again. "Recognize any names on this list?" he asked.

Gwen fumbled for a moment as her hand sought the wall switch. With a click light flooded the room in front of her, revealing rows of shelves filled with bins of various size, shapes and compositions. Two tables were near the door, their surfaces covered with an assortment of brushes, paper tags with strings for attaching them to items, and magnifying glasses for detailed work. Consulting the paper in her hand, she entered the rows of shelves. She scrutinized the labels on the bins, oblivious to the man who entered the room through the open door and slipped into the shadows on the other side of the room.

A third of the way down the length of the room, Gwen crouched and opened a bin on a lower shelf. After looking through it, she stood, empty-handed, and made her way back toward the door. She stopped short at the sight of a man standing by a work table, playing with what looked like a makeup brush. When he met her eyes she put on her best business smile. "Mr. Rivers, isn't it? You're one of the docents here. We met at the reception last week."

The older man put down the brush, but he made no attempt to smile. "Doctor Peterson." He emphasized the title.

"I'm sorry, that's right, it's Doctor Rivers, isn't it? You used to teach at Hudson University. How's retirement treating you?"

The man snorted in derision, but didn't say anything.

"You retired a little early from teaching, didn't you? Something about your research methodology."

"There was nothing wrong with my methodology," he snapped.

"I agree. I've read your papers. You and your colleagues did some fascinating work." Conscious of the silence surrounding her, and the absence of others in the long shadowy room, Gwen realized she had raised her voice.

"My colleagues? You mean the grad students who ran the endless lab tests so I could spend my time on more important things? Stupid children who spent their time drinking and screwing and tweeting and, and...."

"Or in this case not screwing. Your co-author on your last paper, Rachel Jones, rejected Doctor Davidson's advances and had filed a harassment complaint against him."

"So? What good did that do me? Forty years of putting up with petty academics and penny-pinching bureaucrats getting in the way of doing real research. If they'd just given me tenure, but oh no, instead they had to give it to that stupid Doctor Olaf, who was still in diapers when I started teaching, just because his research was more glamorous and brought in more money. And then out of a crop of dim-witted grad students, I had to pick the one who was too stupid to just sleep with her professor and get it over with."

Gwen resisted the urge to cross the room and punch the man in the face. "It was not Ms. Jones' fault that Doctor Davidson harassed her. Nor was it her fault that he attacked your paper."

"She wasn't even the lead author! Her name should've been a footnote, not a credit. Any of those idiot grad students could have run the data. But thanks to her, my career was ruined. Do you know how long it took me to find this job? I don't even do research. I just give the same speech every single day to tourists who think Indiana Jones was a real person."

"You must have been upset when you found out who was

organizing the exhibit."

Rivers picked up a metal palette knife and scraped it back and forth across the work surface of the table beside him. He stared off into the distance, not seeing Gwen. "I tried to tell him it was a bad idea to let the patrons near the artifacts. But oh, no, Mister Big-time-fundraiser had to have everything just so. That idiot mixed the Aztec pottery with the Mayan funerary urns. And do you know what he said when I tried to correct him? 'Stick to giving tours, gramps.' Gramps! The man ruined my life, and he didn't even know who I was!"

"So you decided to kill him?"

Rivers looked at her then, his eyes clear and murderous. "It was perfect. A room full of people who hated him, with an item that anyone could have grabbed off a table."

"Except that you didn't grab it off the table, did you? You brought it with you."

"Clever girl." His knuckles whitened as he gripped the handle of the palette knife tighter. "I didn't know when I'd get him alone, did I? So I had to be ready. But that pretentious twit wouldn't go anywhere he didn't have an audience to admire him. I finally had to slip him a napkin with a note signed 'an admirer' asking to meet him. Idiot actually thought some woman wanted to make out in a closet."

"And then you took the ceremonial dagger from the display when everyone heard screaming. You'd already placed the wrong card, so no one would realize the murder weapon hadn't been part of the exhibit."

He snorted. "Those rich snobs at the reception had no idea what they were looking at. As long as they got their champagne and caviar, it could've been a plastic spoon on that display case and they wouldn't know. And the police wouldn't care. One knife looks like another. But you noticed." His gaze was locked on her face, his eyes emotionless. "Did you come down here looking for the dagger?"

"I thought you might've returned it to storage."

He shrugged, but his eyes never left her face. "Why bother? No one's ever going to notice it's missing. And I'm entitled to something after all my work. It's just too bad you're here. Those shelves are pretty rickety. Maybe the museum will finally do something about them after they find you buried underneath them with your head bashed in and a cleaning knife in your throat."

He lunged toward her, the palette knife raised high above his head to stab her, and the other hand out to grab her. Gwen sidestepped the lunge, grabbed his outstretched arm and twisted it up behind his back. When he cried out she forced him to his knees and grabbed the hand with the knife, twisting it and pressing hard on the nerves below his thumb to force him to drop the tool. She had both arms locked behind him when a figure rushed into the room, gun drawn and pointed at her.

Detective Knutson blinked in surprise, then holstered his weapon. "Need any help?"

"I'm good, although if you've got handcuffs they'd be useful." She yanked her prisoner's arms up higher. "Stop squirming!"

Knutson pulled out his handcuffs and latched one onto the older man's wrists. He untwisted the man's arms and attached the other one while launching into his speech about silence and lawyers. He hauled Rivers to his feet before turning to Gwen. "Nice moves," he said, surprise still evident in his voice.

"Thanks. When you travel around the world looking for abandoned corners of it, you need to be able to handle yourself in a fight."

The detective nodded, considering. "So, what, you left your bullwhip at home?"

Gwen rolled her eyes and the prisoner muttered something under his breath.

"I'll need you to make a statement about your conversation here. But between your testimony and mine it should be a solid case. It's a good thing you invited me to come with you to look for that dagger." Gwen nodded. "I think you can tell Doctor Lopez her lawyer should be getting the paperwork soon showing we've dropped the charges against her."

"So I'm free?" Maria sighed and slumped back in her desk chair. She'd been putting her books into boxes when Gwen came into the office.

"Detective Knutson said they found the suit Doctor Rivers was wearing at the gala. The inside pocket had a cloth napkin in it that was stiff with what may be blood. They think he used it to brush against you and get blood on your dress. They'll know more when it gets back from the lab, but it looks like you're in the clear."

"So now what?"

"I beg your pardon?"

"Now what do I do? Is the university still going to want to keep me after this?"

"They'd better. I'm already working on a grant proposal, and I need your expertise to meet all the criteria. C'mon. I'll buy you lunch at the Alumni club. We can celebrate our paper being accepted for publication and your newfound freedom at the same time."

Maria smiled. "Great! But no champagne. It reminds me too much of fundraising."

Summer of the Black Madonna
By Alice Fitzpatrick

Alice Fitzpatrick's short fiction and personal essays have been published in Canadian and American literary magazines such as The Dalhousie Review *and* The Antigonish Review. *Her traditional mystery series, set on an island off the coast of Wales, features historical novelist and amateur detective Kate Galway. The second novel in the series,* This Thing of Darkness, *was a Top 10 Finalist for the 2015 Killer Nashville Claymore Award. The traditional mystery appeals to her keen interest in psychology as she is intrigued by what makes seemingly ordinary people commit murder. When she is not writing, Alice can be found either singing, or reading with her cats.*

It was the summer my father rented the villa in Tuscany that I killed my mother's lover.

For each of my fourteen summers, my father sought out the other British families at our holiday destinations and established himself at the centre of a whirlwind of entertaining: dinners, cocktail dances and card parties. My mother was the perfect hostess, topping up everyone's drink and laughing enthusiastically at her guests' jokes, no matter how often she'd heard them. Everyone adored my parents' parties. But while my father rested in anticipation of the evening's amusements, my mother spent much of her day planning menus, overseeing the cooking and cleaning, and shopping.

In the past, Mother had ordered the food and spirits and had them delivered to our holiday home. But this summer, she complained that the local shopkeepers were not only sending inferior produce, but overcharging. There was nothing for it but for her to select the merchandise and negotiate the prices in person. Since my father believed that most foreigners were basically dishonest—especially those we'd been at war with fewer than ten years before—he wasted no time in procuring a car. Our gardener, Giancarlo, was enlisted to drive my mother to remote farms, olive groves and wineries.

The previous year, the aunt of my friend Sarah had been routinely absent from home, supposedly to indulge a desire to learn

191

French cooking. But when her soufflés failed to improve, her husband discovered that her desire lay elsewhere. She'd taken a lover. So when my mother began to spend long hours away from the villa, I suspected she might be up to the same thing.

But the only way I was going to confirm my suspicion was to catch her with her admirer. The next time she was preparing to go on one of her excursions, I asked if I could go along.

"You won't enjoy it," she said to her reflection in the dressing-table mirror. She was applying the expensive red lipstick—ironically named Forbidden Passion—that she saved for special occasions.

"Where are you going?"

"Your father has developed a taste for goats' milk mozzarella. Luckily Giancarlo knows of a dairy only an hour's drive from here. But first we're visiting the church in the next village. Apparently it has a carving of a Black Madonna." She blotted her crimson lips.

"We've studied the Black Madonna in art class. It dates back to pagan times, to the all-powerful goddess...."

My mother held up her hand. "While it's reassuring to know that the money we spend on your education doesn't go to waste, I really don't want to be subjected to an entire lecture."

"Does that mean I can come?"

She stared at me, obviously weighing up how much I would interfere with her plans. "The carving is only a hundred years old and done by a local artist."

I knew what she was doing, and I wouldn't be put off. "Please take me with you." I ended the sentence with a whine that had driven my mother mad when I was a child but had always got me what I wanted.

She slammed her makeup case shut. "You're too old to be acting like this, Isobel."

"Then I'm old enough to explore on my own." I hoped that this would reassure her that I wouldn't interfere with her rendezvous. "Please, Mummy." I ran my hand over her perfumed shoulder and added a pout.

"All right, but keep out of trouble."

I flashed my most endearing smile and kissed her powdered cheek before running off to get ready.

Within the hour my mother and I were sitting side by side in the big back seat of the grey sedan, as far apart as possible to make room for the wide-brimmed straw hat that she'd placed between us.

Tall, thin trees lining the road, straight as arrows, whizzed past. Square houses that looked like they'd been standing since before the fall of the Roman Empire, shimmered under the hot sun, with their red-tiled roofs and yellow stucco walls. Red and white flowers crowded together in large clay pots guarding doorways.

But my mother saw none of this. Her eyes were fixed on the back of Giancarlo's head, his black hair glistening with hair oil. She gripped her white-gloved hands together on her lap. Her obvious discomfort only confirmed my suspicions.

The church sat unassumingly in the centre of a nondescript village. It was larger than I'd expected, and weary from centuries of masses, weddings and funerals. No doubt the villagers attended services here due to its convenience rather than its beauty as it had very little, at least from the outside. The only ornamentation was a crude engraving of three saints over the door. I didn't know how many pilgrims came to see the Madonna, but they obviously left little in the way of offerings.

But once inside, I realized its potential for a clandestine meeting. It was empty except for a shuffling priest and a few old women in black, heads bowed over their rosaries, oblivious to the presence of a pale English woman, her face hidden by a large straw hat.

Rather than leaning against the car in anticipation of our return, Giancarlo had escorted my mother into the church and was pointing out areas of interest, whispering in her ear so as not to disturb the contemplation of the women.

I was tempted to trail along to listen to his commentary but instead hung back. I hid in a far corner behind the crypt of a medieval noblewoman, hoping my mother would let her guard down once her lover appeared.

Strangely enough, I wasn't upset at the thought of my mother being involved with a man other than my father. It was an innocent time and girls my age weren't familiar with the mechanics of sex. To us, an affair was what we read about in novels and saw at the cinema: knowing looks and tender caresses accompanied by violin music, none of which, to the best of my knowledge, my mother received from my father. In fact the idea of my mother's illicit liaison brought some excitement to my otherwise monotonous life.

During my parents' parties—or soirées, as my mother referred to them—I would sneak down and sit quietly on the stairs, watching every smile and glance. Whose fingers did she touch while passing a drink, whom did she allow to partner her more than the others during the dances, and whose well-tailored pant leg did she rub with her stockinged toes under the card table? No weepy violins for my mother. Clinking cocktail glasses and the latest Frank Sinatra ballad provided the musical accompaniment to her affair.

I peered over the edge of the dusty crypt. Mother and Giancarlo were huddled together in front of the life-sized carving of the Madonna. Giancarlo's rough hand was pressed against the small of my mother's back, creeping down toward the curve of her bottom. I expected my mother to step out of his reach, bark her outrage and slap him. But she did nothing. She just stood there and allowed it to happen.

I couldn't—no, I didn't want to—believe it. My mind frantically searched for another explanation for what I was seeing. Surely it meant nothing, otherwise Mother would never have allowed it. Perhaps this was acceptable in Italy. After all, if it was shameful, they wouldn't be so public. But no matter how much I attempted to rationalize it, I couldn't avoid the obvious. Giancarlo was my mother's lover.

I ran from the church and walked back to the villa.

For days I avoided her. I shut my book and left when she entered a room. I retreated into the shade of the house when she came onto the terrace in her red floral swimsuit to sunbathe on the lounger. During meals I made sure to keep my mouth stuffed with food in order to avoid having to participate in conversations.

I had to find a way to convince Giancarlo to leave Mother alone. He looked like the sort of man who could be easily bought, not that I had any money. Maybe I could threaten him. But what could I say that would intimidate a man like that? Sadly Miss Lightburn's School for Girls hadn't taught us the truly practical skills of coercion, blackmail and bribery.

Still...

I found him in his mucky boots and grimy cotton workpants deadheading the roses with a lethal-looking pruning knife. At my approach, he regarded me as he might a weed that needed uprooting.

I would deal with him in a businesslike manner. If I treated him as our employee, which he was, in spite of his intimacy with my mother, he should be more inclined to do my bidding.

"Giancarlo, I want you to drive me to see the Black Madonna." I needed to get him somewhere quiet to confront him with what I knew.

"You go last week." He beheaded another rose.

"I left early because I felt sick. I didn't get a chance to study it properly." I shouldn't have to explain myself. After all, his wages were part of the rent that we were paying for the villa, and he was using my father's rented car for his assignations with my mother. You would have thought that he'd want me on his side.

"Too much to do in the garden."

"You're able to make time to drive my mother." I expected him to look up, but he didn't.

"She is a nice lady. You are a little girl."

A little girl? He would soon learn how very much mistaken he was. "All right, stay in your garden. I'll just have a talk with my father about all the driving you do for my mother. Where you go," I paused. "What you do."

This time he did look up and shaded his eyes with his coarse hand. "When you want to go?"

"After lunch."

"Fine, I take you. Do not be late," and he returned to his roses.

That afternoon I sat in the back of the car wishing I had my mother's hat to keep off the hot sun. I stared at the back of Giancarlo's head, but his hair didn't glisten today. In fact it looked in need of a wash.

The car drove quickly along the twisting roads, and I had to grip the armrest to avoid being tossed about. It was obvious that he wanted the visit to be over as soon as possible.

The church was deserted. Even the old ladies were counting their rosaries somewhere else. Giancarlo accompanied me to the statue, no doubt hoping that his presence would hurry me along.

The Madonna stared down at us. I could see where the sculptor's knife had dug into her face. It made her appear old and worn, not at all like the angelic face of the Virgin depicted in Renaissance paintings. She looked well beyond child-bearing age, yet women came to her to pray for babies. Did she really have God's ear?

"Not much to look at," Giancarlo said. "My *nonna* looks better."

"How can you say that? She's the mother of Christ."

He shrugged. "She is a woman. All women have are their looks."

Is that what had attracted him to my mother? Her slim body and soft face?

He took a step closer, and I could feel the heat coming off him and the stench of stale cigarette smoke and sweat, a musky masculine smell. My father and his friends were surrounded by the aroma of hair tonic and shaving cream and freshly-laundered cotton shirts. Giancarlo smelled unclean.

His hands ran down the side of my body, stopping at my bottom. "Don't touch me," I told him sharply, "or I'll tell my mother."

But he didn't move away. He smiled—no, he smirked—confident that I was powerless to stop him. "Mother, daughter—you rich English bitches are all the same." He spit the words into my ear. "No English man satisfies his woman so you come here looking for..." and he grabbed the bulging crotch of his blue workpants. "You want to see what a real man can do, *bambina*?"

His thick body pressed me against the stone wall. I couldn't push him away. He was too close to get any leverage. I tried to twist left and then right, frantic to pull away from the hand that gripped my small breast, causing me to cry out in pain.

"Scream all you want, *bambina*. Today the priest visits the old people. No one hears you. No one helps you."

Then he started to lift my skirt. His touch, his mocking voice filled me with disgust—and anger. I brought my hand back and raked my nails across his face. His head jerked, his eyes wide at my audacity. He stepped back and slapped me hard across the face. The force of his hand knocked me to my knees.

He stared at me as if debating whether to finish the job. If I were to escape, I had to do it now. I reached forward and pushed against the edge of the Madonna's pedestal in an effort to get to my feet. But my exertion tipped the pedestal off-balance. The Madonna fell forward. Giancarlo raised his hands to protect himself, but the statue struck his head. He collapsed onto the floor.

He lay still, blood seeping from his temple and puddling on the worn tiles. All I could think was that I'd killed him. I should try to help, but what if he was only pretending? What if I reached out and his hands suddenly grabbed me? This could be my only chance to get away. So I ran.

There was no one on the road. No one had seen me leave the church. No one could blame me for Giancarlo's death.

But I knew that ultimately I was responsible. I would never be able to erase from my mind the sight of him lying on the church floor in a pool of his own blood.

My parents accepted my story that Giancarlo had abandoned me at the church, that the mark from his slap was the result of my own clumsiness when I'd tripped and fallen against a tree on my walk home.

The next morning, when my father realized that the car had not been returned, he begrudgingly made his way to the church to collect it. Over the next few days, he repeatedly inquired after Giancarlo with the agent who had rented us the villa, apparently more concerned with securing compensation for Giancarlo's remaining wages and his irresponsible abandonment of the car than with any misfortune that might have befallen him. Mother spent hours staring out across the garden into the distance and quarrelling with my father at the slightest provocation.

I held my breath at the sound of every telephone ring and every car coming up our drive, expecting the police to appear at the door. But no one ever came for me.

Barely a week after my visit to the Black Madonna, we returned the rented car and flew back to the familiarity of our Georgian town house. The Italian gardener was never mentioned again.

Nine years later my husband and I were walking along a narrow street in Rome, looking for an out-of-the-way *ristorante* that our hotel concierge claimed prepared the best spaghetti carbonara in the city. Our Roman honeymoon was a gift from my father, made poignant in light of my parents' recent divorce.

But I hadn't wanted to come. For years after we returned from Tuscany, I was frightened by olive-skinned men in blue work clothes, imagining that Giancarlo had followed me to take his revenge. My sleep was disturbed by terrifying visions of him forcing me to the hard floor of the church, his coarse, dirty hands ripping my clothes. The last thing I wanted was to return to Italy. But my husband was so excited about the trip that I reluctantly agreed.

We'd been walking along the narrow street for what seemed like an eternity. The sun was beating down on my head, and I was just about to suggest that we abandon our search for the restaurant when I caught sight of a man up ahead with familiar glistening black hair now flecked with grey. At his side a fat woman was struggling to control three boys who were squabbling and chasing each other down the street, deaf to their mother's threats.

"Is something wrong?" my husband asked.

I'd stopped walking. "No, I mean, I just thought since we haven't found the restaurant yet, we must be going in the wrong direction."

He squeezed my hand and pointed to the man and his wife. "Let me ask these people."

"Simon, please don't." I tried to keep hold of his hand.

"Don't worry."

He ran ahead, calling out, *"Mi scusi."*

Simon and the wife launched into a conversation, both seemingly amused by my husband's schoolboy Italian and animated gestures.

"It's all right," Simon said as he rejoined me. "We just haven't gone far enough. A few more minutes should do it."

Up ahead the husband was alone now, leaning against the ancient wall where the street intersected with an alleyway. He was in need of a shave and was wearing a shabby suit jacket with pants that didn't match and a blue shirt faded from the sun and repeated scrubbing.

I stared hard at his face, fleshy from middle-age and his wife's cooking. There was something vaguely familiar about him, as in a dream the dreamer instinctively knows who people are, even though they don't look the way they should. I began to walk toward him.

"Isobel, where are you going?"

"Wait here. I won't be long."

My heart was pounding. I had no idea what I was going to say. I had no idea what I was going to do. The only thing that I was certain of was that I had to know if it was him.

My hand reached into my straw shopping bag and found one of the kitchen knives we'd bought only this morning for our new home. I slipped the knife from the newspaper protecting its blade.

The man watched my approach as if waiting for me. I stopped in front of him. He smelled of stale cigarette smoke and sweat.

I held the knife between us where no one else could see it. The point pushed against his worn shirt just above the waistband of his ill-fitting pants, forcing him back against the stone wall.

I could see no marks from my nails across his cheek, but there was a pale scar emerging from his receding hairline and trailing down the side of his temple. My hand reached up as if to touch it. He flinched. "I see the Madonna showed you mercy," I whispered.

He kept his eyes on the knife, looking as if he might smile. But there was only a nervous, apprehensive pursing of his lips.

"You remember me," I said. I'd meant it as a question, but it was spoken as an accusation.

His eyes grew large, and he looked into my face as if for the first time. "No, *Signora*."

I still couldn't swear that it was him. After all, lots of working men had scars from their jobs or drunken brawls.

The wife called out. "Giancarlo, *andiamo!*"

He looked toward the alleyway and then back at me. His focus returned to the knife as if expecting me to respond with a thrust of the blade. It would have been so easy to fall forward against the handle and push the knife into his soft stomach.

"Please don't hurt me, *Signora*. My boys."

I paused as if considering what to do next. But I already knew the outcome.

I stepped back and gave him space to leave.

His eyes were still on the knife as if unsure he could trust me. Then with a quick nod, he turned and walked quickly down the alleyway. I watched as he joined his family. He never looked back.

I managed to slip the knife out of sight as Simon came up beside me. "Is everything all right?" he asked.

A breeze was blowing across my arms and face, a welcome relief from the relentless heat. Above the chatter of passersby and the laughter of children rose a passionate tenor voice in a spontaneous serenade of a traditional Italian love song. I looked up into my husband's face, so full of concern. "I'm fine. Really, everything's fine."

"Hungry?"

I put my arm through his. "Ravenous. Let's find that restaurant."

He smiled, and we continued down the street.

Accidents Happen
By Darlene Ryan

Darlene Ryan is an award-winning writer of six young adult novels. As Sofie Kelly she is the author of the New York Times bestselling Magical Cats mysteries, including Curiosity Thrilled the Cat *and* Faux Paw. *As Sofie Ryan she writes the national bestselling Second Chance Cat series. She lives on the East Coast with her husband and daughter, where she likes to work on mixed media art projects and prowl around second-hand stores.*

A dead body really wasn't that much of a novelty at Pinewoods Senior Living—or Shady Pines, as the residents referred to the former shoe factory—so no one paid much attention to the ambulance that pulled up to the front entrance one Tuesday in early February. It wasn't until the police cars and the forensic van arrived that the whispers began and the news moved from floor to floor, room to room, faster than a fibre optic internet connection: Suzanne Jennings, Pinewoods' activity director, was dead.

Charles Cunningham was in his room, sitting at the small wooden table by the window, working on *The Globe* crossword puzzle, when Pinewoods' director Kim Wang knocked and opened his door before he even had time to say, "Come in," or get to his feet. A middle-aged man, blond hair cropped close to his head, stood next to her. He wore a black jacket, unzipped, over a bright blue shirt with a striped blue and black necktie and dark trousers.

Charles put down his pen, stood up and walked over to them.

The director was wearing her usual uniform of slim black skirt and white blouse, her hair pulled back in a tight twist. But instead of the professional smile she usually gave the residents, two frown lines knotted her forehead between her eyebrows. "Charles, I'm afraid Suzanne has had...an accident," she said. She indicated the man standing silently beside her, feet apart, a small spiral-bound notebook in one hand. "This is Detective Scott."

The policeman offered his hand. "Mr. Cunningham, I have a few questions, if you don't mind," he said.

"Of course not," Charles replied. "Please come in."

Detective Scott looked at the director. "Thank you for your help, Mrs. Wang," he said. "I'll stop by your office when I'm finished."

The director was being dismissed, and by the way her mouth pulled into a tight line she wasn't happy about it, Charles thought. She nodded curtly and looked at him. "If you need anything just press your call button," she said before turning and heading down the hallway, her heels making a staccato tattoo on the faux-wood floor.

"Have a seat, Detective," Charles said, gesturing at the small table in front of the window. He noticed the officer checking out his surroundings. He wasn't being overly nosey but he wasn't trying to hide his curiosity, either.

Charles had one of the larger one-bedroom units in the converted shoe factory. The corner apartment had windows in both the living room and the bedroom that filled the space with morning light.

"Would you like a cup of coffee?" he asked. "I just made a pot." He smiled. "I ground the beans myself."

"I would. Thank you," the detective said. He was several inches taller than Charles' five foot ten; six one or two, the older man decided.

Charles reached for his own stoneware mug on the table next to the crossword puzzle, and got a second one from the cupboard over the tiny sink in the equally tiny kitchenette. He filled both cups and got a small carton of cream from the refrigerator. At the table he took his time adding cream and sugar to his coffee, watching the detective doctor his own, take a sip and then nod in satisfaction.

"You make a good cup of coffee, Mr. Cunningham," he said.

Charles smiled again. "I'm a bit of a coffee snob. In the dining room all they have is those little plastic pods that make a cup at a time." He made a face. "And it's decaf. So I brew my own." He took a sip from his mug, then leaned back in the chair and eyed the younger man across the table "Suzanne Jennings is dead, isn't she?" he asked.

Detective Scott nodded. He didn't seem surprised that Charles knew.

"What happened to her?"

The detective picked up his pen. "That's what I'm trying to determine. When did you last see Ms. Jennings?"

"After lunch. There was an activity in the dining room." Charles took another sip of his coffee.

"How many other people were there?"

"Four. Ava West, Genevieve Culligan, Artie Hanover and Meridee Young."

Detective Scott wrote the names in his notebook. "You said activity. What exactly were you doing?"

"Making Mardi Gras necklaces out of macaroni that had been spray-painted gold," Charles said. "It's supposed to help us maintain flexibility in our hands." Without really thinking about it, he flexed and clenched his left hand. For years his fingers had put together complex electronics. Making pasta jewelry wasn't exactly a challenge.

The activity director had poured a pile of the spray-painted pasta onto the table and handed each of them a blunt-pointed plastic needle threaded with a stretchy cord that was knotted at one end. Then she'd showed them how to string the rigatoni and penne noodles.

"You can make more than one necklace," she'd said brightly in her singsong voice. As soon as her back was turned Artie had tied his cord into a mock noose and pretended to hang himself.

"How long were you in the dining room?" Detective Scott asked.

"About an hour." Charles wrapped both hands around his mug. "We were finished about quarter to two but I stayed to help put everything away."

"What about the others?"

"Genevieve said she was going to have tea up on the second floor." Charles cleared his throat. "Tea is actually gin and tonic."

The detective raised an eyebrow.

"With an occasional menthol cigarette," the old man added, "but only when it's warm enough to open the window."

The policeman stifled a smile and made a note on his pad.

"Artie left with Meridee and Ava. I'm not sure what they did."

"Do you usually stay to help clean up?"

"Sometimes," Charles said, smoothing a hand over his bald head. "This time I wanted to talk to Suzanne—Ms. Jennings. I was hoping she'd be interested in starting a book club."

"Was she?"

"Yes. She liked the idea." Suzanne Jennings had liked the idea of a book club, just not his suggestion that they start with Dickens' *A Tale of Two Cities*.

"I have a box of large-print *Chicken Soup for the Senior Soul* in my office," she'd said, giving Charles a smile that he felt she would have given him if he'd been five and just figured out how to tie his own shoes. "It's a much cheerier book than Dickens."

Detective Scott reached for his mug, realized it was empty and set it back down again. "You talked about the book club. Then what did you do?"

Charles got to his feet, retrieved the coffee pot and filled the detective's cup, topping up his own as well. "I came back here," he said. "Ms. Jennings walked about halfway with me. I stopped to speak to Gavin—Gavin Henry, he's head of maintenance—to thank him for fixing my showerhead and she headed toward the back of the building."

"Did Ms. Jennings say where she was going?"

The old man took his seat again. "No, but I assume she was going down to the basement. She had a shopping bag filled with rolls of tissue paper and she was carrying all of the supplies from the necklace-making."

He reached for the carton of cream. "I'm not trying to suggest that she was helpless in any way. I just thought she was carrying too much and she was wearing those high, skinny heels that women her age seem to like. She kept spilling bits of macaroni out of the bag as we were walking. There was a little trail of it going down the hall like Hansel and Gretel leaving bread crumbs through the woods. Gavin said he'd take care of it." Charles stopped, blue-grey eyes fixed on the officer across the table from him. "You can't think Gavin had anything to do with..." He left the end of the sentence unspoken.

The detective shook his head. "No." He swiped a hand over his chin. "I guess there's no harm in telling you, Mr. Cunningham. I still have to talk to a couple more people, but from what I've seen it looks like what happened to Ms. Jennings was just an accident. As both you and Mr. Henry noted, there seemed to be a hole in the bag of macaroni she was carrying."

"The macaroni," Charles said, softly. "It spilled on the stairs and she fell." He closed his eyes for a moment. "I should have helped her carry things. I should have insisted."

The detective shook his head. "It was an accident, Mr. Cunningham. Not your fault. Accidents happen."

The old man cleared his throat and nodded. "I know. It's just in a place like this, you expect them to happen to someone my age."

Detective Scott got to his feet. "Thank you for answering my questions, Mr. Cunningham," he said. Then he smiled. "And thank you for the coffee."

"You're very welcome," Charles said. "I'll take you to Mrs. Wang's office. This building is like a rabbit's warren."

He walked the police officer back to the main entrance of the building. They shook hands. "Don't blame yourself, Mr.

Cunningham. Accidents happen," the detective said again.

Charles started across the lobby. Pinewoods' chef, Bryan Smythe, was just coming from the dining room. "Good afternoon, Charles," he said in his booming voice. "Kale and feta egg white omelets for breakfast tomorrow." Thankfully he didn't wait for a response.

Charles sighed and wondered if Meridee had any Pop-Toasts left in her stash as he watched the chef head down the main hallway.

He thought about how good a stack of pancakes with maple syrup and sausage would taste. He thought about how sick he was of kale and feta egg white omelets and green smoothies that smelled like feet. He thought about how sick he was of Chef Bryan and his booming voice. About as sick as he'd gotten of the activity director's singsong tone and kindergarten activities.

Charles reached in his pocket and fingered the handful of rigatoni and penne he found there as he watched the chef disappear down the hallway. He remembered Detective Scott's words: Accidents happen.

Disaster Planning
By Miriam Clavir

Miriam Clavir grew up in Toronto and her interest in museums began in her childhood during many visits to the Royal Ontario Museum. Today she is both a writer and a professional art and artifacts conservator. Miriam's first mystery novel, Insinuendo: Murder in the Museum, *was published in 2012 by Bayeux Arts. Other publications include a mystery short story in the* The Whole She-Bang 2, *several short personal essays, and literary short stories in* The Antigonish Review, The Nashwaak Review, *and* Grain. *Miriam divides her time between Vancouver, B.C., and Garter Lake, Ontario.*

In the museum's pioneer display the upper thick round millstone was turning, scraping against the lower one, the noise finally registering in Gena's brain. But today the building was closed to the public. Why was the historic mill running? Why was the old farm tractor, on exhibit beside the mill, pitched on its side? Gena had to solve this problem. Because if she didn't, she would have to accept that the turning millstone dragged around a tangle of clothes, and that meant the red and sodden parcel crushed by millstones and the tractor had once been a man.

With a distinctive chartreuse tie.

A man she hated. A scrawny dork with a soul patch and a too-white toothy smile, but on staff here at the museum, like her; he was in Human Resources and she managed the museum's artifacts. The dork incensed not just her with his enjoyment of manipulating decisions in every department's hiring, firing, benefits and vacations. Even so, at the sight of the millstone, Gena's knees hit the floor and she vomited. Some pioneer something on exhibit got spattered. It didn't matter. Not now.

Suzy, the intern in Exhibits Design, was leaning against the wall, pulling at her straggling curls, sobbing. "Please, please call the guards."

The screams from the young voice had sent Gena racing down a narrow path around half-lit dioramas of settler life: stilted, beautifully dressed mannequins conversing under fake oak branches as if the world were bonny.

Now on one knee, Gena couldn't throw up the fact that as Collections Manager she'd been put in charge of today's Annual Emergency Preparedness Drill at the museum, and here was a real disaster. She staggered back from her muck.

Gena punched numbers into the security walkie-talkie she'd been given and shouted her news to the guard at the other end. He warned her not to touch anything and clicked off immediately. For a few seconds Gena's fingers raked through the grey of her hair while she hid her head in her sleeve, wiping and re-wiping her mouth.

"Who is it?" Suzy whimpered as they waited, backs turned, for Security. Suzy's hands were balled into fists over her wide-open eyes and mouth.

"The guy in HR." Gena's belly knew this without question.

"Skinny Ernie, the guy you couldn't stand?"

Gena's cubicle was opposite the Human Resources office. As manager of the museum's artifacts, she had a desk in the windowed office area as well as one in the closed collections storage downstairs.

"Skinny that you hexed the other day? When the guys installing the new exhibit were brushing their clothes off in the coffee room and those fake twigs landed all over? You grabbed our snacks and stabbed them with the twig wires." Suzy punched out her arms in exaggerated imitation, already on a mercy flight lifting her away from the grinding millstone scene behind her. "You kept stabbing and humming the words 'chanted forest, chanted forest' and his name and something else that rhymed. So cool."

"You heard him say my leave was denied. Out loud in front of everybody at coffee."

"What'd you chant exactly? About lightning?"

"Beware the oak. It draws the stroke."

In the museum classroom the police had commandeered, Gena huddled inside a clean lab coat, sipping hot sweet tea, saying nothing. A pukey aroma hung around her like fog, and her neck seemed to flinch from the still-damp straggles of hair. Gena knew the police had already searched her office and workroom for bloodstained clothes, and she had handed over her apartment keys so they could see she had no secret plans. Someone would have told the cops about the hex scene in the coffee room. *As if it really threatened Ernie.* At one point Gena roused her brain to ask to call a lawyer.

206

The policewoman said to wait for Detective Jamieson; they might not even be taking her to the station. This was good. Gena knew no lawyers.

She remained sequestered in the classroom all afternoon, a knock on the door bringing a cheese and tomato bagel sandwich left over from the catered lunch the museum traditionally provided for the emergency drill's participants. Gena saw two flat millstones with red squashed in between.

At 5:30 Detective Jill Jamieson showed up and proffered a short list of items the officers had taken from Gena's apartment: minor stuff like a wall calendar, and the more important download they'd made of her computer data. They had left the computer. For now. Jamieson read out notes various officers had made during the day and jotted down Gena's responses. The notes said she disliked HR officer Ernie Spall. That she had told him to beware of her, and had made an angry gesture against him. Detective Jamieson commanded Gena to sign the list.

"I wasn't the only one having problems with Ernie," Gena said, the pen stopping in her raised hand. Jamieson's eyes narrowed.

Gena stared back. Jill Jamieson had the appearance of a young and militant bureaucrat. After a long few minutes that were probably no more than thirty seconds, Jamieson said, "Your assistant Ted's been adamant we ask everyone if they hated Mr. Spall. We have."

"I didn't say I 'hated' him." At least she hadn't used that word out loud. Silently, Gena waited for the detective's next move.

"You're a person of interest to us. Sign these and you can go home." Jamieson dangled Gena's apartment keys. "But we're keeping an eye on you."

"I didn't kill him! Suzy's my witness. I got there after her and she saw how upset I was. And you can check the records how early I arrived at work. Spall probably wasn't even here yet. I must've talked to a dozen people about the emergency drill before we started. They're witnesses. Put that in your statement."

"Mr. Spall *was* here, for your information, since his morning would be used up with the drill."

Gena hadn't paid attention to the HR office this morning when she'd rushed in. But she remembered that Ernie Spall was the only permanent staff member who hadn't turned up for the drill assignments at quarter-to-ten. She'd made a point of calling out his name several times in front of the assembled participants, until someone at the back yelled, "Mr. Bean Counter's probably in his office counting the minutes 'til we start. Want me to get him?" If only she'd answered yes.

A loud, persistent voice was saying, "It's time for you to sign and leave before we organize a test to see who can push over a tractor."

Gena signed and scooted out the door, straight toward her relieved assistant, Ted. Strong arms hugged her and she hid her embarrassment and tears in his smooth T-shirt.

Ted drove Gena home, then left to get some take-out Chinese for both of them. This morning her nest had seemed comfy, with its brass bedstead, stuffed old furniture, funky fifties kitchen and light streaming in on both sides. Now her apartment looked shabby, small, in the kind of old building that needs constant cleaning. Gena had worked in museum collections management for close to twenty years, gained thirty pounds, her hair was already thinning and here was her life. With a slide today into home plate, when she was almost fifty years old and almost accused of murder.

Ted found Gena crouched in an armchair, swearing as her tears fell and a fist pounding the wet upholstery.

"I know something that's going to make you feel better," he said. "I'm not here just 'cause I love you."

"Damn."

"But you've had a hard day, boss, and I do love Chinese food. Kevin's always complaining I never cook, and I say, why cook when there's shrimp and lobster sauce? Besides," Ted's dark hair and tight T-shirt disappeared behind a cupboard door as he searched for plates. "Like I said, there's something to tell you."

"Calm and food first."

They were halfway through the meal before a fidgeting Ted blurted, "Don't you even want to ask what I know that's going to make you feel better? Or in your dotage can't you remember I said that?"

"Dotage, hell. I'm about to be hanged in the prime of life."

"No way, boss. When you called out Spall's name this morning for his big drill assignment, and when he wasn't in the room, you growled about how important the drill is. But you imitated him! The tone of voice exactly, even the words. 'I have difficulty with people being late. You can't just determine your own schedule, you know. The museum comes first.' You must have heard the guffaws."

Gena tried to remember but the emotion of the day had drowned the details.

"So, I know you didn't mean to make fun of him deliberately. Or at least, that's what I told the police. Because the person sitting next to me was the Dowager Empress, and she was laughing along with the rest of us. So even his own boss didn't like Ernie Spall."

"It's years they've worked together, Mrs. Dr. Frankenstein and Igor. Inhuman Resources."

"Only five. And," Ted beat a drum roll on the table, "I saw The Empress around nine in the back hallway with Spall."

"The corridor to the pioneer gallery?"

Ted tried to swallow his mouthful and grin back at the same time.

"You're saying she did it?" This was better than comfort food.

"I sure hope so." But his tone was glum.

"Ted?"

His voice was barely audible. "The Empress came up to me and said, 'Ernie was showing me what he called staff negligence this morning. Someone left the mill on. Turned it on and went away. A safety issue—which job oversees it?' I gave the police the information, and I'm sorry to say I had to tell them also you were the only other person I saw in the vicinity."

Gena frowned. "I don't get it."

"I think she killed him, and she's shifting the blame to me when they realize you didn't do it."

Studying the drawn face perched on a thick neck and buff body, Gena knew Ted could push over a tractor. "I don't feel better," she said.

"You will when we prove The Empress is a murderer."

The conspirators put their plan together. Gena dressed for business in her good pants, small heels and museum-shop earrings, and used her status as a suspect to talk to staff members, starting with the guards at the entrance desk about who had arrived when, and what they'd seen on the screens of their security monitors before the drill began. But the guards who man the museum's entrance had been concentrating on signing in a line-up of drill participants. All the staff, the sixty museum volunteers, even some of the board members had come in. The guards had had little time to look at the security monitors scanning the building's rooms.

"But does it really matter?" one guard had asked Gena. "The only people inside all signed in at our desk." He had shoved the ledger book toward her.

"Isn't it true," Gena had sighed, "that just the cameras which focus on the main museum areas record?" The Empress and The Dork together at 9 a.m. in a back hallway would be only hearsay, not evidence. No images could be replayed. But it was hearsay Gena trusted.

Ted found an excuse to survey staff about who knew how to turn on the mill. All the Collections people did: that went without saying, because the millstones were in the official museum list of artifacts they inspected annually for new damage. Security knew how to work the mill in case it had been forgotten by closing time. The history curator and all the Educators and their volunteers who gave the school tours used the mill in their programs. So the question became, who at the museum did *not* know how to turn on the mill? Ted could have kissed the feet of the Education volunteer who told him Ernie Spall had asked last week how the mill functioned, "...so HR could include the skills in a job description."

Questioned again by the police, Gena had prepared her research. She'd talked to enough people to do a timeline of whom she'd seen, where, and when, on the morning of the disaster. From her discussions about the morning's drill, she now had complete notes documenting every quarter hour. Gena signed more statements and hoped she was off the list of suspects. Detective Jill Jamieson gave no indication of who was on it.

Gena spent the next lunchtime alone, reviewing and reconstituting each detail of the plans for the drill and every conversation with the staff. She could not find solid evidence that the Dowager Empress had been in that far hallway before the meeting. What she knew was that The Empress had shown up at a quarter to ten at the pre-drill meeting, easing regally out of her office according to one witness, with others adding the telling detail that The Empress had remained immaculate all day. Rosie the guard, who had signed The Empress in when she first arrived at the museum, described her as wearing a flowing turquoise "Full-Bodied Woman" draping jacket and skirt. Many confirmed she'd worn the same outfit all day, creased but clean, and no one had seen red or brown stains. And no one apart from Ted had seen The Empress heading to the gallery with Spall.

In planning the emergency disaster drill, trying to keep at least one person in HR on her side, Gena had assigned the old Empress the calm task of recording what time each staff member and their charges arrived after the drill at the assembly point outside. Everyone had seen The Empress at her station, the large raincoat from her office thrown over her shoulders, coffee in hand.

That evening Gena reviewed again what staff said they had been doing between their time of arrival and the meeting at a quarter to ten. And who might confirm it. She saved asking about Ted until the last, since she would have to ask The Empress if she'd seen him in the corridor near the mill.

The other glaring problem was Suzy. She had no one who could back her up that early in the morning she was in the ceramics gallery measuring display cases for an upcoming exhibit. This wasn't surprising, as the gallery was off in another corner of the building, but it still made for a gap.

And then one gap was filled. A gap in Gena's mind. There were no display cases in the ceramics gallery. Not in the proposed exhibit. As Collections Manager, Gena had the list of objects for "Yesterday's Asian Imports" and it was an open display. The design plans were for large, out-of-public-reach platforms, one with a replica kiln and stacks of blue-and-white porcelain and the others with textiles and collectible *oriental objets d'art* secured to plinths. The next morning Gena caught Suzy before she could get inside the museum's door, and took her for a little walk outside.

Suzy's fingers were fiddling with her streaked curls as they strolled further from the building. Under the red oaks that shaded the museum grounds, Gena said, "You weren't in the ceramics gallery that morning, were you? Now that I think about it, you weren't even at the drill meeting. Since you aren't on permanent staff, you weren't in charge of anything and you weren't missed. You were in the pioneer gallery along with Ernie Spall."

Suzy twisted but Gena was stronger.

"If you tell me first, before the police, I can work along with you." Gena looked at the thin wrist she grasped. "I don't believe you shoved that tractor over."

"I didn't! The police know already why I was there."

"Know what?"

"You won't tell?" Suzy bit her lip and scowled. "If they charge me I'll get fired anyway."

"Charge?"

Suzy's dark eyes fixed on Gena. "I needed my medicine. I went to where I could be alone. The old washroom at the end of the pioneer display. Then the police found my 'juice box.' They must've smelled it."

To Gena's puzzled face she said, "It's for dope. It looks like a cigarette case with a straw. It's better for you than smoking; you suck on it. It absorbs the smoke. Marijuana's medicinal, Gena, and I'm giving the police a letter from my doctor to prove it. I get really anxious, you know that."

Gena gave Suzy a warm squeeze but left her arm companionably around her shoulder. "Thanks. It explains why you were at the far end of the pioneer gallery."

"Ow! You're hurting me."

"Sorry. My hand is acting out my stress. Suzy, what's really crucial for me right now is, did you hear any voices, any conversation before you... saw what you saw?"

"I don't want to. I can't!" Her voice disappeared into a high wailing mew. "Not to a judge. Say anything. They took my grandfather in Chile to court and he didn't do anything and then they killed him."

"That's so awful!" Gena enfolded Suzy in her arms. "I'll stay with you, I promise." Pausing, she said, "Look, it's going to come out anyway. Tell me first. It's easier than talking to the police."

Suzy was sobbing, bending over as if her whole body cramped. "I came out of the washroom and I heard him say, 'I'll kill you.'"

"Who said?"

"Skinny Ernie. But I was in the dark and he was threatening someone in the gallery. You know who, too. 'You old bitch, you won't promote me but now I'll get your job.' There was a lot of grunting and scraping."

"Like they were fighting?"

"Yeah, pushing and shoving. Then came this big crash."

"The tractor? Was there any screaming?"

"Skinny yelled, 'Come back you bitch.' And then, 'Shit,' and 'Help.' So I ran over. The tractor was kind of tipped against the pile of flour sacks there and he was trapped."

"But alive?"

"I don't think he was really hurt, he just couldn't get out, the way the tractor had fallen. I said I'd go for help. Outside, Ted was in the hall."

"And?"

"I don't know. Ted went in but I couldn't handle it. I ran. I did almost go to the ceramics gallery. Then I ran back. For more juice.... Ted must've tried to help. The tractor had slipped. The millstones...."

Gena hugged the limp Suzy as if she were her child.

If she were still a person of interest to the police, Gena figured she would at least be lower on that list than Suzy. And the Dowager Empress. And Ted. And who knows who else. Someone had turned the mill on, and when? To look out for Suzy as she had now promised, Gena had to confirm her story about meeting Ted in the hall. And confront The Empress about her presence in the pioneer gallery.

In the HR office, Gena didn't take the offered chair but perched on the edge of a now-empty desk. "I hate to be this blunt, but I know you were in the pioneer gallery with Ernie Spall. When the tractor tipped. Would you tell me in your own words?"

The Empress settled her bulk more comfortably in her high-backed chair, smiled, and closed her eyes as if in meditation. "I could use you and your investigative abilities in my department if you ever want to switch."

After a long minute she continued. "Ernie tried to kill me. I'd marked something in his file he didn't want down in black-and-white." She looked up to catch Gena's shock. "I've told the police this. He lured me into the pioneer gallery with an excuse about the mill running. He turned it off and on again, showed me how easily it could be done. It wasn't safe. He wanted it only in certain job categories. I stepped closer to examine the whole set-up, and then he pushed. We tussled. I'm bigger than him. It didn't take long. The tractor got pushed toward the flour sacks, Ernie was trapped, and he was swearing, but he wasn't hurt. He showed no pain. I went for help."

"Or to give him time to stew 'till we found him in the emergency drill."

Another smile flickered on The Empress' face. "That's your interpretation."

Gena looked at the stout woman a number of years her senior, and said, "Mind if we arm wrestle?"

The smile broadened as The Empress rolled up her right sleeve and planted her elbow on the cherry wood desk. She beat Gena easily.

Gena grinned. "I'd live in fear if I worked for you."

"Good. Remember this when you get to be my age. Don't let anyone think you're just a fat old woman."

"Share your training program?"

"Just grow up on a farm and keep at it. And you, as Collections

213

Manager, might want to remember just whose family donated that tractor to the museum."

Gena gave her a thumbs-up. The Empress knew what was going on in her kingdom. Gena said, "So was it an accident or was he murdered?"

"Everyone disliked poor Ernie, and for good reason. Very convenient for me, I'll have to say, having a bad cop so I'd look like the good cop. But there was one person who hated him intensely."

"Me?"

The Empress raised her eyebrows and shrugged. "Ernie hated himself, especially because his religion didn't admit to people being gay. Staying gay."

"Ernie was gay?"

"Nobody guessed except those with gaydar. Or men who get turned on by a chartreuse tie."

"A gay man with bad taste? Say it ain't so."

"What it is," The Empress said without smiling, her voice quiet, "is trying to be one thing when your body and soul are saying you're another. Ernie was extra harsh on our gay staff. That's what I'd marked in his file and the implication was he did it not because of the individuals, but because he had trouble with the concept of 'being gay.' Ask your assistant Ted, he would know how Ernie treated him. Now it's your turn—murder or accident?"

Gena knew Suzy had asked Ted to "help" Ernie Spall. And later that day, over Chinese food, Ted had tried to convince Gena that the Dowager Empress had killed Spall, on the basis of seeing her come out of the pioneer gallery. Either accident or murder, Ted knew exactly what had happened in that gallery, and he'd tried to shift the blame.

This secret was for her right now, not the Dowager. Gena answered slowly. "I don't want to know if it was murder."

"Gena, if I'm called to the witness stand and it's for one of our staff members, I'm going to argue for extenuating circumstances. Could you help? Somebody like Ted might talk to you sooner than me. He might be happy to say in court what Ernie was like. Would you ask him? I think it might be a case of justifiable homicide. Himicide."

Gena tried to laugh but it sounded raw. "Let's hope first they show it's an accident. Like a lightning strike is. We could practice emergency procedures every day but you can't out-plan every disaster." She swallowed hard. "I think Ted hopes they show it's an accident, too. If they prove it's murder, none of us will be very happy."

But she knew the real question was not happy or unhappy; the question was murder or accident. Gena needed to corner Ted before the police investigation narrowed down to focus on his pivotal role. As soon as possible, she had to share with Ted what she had concluded and what museum personnel would testify to, including Ernie Spall's prejudiced treatment of gay staff. Ted needed, as well, to know that whatever had gone on in the pioneer gallery, both she and The Empress were committed to his support.

But Ted didn't come back to work. He called in sick. Rather, his partner, Kevin, called in for him, and the next day delivered a note to HR from Ted's doctor saying Ted was undergoing tests (unspecified) and might be off work for an extended period of time (unspecified).

Gena had museum staff sign a card, bought a large bouquet of flowers, and disguised her voice when she buzzed Kevin and Ted's apartment intercom. Upstairs at the door she hid her face behind the flowers, and as soon as the door opened, Gena barrelled in, yelling, "Ted, I love you!" Kevin grabbed the flying bouquet. Scuttling into the living room, Gena grasped Ted's startled hands with both of hers, took a slow, smiling breath and said in the calm voice she had rehearsed, "Please Ted, just let me know how you are." She figured they wouldn't throw her out after that.

Next she had to carry off the hardest part. Gena planned to learn exactly what Ted had done in the pioneer gallery that disastrous morning, in addition to the current state of his health. Seeing him lying on the couch, it was clear he did look sick, and Ted described, in brief detail, for which Gena was grateful, a stomach ailment the doctors hadn't yet pinpointed. He was now eating only the softest foods, and in small portions. No, didn't look like cancer. Yes, feeling low, kind of frightened. No, no other help needed, thanks anyway. Yes, gorgeous flowers. You made my day.

"Ted, I found out you're a police suspect. Look, even The Empress, Spall's boss, supports you, not him. She knows he treated you badly. I do, too." Gena paused. She could think of no way forward except to ask outright, "What happened when you went into the pioneer gallery when Spall was trapped behind the tractor?"

Ted opened his mouth, gagged, and vomited into a bowl beside the couch, barely missing Gena.

Kevin glared at her, signalled toward a chair across the room he wanted her in, and cleaned up. When he finished he hugged Ted and used this closeness to whisper in his ear. Gena saw Ted shake his head.

"Ten more minutes," Kevin said gruffly, "and no more about the museum."

Gena had not sat down. Standing by the designated chair, she looked Kevin in the eye. "Don't kid yourself." Her voice remained steady but bitter. "It's all about the museum. Ted could be charged with murder. The museum sent the flowers. What do I tell them? What's the story?"

"I don't know!" came a hoarse whisper from the couch, and Gena saw tears sliding down Ted's face. "Except they'll shove me in jail."

Kevin sat quickly on the wooden coffee table in front of the couch and began massaging Ted's shoulders. Gena squeezed in between the table and the couch, knelt, and covered Ted's hands with hers. No one spoke.

Ted's fingers curled to grip Gena's. "I went in to help. Honest." His voice caught in his throat and words that began as a trickle started tumbling as fast as white water. "He yelled for me to move the top flour sacks so he could get out. But I knew it might make the tractor wobble. We were shrieking at each other. Then he called me a pervert. Said I'd want sex for freeing him and I was disgusting. He started shoving and pounding at the sacks and calling me more names." Ted's hands flew up and slapped over his eyes. "And the sacks slumped. The tractor slid. It took, like, a second. He screamed. Once. So hard." Ted's voice trailed into a desperate whisper. "I saw him crushed up against the millstones.... I heard...just...scraping." Slowly Ted's eyes opened wide, scared, imploring. His fingers slid rapidly to cover his mouth, as if he was trying to stop words compelled to surface. "And I was too chicken to turn the millstone off. I panicked. I thought, they'll see my fingerprints and think I turned it on. I ran."

Ted turned his face into the couch pillows, sobbing. "I killed him by not turning it off!"

Kevin was whispering, "Noo," reaching to lay his head on Ted's shaking back, his arms around him. "Ted. I told you, when he hit the millstones, he stopped screaming. That's the evidence he died instantly."

"People'll think I pushed him."

"But you didn't." Gena stayed very still. "Everyone'll believe what you just said. I just look at you and know it's the truth."

Gena rose to leave Ted and Kevin alone, said she'd give the museum Ted's thanks for the flowers, tell people he was sick, that doctors were looking into stomach ailments, and that Ted was still very upset about seeing Spall's body on the turning millstones. "Period. Okay?"

Kevin nodded and quietly Gena let herself out.

All the same, Ted would need a top criminal lawyer for his best chance of being exonerated. Gena was determined that no one, on her watch, would be hanged in their prime of life from an old oak tree, despite their arboreal presence on the museum lawn.

She buckled down to researching good lawyers for her valuable assistant. Besides, a key part of Gena's job, the "emergency prepar-edness planning," focused on warding off disasters.

Goulaigans
By Judy Penz Sheluk

There's a place about thirty-five kilometres north of Sault Ste. Marie, Ontario, called Goulais River. Now, you might be tempted to pronounce it the French way—Goo-lay—or the way it reads phonetically—Goo-lays—but either way you'd be wrong. You see, up in these parts, it's Goo-lee, and the residents are known as Goulaigans, rhymes with hooligans, just so we have our facts straight.

I'm telling you all of this because not much happens in Goulais River, which is what you'd expect for a town with a population of thirty-six hundred people in twenty-three hundred dwellings. Oh sure, there's the occasional bear spotting, a bald eagle here and there, solitary paddlers in kayaks and canoes, not to mention the summertime sensationalists who seem to enjoy thrashing about Lake Superior on their jet-skis. But overall, it's a quiet place where folks tend to mind their own business, which brings me to this particular story.

The waves were rolling in hard and rough that day, the way they do when the wind is from the northwest, leastwise where my camp is situated. Wind from the south, Superior's flat as a mirror, though that can change faster than my ex-wife, Gilda's, most recent unreasonable demand.

I was sitting on the dock, alternating between reading the latest Clive Cussler and attempting to toss a fishing line into the swirling water, when I spotted a swatch of bright orange fabric a few yards down the beach.

I pulled myself up out of my Muskoka chair with a grunt. Darned things are comfy enough when you're sitting in them, but the way the back is slanted can make them a bugger to get out of, especially if you're carrying a few extra pounds around the middle. I slid my feet into a pair of well-worn water sandals and inched my way over, careful not to slip or stumble on the rocky shoreline.

It was a Personal Floatation Device, firmly jammed into a crevice in the rocks. I'll admit to feeling relieved that it wasn't attached to a body. We'd had a decent summer so far, more hot days than not, so the water temperature was hovering in the mid-teens, though that could slide a few degrees on either side depending on the depth of the water. Get out deep enough and a body could get hypothermic real quick.

My first thought was that someone had either tossed it or lost it; nobody around these parts is crazy enough to navigate Superior without wearing some sort of PFD.

And then I spotted the canoe.

It was a yellow canvas-covered cedar strip canoe, weather-beaten by time and water, the sort of canoe Joe Tucker rented at Tuck's Trading Post. It had been pulled up on shore and tilted carelessly on its side, paddles and a plastic baggie with maps spewed out onto the ground, as if someone had left in a powerful hurry.

A quick inspection of the canoe revealed Tuck's moose head logo on the side. I didn't see a flashlight or a compass, which led me to believe that the paddler had taken them with him. Either that or they'd been sucked into the bowels of Superior, two more artefacts to add to its collection.

Whoever had paddled here knew the area. The cabin on the property had burned down five years ago, the charred remains of wood, concrete and shingles strangled by weeds and scrub brush. The rest of the two-acre lot was heavily treed, making it all but invisible from the water or the road. Every now and again a For Sale sign would go up at the end of the narrow, rutted driveway, only to come down again when the listing expired a few months later.

It could have sold, despite the condition, frontage on Superior being a real selling point, but there was a long history of violence, starting with a prospector who'd been found frozen in the woods, to the not-so-accidental fire that had left a husband and his cheating wife engulfed in flames. Murder-suicide—that had been the verdict, and I thought, at the time, that there had to be a better way.

There were plenty more incidents in between, if local legend was right, but you should be spared the gruesome details. Suffice it to say that some folks thought the property was haunted. Others would tell you it was cursed. Either way, this was one unlucky place, and I didn't plan to linger longer than was absolutely necessary.

That made it time to go to Tuck's.

Tuck's Trading Post is a one-stop shopping general store, should you be willing to pay moderately inflated prices for the convenience of not having to make the forty-minute trek into the Soo for your supplies. Within those rustic walls you can find everything from five-dollar packages of no-name hot dogs to fishing and camping gear, basic hardware supplies—nails, screws, that sort of thing—bird seed, dog and cat food, and the usual assortment of cheesies, chips, and chocolate bars. There was also a propane bar, two gas pumps—one diesel, one regular—a small lumber yard at the back of the property, and, of course, the canoe rentals.

Joe Tucker was the sort of guy that men liked and women loved. I happened to know this firsthand because I used to like him, at least until my ex-wife Gilda fell in love with him. He ambled over to me, his grey eyes crinkled with curiosity. It shouldn't surprise you that I'd stopped shopping there. Hadn't seen Tucker in a good three years. It pleased me to see how much Gilda had aged him.

"I found one of your canoes," I said, sparing us both the "hey there, how's it going" pleasantries. "A yellow one. Out at the old Donaldson place." Donaldson was the name of the frozen-in-the-woods prospector. Didn't matter the property had been bought and sold a dozen times since, didn't matter how many bodies the land claimed, to us Goulaigans, it would always be the old Donaldson place.

"I didn't think I'd see it again," Tucker said. "Fella rented it a few days ago, guy with a beard. I haven't seen him or the canoe since. Is it in one piece?"

"It is. Found a PFD, too, though it's a bit worse for wear." I explained how I found it lodged into the crevice of a rock.

"Appreciate you stopping by to let me know. I'll head over there later on, collect everything." He started to walk away.

"How's Gilda?"

If Tucker was surprised to hear me ask about my ex, he didn't show it.

"If you must know, she left me. Said she was tired of being a Goulaigan. Now if you'll excuse me, I've got a store to run."

Gilda's body washed up on shore three days later, about a mile from the old Donaldson place.

"Whatever happened to Superior not giving up its dead?" Tucker asked me. We were sitting in my cabin, sipping on twelve-year-old whiskey. Now that Gilda was gone, we could be friends again. Or at least pretend to be.

My mind replayed the lyrics to the Gordon Lightfoot song, "The

Wreck of the Edmund Fitzgerald." It was a favourite on the radio up here, seeing how the Fitzgerald sank in 1975, not ten miles from Whitefish Bay.

"I think that's only in November," I said. "It's August...there was no fella with a beard, was there?"

Tucker shook his head. "Do you think Nolan will suspect foul play?"

Nolan was the cop in charge of the investigation. What Tuck was really asking me was whether Nolan would suspect him.

"He'd have to get his head out of his ass first."

Tucker summoned up a weak smile. "It was supposed to be a good day. The water was calm and the marine forecast promised more of the same. We drove over to the old Donaldson place, parked at the end of the driveway, and started to paddle over to the Sandys."

The North and South Sandy Islands were designated as a nature reserve by the provincial government. On a clear day, I could see them from my dock. "Go on."

"We started to argue. We'd been doing that a lot lately. Gilda was griping about the long hours I put in. I tried to remind her that those long hours paid for the lifestyle she'd grown accustomed to, manicures and pedicures and massages and who knows what other nonsense, and besides that, wasn't I taking time off to be with her now? But you know how Gilda could be, once she started in on something."

I'd been on the receiving end of Gilda's drama more times than I cared to think about. Even after our divorce, I'd never really been free of her.

Tucker was still talking. I pulled back my thoughts and forced myself to listen. "I paddled back to the old Donaldson place and left her there," he was saying. "I figured she'd find her way home, maybe go to your place."

He gave me a hard look. I gave him a harder one back. We sat, eyes locked, for a few seconds. Tucker looked away first.

"When she didn't show up a few hours later, I went back," he said. "The canoe was lying where I left it. I'd already grabbed the compass and flashlight when I left the first time. I didn't want to make it easy for her, you know? Not after she'd made my life so difficult."

I nodded. I'd figured as much. Tucker took it as his cue to continue.

"I searched everywhere, didn't find a trace of her or the PFD.

When I was satisfied she was nowhere to be found, I went back to the store and waited for her. Two days later, you came by."

I took another sip of whiskey, remembered Gilda standing at my dock, PFD in hand, tears streaming down her lovely face. The sort of face that could break your heart and keep on breaking it. Thought about the way my hands felt when I pushed them into her heaving chest after she begged me to let her come back, this time for good. The way the jutting rocks had cracked her skull as she fell backwards into the water, her blond hair turning pink as the blood swirled around. The shocked look in her emerald green eyes as she watched me turn away.

Not that I killed her. I let Superior take care of that.

As for Tucker, even a knucklehead like Nolan might eventually connect the dots and arrest him for murder. If not, Tucker was bound to blame himself for Gilda's death until the day he died.

I took another sip of whiskey and smiled.

Served the man right for stealing his best friend's wife.